SWITCH HITTER
A HIT AND RUN NOVEL

E.M. LINDSEY

Switch Hitter
E.M. Lindsey
Copyright © 2022

All rights reserved. This book or any portion thereof
may not be reproduced or used in any manner whatsoever
without the express written permission of the publisher
except for the use of brief quotations in a book review.

This book is a work of fiction. Any events, places, or people portrayed in the book
have been used in a manner of fiction and are not intended to represent reality.
Any resemblance is purely coincidental.

Cover by: Sleepy Fox Studio
Photographer: Golden Czermak/FuriousFotog
Model: Grant Mims
Editing: Sandra with One Love Editing
Proofing: Cindi Livingston

Content Warning: This book contains past mentions of violence, minor harassment/stalking, mild use of ableist language, and a permanent injury due to a gunshot wound. Please take care with any triggers you may have.

FOREWORD

The Major League Baseball portrayed in this book is made up of entirely fictional teams and exists in the world where LGBTQ+ players are comfortably out and accepted by the majority. While the rules are generally the same, I have made some adjustments in order to fit it into the world I've written.

That being said, I have done my best to keep the spirit of the MLB alive in this book. Baseball, while not without its issues, has a long history of accepting players with disabilities, and I have attempted to portray that here in the Hit and Run universe.

For more content like this, please subscribe to my newsletter.

SWITCH-HITTER

a Hit and Run novel

E.M. LINDSEY

You taught me that there is such a thing as unconditional love; when you found a way to love me, in the condition I was in.—
William Chapman

PROLOGUE

Rubbing his temples, Pietro did everything in his power to ignore the sound of his soon-to-be ex's voice. Hervé wasn't always so grating. Pietro wouldn't have lasted that long with him if the man crawled under his skin like this every single time they were together. In fact, Pietro kind of liked the way he whined—so long as they were in bed with Hervé writhing beneath him.

But these moments—the ones where Hervé's voice had reached some sort of hysterical pitch as he threw his clothes into suitcases, screaming in some hellish mixture of French and English about what a piece of shit Pietro was—those were the ones he could do without. Forever.

It didn't help that his mouth was still throbbing, his gums swollen from all the emergency dental work. Pietro had suffered plenty of injuries in his line of work. Baseball didn't come with as many risks as the contact sports, but he'd taken a couple of strays to the ribs, and once to the side of the jaw where he'd lost a molar.

But he'd never been sucker punched before. At least, not in the goddamn teeth.

It had been forty-eight hours since the club—since he was on his knees spitting rivers of blood onto the polished floor—and he still didn't know what the fuck he'd done wrong. He had been drinking, which wasn't exactly out of the realm of ordinary during the off-season. He was dancing with his friends. Scooter's twin sister had bet him that he wouldn't be able to perform the *Dirty Dancing* catch, and everyone had given them room.

He nearly missed, but he caught Janelle before it was a disaster.

Then suddenly there was a massive, bulky French bodyguard all up in his face. And then there was a fist flying.

His vision had gone double, and then there had been screaming and the sound of Hervé crying. James loaded Pietro up into a car, and the next thing he knew, he was sitting in some after-hours dental surgery office being flooded with nitrous oxide. It had taken the edge off, but the pain had made him nauseous. His broken teeth were filed and capped, and he was sent home with a nice bottle of Vicodin and a bunch of unanswered questions because what the *fuck* had actually happened at the club?

Being surrounded by French strangers was nothing new, of course. He'd gotten used to it after dating Hervé, who traveled with an entourage. He was relatively unknown in the States, but he was one of the most popular French models and actors the country had seen in years.

And of course, Pietro also knew who the fist belonged to: Thierry Bourget, Hervé's hired bodyguard and best friend since they were kids.

Thierry never ever spoke to Pietro when he was around, but over the course of his off-again, on-again relationship with the model, Hervé had told him that Thierry had always been there whenever shit went down.

He just...still had no idea what the hell went down and what he'd done to deserve the pain he was currently in.

"...and you still have nothing to say to me?"

Pietro blinked away some of the opiate fog and the fact that his ADHD was riding high from all the adrenaline and pain, and he stared across the counter at his now-ex, who was standing in the middle of the kitchen with his arms crossed. He'd been tuning Hervé out all morning as the man packed his shit, but he was impossible to ignore now.

"Mm?" Talking still hurt like a bitch, so he just adjusted his ice pack and narrowed his eyes.

Hervé huffed. "I know it doesn't hurt that much. You were always so dramatic."

Pietro swallowed and swore he could still taste blood, which made the whole situation worse. He half wished Thierry was in the house instead of waiting in the driveway for Hervé to finish packing his shit. He didn't have words for him, but he did have a point to make. With a fist. Because he was still furious and pretty sure he always would be.

"Come on," Hervé goaded. "Out with it."

"I want to know what the fuck I did to deserve that," Pietro finally mumbled. "I know he didn't punch me for fun."

Hervé scoffed. "He's always hated you."

"Yeah, well, he's always resented you for making him your bodyguard and *bitch* instead of letting him go off to live his own life and be a chef or whatever," Pietro shot back. A low blow—another fact he'd learned from Hervé when he'd been feeling talkative. He'd confessed one night over three bottles of merlot that Thierry had always wanted to cook for a living— something Hervé found both amusing and disgusting. Fuck, he was such a snob.

Pietro squared his shoulders. "But I don't see him knocking you on your ass, so..."

Hervé's cheeks pinked. "You don't know what you're talking about, you..." He trailed off into another string of long French that Pietro was too high-strung to follow. "In case it wasn't obvious, I'm leaving for good."

Pietro couldn't help his laugh. He dropped the ice pack on the counter and half stood from his barstool. "Promise?"

Hervé blinked, and then his eyes filled with tears. "Five years and this is all I get?"

"He punched me in the fucking face," Pietro bellowed. "He knocked out two teeth because you asked him to, and you don't even have the courtesy to tell me why?"

Hervé went quiet for a long time. "I couldn't find you. He said men like you always cheat. He said I deserved better. Then we saw you with *her*..."

"James' sister? Who's practically *my* sister?" Pietro growled. "Fuck me! You told him to clock me because I was doing eighties dance moves with my best friend's sibling?"

For the first time, Hervé looked almost...reluctant. "I didn't know who she was."

"And you didn't ask. Instead, you sicced your little guard dog on me." Pietro sank back down and tried not to let himself feel hurt because fuck that. Fuck Hervé. He shouldn't have the power to do that.

"Maybe we should talk about..."

"Get out," Pietro said tiredly. "You want this to be over, fine. It's over."

Hervé made a wounded noise and took a step closer. "Just wait. Thierry was the one who said I should leave if you were cheating..."

"I don't cheat," Pietro said. His voice was dull now, exhausted. He was just so done. "That's all you—breaking up with me every six months so you can go fuck whatever up-and-coming piece of ass just hit the big screen. I'm just the dipshit who keeps taking you back."

"That's not cheating," Hervé started to defend, but Pietro just laughed.

"Whatever you say. Look, you want to be free, be free. Just get the fuck out and lose my number. Tell your friend that he wanted me gone, so he got his wish. But if I see him again, I'm not going to be polite about it." He picked up his ice pack, pressing it to the front of his mouth, then breezed past Hervé and into his bedroom.

He heard his ex coming after him, but he quickly turned the lock, then flopped over on his unmade bed. It smelled like him—just him—which was a blessing. Hervé had slept at a hotel the night before, and housekeeping had brought in fresh bedding before he got home that night. Pulling a pillow over, he pressed it against his ear, and eventually the muffled sounds of Hervé crying faded into silence.

Enough was enough.

He was done.

Thierry got his wish, and Pietro would never have to see either of them again.

usual thanks to the hours under the unrelenting desert sun. "There's a vending machine right next to the laundry room."

James stared, then burst into laughter. "Go to the fucking store."

Pietro huffed and crossed his arms. "I can't cook, dude, okay? You and I both know this."

It wasn't a lie—though if he was getting technical, he hadn't actually tried to cook for James. The two of them had gotten a little buzzed two seasons back and decided to make their rookie pitcher, Bruce, a birthday cake.

It...hadn't gone well.

It was mostly that Pietro was bad at cooking, but the reason behind it he now knew was the fact that his brain just... couldn't focus on recipes more than three or four steps. He'd been diagnosed with ADHD three years before, and his therapist had explained that most people had an internal secretary keeping track of everything that needed to get done, and when, and how. But Pietro's took a lot of vacations and got lost watching ESPN, leaving everything else behind.

The new meds helped, but not enough, and his therapist said that sometimes that was just reality. Sometimes, things would just fall apart. His life as an MLB player was chaos even when it was calm, and sometimes balls would drop.

But try as he might to function more in his own home, the fact remained: Pietro was a disaster in the kitchen.

Pietro ran his tongue over his front teeth which—even after a year and a half—still felt so fake. He'd kind of always wanted to be that guy who slipped into retirement without plastic surgery or veneers from getting clocked in the face.

Unfortunately, his ex had made sure he couldn't check off that little bucket-list item.

It was fine though, most of the time. Mostly because it had been over a year since Pietro had heard from his ex. Hervé had called just once, three months after they split for good, letting him know there had been an incident.

"Someone attempted to shoot me," Hervé had said, his tone clearly angling for a reaction.

Pietro had closed his eyes and told himself it wasn't his fucking problem. The last thing he wanted was for his ex to be hurt, but he wasn't going to let him come running. "It sounds like you're okay."

"Yes, but Thierry isn't. I guess you got your wish."

For a moment, Pietro had thought the man died. He didn't get the chance to ask Hervé about it though. The little shit hung up and refused to answer his call back, so he was forced to google and wade his way through French articles on the pathetic vocabulary he'd picked up from his time spent with his ex.

It turned out, Thierry hadn't died at all. He'd been shot and paralyzed. Hervé had made a public statement about how much he was going to miss working with him. It had been cold and distant, and for the first time since that sucker punch, Pietro felt sympathy for the man.

Of course, he wasn't surprised by the way Hervé had handled it, and he supposed—in a kind of fucked-up way—he owed Thierry a thank-you. After all, if it hadn't been for him wailing on Pietro in the club that night, God only knew how long he would have stayed in the orbit of Hervé's circus.

Life was quiet now though. At least, as quiet as his asshole teammates would allow.

He reached forward for his little ramen container, shoved the fork in, and took a massive bite. "Are you going to let me shame eat in private?"

"No," James told him. "I'm going to make you do something about this mess. Take some cooking classes."

Pietro snorted a laugh so hard he choked on a noodle, and

it took him a full thirty seconds to compose himself. "Right, yeah," he said through a cough, thumping his chest. "With all this fuckin' free time I have."

"Isn't your brother married to some kitchen prodigy?"

"If you mean a high school foods teacher, then yes," Pietro said, then felt guilty because his brother's boyfriend, Ezra, was more than that, and all the guys knew it. He'd sent over enough holiday cookies for the team that he was already half-famous. "And Gabriel would cut my balls off if I tried to bogart any of Ezra's free time."

"Then hire a private tutor. Hire a personal chef," James said, ticking fingers off his hand like he was counting a list. "Hire Gordon fucking Ramsay to teach your ass how to poach an egg. Or, at the very least, make spaghetti noodles with butter."

Pietro cringed at the insult. He wasn't very Italian, but he was Italian *enough*. He just...hadn't gotten the gene the way his siblings had. Even Gabriel knew how to make their nonni's sauce.

Pietro was just the back sheep—the genetic fuckup.

Maybe it was the price he paid for living out his dream while Gabriel's MLB career was flushed down the toilet thanks to being in the wrong place at the wrong time. Pietro didn't want to think that his messy brain was karma, but sometimes he wondered. Knowing Gabriel—who had once been just as good as him, maybe even better—lost it all from a single accident.

But Gabriel was also ridiculously happy. Still an asshole, yes. Still a grumpy dick on his best days, sure. But he was also in love and content in his new career.

And Pietro was left in a shitty hotel lobby in fuckin' Arizona, eating vending machine ramen.

So, who was the real winner?

"A personal chef doesn't sound like the worst idea," he mused after shoveling the last bite into his face. He felt tragically unsatisfied, but there wasn't much he could do about it.

James shook his head. "Fucking diva. But in your case, I'd probably recommend it. Now throw your garbage away. We're heading into town tonight to get a little tipsy and see what desert flowers come out to play."

"You're a fucking joke," Pietro complained, but he didn't hesitate as he followed him down the hall, tossing the leftovers in the trash and eager to erase the taste of Styrofoam and sadness out of his mouth.

They had three more days before he was heading back to the cool mountains, and he was going to make the best of them.

TIME PASSED IN A BLUR, and before Pietro was really consciously aware, the season was almost over and he was staring down the line at playoffs. The weather was creeping into the cold season, the night games a little more unbearable with the frigid Colorado wind, but it also meant he was close to tasting victory again.

Of course, it also meant facing another year of his life where nothing had changed. James had given him a good starting point, but back home, he tripped and fell back into old habits. He felt like the ultimate fuckup, but the only person he was hurting was himself.

So, it was hard to give too much of a shit.

Pietro sighed into his pasta, knowing full well he looked like a goddamn barbarian with sauce smeared across his cheek, but it had been months since he'd had a real home-cooked meal.

He was feeling a little better though, finally having sold his house and setting up in a more secluded part of Denver. It was mostly just to erase any lingering memories of Hervé, but his therapist had also accused him of running away from problems instead of trying to learn better coping skills, and he couldn't bring himself to deny the accusation.

He was grateful the only one at the table to see his barbaric eating habits was his brother, though making an ass of himself in front of Gabriel wasn't exactly high on his priority list.

Still, humbling himself helped ease some of the tension that lingered between them. Pietro had never quite been able to shake his guilt at the fact that Gabriel had lost everything right when Pietro's career was hitting its peak. Every single award won, every time he came up to bat with the World Series riding on their games, the victory was bittersweet.

He almost preferred it when he lost because at least he wouldn't have to meet Gabriel's eyes and know that his brother would never get there.

"You're getting your melancholy all over my table," Gabriel said.

Pietro looked up, then wiped his mouth with the back of his hand. As predicted, Gabriel let out an annoyed scoff and tossed one of the linen napkins at him, hitting Pietro in the face. "Thanks."

"You might want to pace yourself," Gabriel said mildly. He'd barely touched his own food, but that wasn't out of the ordinary. "Ez left dessert."

Pietro perked up, and his brother let out one of his rare laughs. "What kind?"

"Some sort of mocha pie thing he's working on for next week. I had the first few versions. They're nice."

Pietro rubbed his hands together, then went back to work

on his pasta while Gabriel sipped at his wine. "Is there any chance Ez wants to leave his job and come work for me?"

Gabriel made a growling-choking noise. "Is that a serious question?" Pietro dropped his fork, made a show out of wiping his mouth with the napkin, then folded his arms over his chest. "Yes and no. I know you wouldn't part with your precious chef, but it's getting kind of dire at my place. Does he know anyone looking for a job?"

"Don't *you*?" Gabriel fired back. "You have an entire league of rich sports stars. Surely one of them has a contact that can help you out."

"I'm already signed up with this employment service that handles shit like housekeepers and personal chefs," Pietro grumped. "So far, nada. Not even an interview."

"And you can't just, like, send out for food?" Gabriel asked, frowning.

Pietro groaned. "What—those fucking disgusting meal services where everything tastes like it came out of an old folks home and is the color of dirty dishwater?" He'd tried the meal services and the delivery companies that sent ingredients and recipes. Most of the time he was too damn tired to bother, and after one month where everything spoiled and turned the air in his house rank, he gave up.

Gabriel lifted a brow at him.

"Fine," Pietro said. "I don't want to ask because it makes me feel like a fucking toddler that I can't do more than microwave canned spaghetti. The guys all think my bad eating habits are hilarious on the road, but I think most of them assume I'm a functional adult."

"You *are* a functional adult," Gabriel said softly.

He was one of the few people in Pietro's life who also knew about his late diagnosis. ADHD sounded like the thing you used to explain away a hyper kid in class—not an executive disorder. Not the reason why he was so goddamn good at some things but the rest of his life was a damn mess. He knew his embarrassment was his own fault. It was from years of listening to mean jokes on the playground, then praying every single night that God make sure he stayed "normal."

His team was his family—his other family. And logic told him they'd understand if he just admitted the truth. But there was a mean, ugly little voice just under that who liked to whisper that it would just give them another reason for them to mock him behind his back.

He swallowed thickly, and his gaze darted away. "I know I should be working on this shit, but I can't. And I mean that literally. Everything goes into the season, and I've been struggling more since Hervé left, and..."

Gabriel leaned across the table until he caught his brother's gaze. "I'll make some calls. I can't promise anything. You know I don't have the same connections you do anymore, but I'll see what I can do."

Pietro swallowed thickly. "Thanks. You know I hate asking."

"Yeah." Gabriel stood up and collected the plates, and Pietro stayed rooted to his chair, stuck with indecision over whether or not he should get up and help. In the end, it didn't matter. His brother returned with an entire pie tin and a fork.

"Are you serious?" Pietro asked, feeling far too eager.

Gabriel rolled his eyes, but he was clearly trying to fight back a smile. "I ate one by myself last week. Go nuts."

With a grin, he dug in and groaned. "Fuck. Marry him, okay? But also make him promise he'll make your favorite brother dessert like once a week."

At that, Gabriel actually smiled, making him look years younger and actually happy, which was almost terrifying. Even after falling in love, his brother was kind of a grumpy dick. But it was nice seeing him like this.

It was in these moments the guilt lifted from Pietro's shoulders—even if it didn't last.

"Actually," Gabriel said, and his voice was suddenly low and serious, making Pietro snap to attention, "I'm going ring shopping next week. I thought you might want to come."

Pietro's cheeks hurt from how wide he was smiling. "Shit yeah, man. But if you tell any of the sisters..."

Gabriel shuddered. His family no longer lived very close, but both brothers knew the moment any of them heard the word "wedding," they'd start to descend like locusts.

"Keep it off Facebook," Gabriel ordered.

Pietro put up his hands in surrender, almost losing his fork. He caught it at the last minute in a small spray of chocolate-coffee drops, and he licked his hand before digging back in. "You know I don't want to deal with any of them, okay? But I am excited. Does Ezra know?"

Gabriel huffed a laugh. "He told me if I don't hurry up, he's going to do it for me."

Letting out a small sigh, Pietro set his fork down and took a long gulp of water. "You know I love that for you, right? One of us had to make this shit work."

"If you quit dating models who literally feed off public drama," Gabriel said flatly, "you might open yourself up for someone a little more..."

"Normal?"

Gabriel scowled. "Able to make you happy."

Pietro let out a slow breath, then leaned his head back and stared up at the ceiling. "That's all well and good for people like *you* who..." He stopped because the next words out of his mouth were going to hurt his brother. Then he realized the silence was just as bad because Gabriel knew what he was going to say. "I knew what I was signing up for when I decided to marry the MLB."

Gabriel said nothing for a long while. "You don't have to resign yourself to misery. And you sure as shit don't have to accept getting punched in the mouth every time your partner gets annoyed with you."

A microscopic piece of Pietro wanted to argue in defense of Hervé, because it really was the first time the guy had incited violence, but he knew better. He knew there was no excuse that could have made what his ex had his bodyguard do in any way right. And Hervé hadn't ever been kind in the course of their relationship, even if he hadn't been violent.

He'd enjoyed taking Pietro down a peg or two every chance he got. He seemed to get off on making Pietro feel like shit about himself.

His therapist had said Hervé wanted to be the source of Pietro's self-esteem, and that had terrified him more than anything, because before the split, he had already started to feel that way.

Pietro knew himself all too well. He knew he wouldn't survive if his self-worth was in the hands of someone else.

"I should probably take off," Pietro said after a beat.

Gabriel looked like maybe he wanted to say something else, but he kept quiet, and Pietro was glad for it. He was tired, and he had a long week ahead, and he was determined to get more of his life back on track. Even if it came at humbling himself to ask for help from others.

CHAPTER TWO

"Fuck yeah, man. That's fucking amazing." Chris grinned at him, his teeth very white and touching his lower lip as he smiled.

Thierry always thought he looked a bit like a demigod the way he always stood in beams of sunlight which made his dark brown skin glow. Thierry might have even let himself fall for the guy, except that Chris was very straight and very engaged. And Thierry hadn't ever been in a serious relationship before, so he had no idea where to even start being a decent partner.

Thierry appreciated his physical therapist's enthusiasm for what were once mundane tasks—like being able to stand on one foot between a set of parallel bars. What was simple for the average man was a massive feat for him only a year and a half after being shot in the stomach.

Especially since a bullet had grazed in his spine and his doctors had all been damn sure he wouldn't have any movement below his navel. It had taken him a year to walk and an additional three months after to balance on his own without Chris' hands on his waist.

But it didn't feel like progress to him—not really.

In fact, the week before, he'd told Chris to go fuck himself and refused to get out of the chair because he realized he wasn't working toward getting his former life back. There wasn't going to be some sappy movie miracle where he'd hurtle through a montage and come out of it running a marathon.

He was paralyzed.

For the rest of his life.

He could move his legs and he could stand, and he could go from his sofa to his kitchen without assistance, and that was... well. It was *fine*. But on particularly bad days, walking felt like he was on stilts made of sandbags. Some days, when he moved wrong, he would lose all feeling from the stomach down, apart from the burning nerve pain that raced from the balls of his feet all the way to his stomach.

The doctors had been very clear it wasn't something that was likely to go away, either. This was just life now.

After being shot, Thierry laid in his bed unable to wiggle a single toe, staring at the pale walls of the hospital room, wondering if there was *living* after all this. He'd been given the worst, most terrifying literature in rehab after he'd come out of his drug fog. It had the best-case scenarios where he was independent and didn't need to piss in a bag and would be able to walk on his own.

And it also had the worst-case—the sort of life where he never moved his legs again and died young from complications of a spinal injury.

Two more surgeries and three months in a private rehabilitation facility just outside of Versailles, and he made progress. Not enough, but some.

His old life was gone, of course. He wouldn't be following Hervé and his entourage of actors and models from club to club. He didn't have the capacity now for running or moving faster than a ninety-year-old man.

Not that it mattered. Hervé had all but abandoned him the moment he realized Thierry's body was useless to him. He'd gotten a single text, and then the man who he'd once believed was his best friend in the world was gone.

It took a few weeks for him to realize it was for the best, but the epiphany that the man was nothing more than a narcissistic piece of shit who only cared about himself wasn't far off. Hell, before the incident at the club, Thierry had been questioning why he'd abandoned all of his personal dreams for a man who treated Thierry like he was nothing more than a wall of muscle.

That, of course, stemmed from the moment his fist went flying on Hervé's orders, cracking into Pietro Bassani's face. Thierry had watched the blood pour from his mouth with a sort of strange detachment, and it wasn't until the next day when Hervé was wailing in the car about how Pietro wouldn't give him a second chance that Thierry started to wonder if the man had any heart at all.

That plagued him as he lay in the hospital bed, and when his father finally came to visit him with an offer of rehab in the States, Thierry knew it was his chance to start over. "It's the highest-rated facility in the world," his father had said, laying a hand on his. "We don't want you to leave, *mon fils*. We just want you to start feeling better."

Thierry understood what his father was trying to say, and the reality was he didn't mind the idea of leaving. There was nothing left for him in Paris now anyway. "Where is it?" he asked, shifting up on his bed.

His father gave him a half-smile. "Denver, Colorado. You were there, yes? When you and..." His father stopped, knowing Thierry didn't want to hear the name of the person who'd abandoned him. But in the moment, the distraction would have been welcome because that was the last place he wanted to go. The city where everything had started to fall apart. The city that was home to Pietro Bassani.

"I don't know," he started. "I..."

His father squeezed his fingers. "If you're too afraid to be on your own like this, I understand."

But that wasn't what it was, and the words were the shock he needed because he didn't want to wallow like this. He didn't want to live a half-life. He wanted more.

He could shed his past with Hervé like an old, rotted snakeskin and embrace all of the things he never believed he could do again.

"Alright. I'll go," he murmured, and that was that. Signed on the dotted line.

He kissed his parents goodbye once the facility discharged him, used the clunky, awkward airport wheelchair, and made his way across the ocean to something new and terrifying.

Thierry embraced his new future though, with both arms. He threw himself into physical therapy, found a place to live that helped cater to his needs, and eventually managed to finish a culinary program at the community college which offered him the chance to sign on with a company that provided well-off clients with personal chefs.

It wasn't ideal. It wasn't what he'd wanted. He imagined himself heading up his own restaurant and taking his talent to the very top of the culinary world—but it wasn't nothing. It was a start, and he felt like he was on the verge of becoming an entirely new person.

Now, standing between the parallel bars, his right leg was starting to tremble. His balance was okay. Until it wasn't.

And he fell.

The sound of his hands slapping the mat was almost as

loud as the shot that had pierced his stomach, and he found himself on his side, breathing heavy. The look on Chris' face said that he knew Thierry wasn't in pain—at least, no more than usual. No, he was just lost back in that dimly lit club with all the screaming, and Hervé crying, and then…

And then the burning sensation.

He took several breaths before he rolled up onto his hands and knees before realizing he'd pinched something, and now his legs were just short of numb. With a frustrated sigh, he rocked himself up to sit. He managed to grab the bars after an eternal struggle, and then he was upright again.

"Hands off," he barked when Chris reached for him.

Chris took a step back, but he stood there with his nose twitching like a wild rabbit ready to leap.

"Stop staring at me like that," he said, first in French, then remembered Chris didn't speak it, so he repeated himself in English.

Chris laughed and put his hands up in surrender as Thierry twisted his hips, dragging his right leg forward, and then his left until they started to limber up.

His chair was waiting for him like a beacon of relief. He never thought he'd be glad to see the fucking thing, but after every PT session, he wanted to hold it tight and make everyone around him promise he wouldn't have to get up again.

The tremors started the moment he was back down, so he quickly did up the leg straps, then followed Chris over to the water table and gulped down the tepid bottle he'd left perched on the edge.

"Not bad, man. You ate shit and got right back up."

Thierry snorted. "Mm."

"No witty comeback today?" Chris asked. There was a hint of real worry in his tone, so Thierry waved him off. "Is there something wrong?"

"No," Thierry forced himself to say. There wasn't really—apart from his complex PTSD from the injury. And how humbling his new life had become. "I have a job interview tomorrow, and I'm nervous. I lost focus."

Chris' brows rose. "Oh shit. So that means you're *staying* staying? You didn't tell me that."

Thierry felt like shit all of a sudden. Chris was more than just his physical therapist. He had become a friend.

They had weekly movie nights with his neighbor Sarah, and Thierry was learning to love American takeout and dessert-only restaurants. He'd gotten so settled, he realized he'd never told his friends that he was planning on making this as permanent as he could, because for the first time since the injury, he was something like happy.

He could get around Denver with little problem, he was in classes learning to drive with the new hand controls the dealership had installed in his crappy little car, and for the first time in his life, he had real friends.

"I'm staying," he confirmed. He drank the rest of the water bottle, then swiped the back of his hand over his forehead.

Chris gave him a hard slap on the shoulder. "Fuck yeah, man. We're going out to celebrate."

Thierry groaned. "No."

Chris grinned wider. "Yes. Hailey's back in town next week, and Sarah promised her a girls' night to celebrate, so you have to keep me company."

Thierry wanted to argue back, but he couldn't bring himself to do it. A small burst of joy had flared to life behind his ribs because not a year and a half ago, he didn't think he could have this. Friends, care, comfort, love. But it was impossible to deny when Chris was smiling at him.

"Fine. You have to pick me up though. I tried to take my car to the supermarket yesterday and almost crashed it." His new life was all still a work in progress, but he no longer felt like a chore to the people around him. "I won't be ready to go on my own by next week."

"It's a deal." He drummed his fingers on his thigh, then straightened up. "Where should we...*oh*, shit! Let's go to the Platinum Cat."

Thierry's brow furrowed. "The...what?"

"That new club downtown," Chris said. "It's fucking lit. My cousin is the bouncer there, so he can get us in. All the local celebrities hang out there. I heard that James Harney from the Vikings owns half the place or some shit. Didn't you know a guy from that team?"

Thierry wanted to scream. He had deliberately not told Chris what had happened the last time he and Pietro were in the same room together. How he'd been feeling bitter and angry and whispering poison into Hervé's ear because he knew the man would react. And how he used Hervé for permission to punch someone.

He didn't deserve to be forgiven for it, and it was the one reason he had truly considered not staying in Denver.

When he first met his neighbor Sarah, he'd brought Pietro up, trying and probably failing to sound casual. "Do you ever see people like Bassani around town? I mean, Denver's not that big, so...is there a chance I'd see him?"

"Babe," Sarah had told him, giving his hand a patronizing pat, "people like Pietro Bassani don't hang out where the plebs do. Unless you can get yourself a pass to the VIP clubs downtown, you're literally never going to see him."

Now he didn't know how to tell Chris no without telling him the whole truth, and he wasn't sure he wanted his friend to look at him as the man he once was.

"Why do you look like I asked you to step in front of a firing squad?" Chris demanded as Thierry rolled away from the table.

Leaning down, he undid the straps on his chair now that his legs had stopped shaking, and he gave them an experimental flex. They were still tingling like they were asleep, but he was pretty sure they would bear weight again. "It's nothing."

"Look, you and I both know you need to get laid..."

Thierry snapped his gaze up at Chris, then eased himself to stand. It took a second to find his bearings, but when he did, he crossed his arms and set his jaw. "I'm not ready for that."

Chris immediately softened and put his hands up in surrender. "Alright, that's fine. That's better than fine. But just so you know—for the future—I'm the best goddamn wingman you'll ever hope to have."

Thierry softened and shook his head before reaching for his folding cane that was lying on the table. He set it down gently and rested his weight against it, taking some of the pressure of his still-aching legs. "Sorry for being an asshole."

Chris laughed and gave him a slap on the arm. "No worries, man. That hot-ass French accent makes it a lot easier to tolerate."

Thierry flipped him off, then turned on his heel and slowly made his way to the changing room. He debated about rinsing off, but it was easier to do at home with his comfortable and posh bamboo shower chair.

Thierry had always been a private guy, and in this place, he felt so exposed.

He took his time changing, and just as he was running wet fingers through his hair, his phone buzzed in his pocket. He didn't bother to check who it was. Sarah had promised to pick him up at the end of the session and then take him to his interview, so he slung his bag over his shoulder, then bypassed the front desk at the fastest speed he could manage that told them he wouldn't be stopping for small talk.

Letting out a sigh of relief when the fresh air hit his face, Thierry carefully made his way around the corner of the building and saw Sarah leaning against her car at the loading curb. He couldn't see her eyes behind her shades, but he could tell from the way her cheek scrunched up, she was winking at him.

"Good session?" she asked.

And that was a loaded question considering he was now roped into going to the Platinum Cat with Chris and officially risk seeing Pietro for the first time since he'd settled in Denver.

"*Comme çi, comme ça,*" he answered her absently as he threw his bag in the back, then dropped into the seat. It wasn't much of a relief, but his legs appreciated it, and he folded his cane up and stored it between the soles of his shoes.

Sarah gave him a side-eye, but she said nothing as she started the car. "Okay, so," she began, and he braced himself, "we have exactly seven extra minutes if we want to keep to your pre-interview schedule, and if I don't get a coffee, I'm..."

"Going to literally die?" he offered, trying and failing to mimic her American accent.

She laughed. "See, you're learning. Promise you're not going to get all worked up if we're, like, a *second* late."

In reality, he didn't mind the delay at all. Hell, a small part of him half wished for some disaster to strike so he didn't have to go to the job interview at all. Of course, he knew that was just the dark place in his brain talking—the place that insisted he wasn't going to be able to do it, that he'd never be ready.

But he was tired of that feeling. He was tired of letting things get in the way of what he really wanted.

"I won't mind," he finally said, and Sarah laughed because by the time Thierry answered her, they were almost halfway there.

In the little café drive-thru, he ordered a café au lait with a single sugar packet. He ignored Sarah's smirk as he added it to his drink—knowing she was replaying his lecture he'd given her once about how Americans drank coffee so wrong. Sue him—he liked it this way. He was embracing their culture because as far as he knew, he was never going home.

He sipped on the hot drink and rubbed his thighs, which were starting to tremble again. "Just ask," he said after a long silence after he caught her staring.

"How many times did you fall?"

"Just the once." It was technically a triumph, but he didn't want to tell her how the sound of his hands hitting the mat had catapulted him right back to that night. He could still feel the last vestiges of that panic rippling over his skin. "Chris was right there."

"That's good. He's probably going to send you home with a more permanent cane next week," she said as she turned to corner toward his condo. He grimaced, and she reached over and smacked him over his pec. "Make that face all you want, but it'll be good for you."

"*Ben voyons*," he said, sarcasm dripping from his tone. "It's just a nice reminder that I'm not even forty but living like I'm ninety-eight."

She laughed and shrugged. "Better than last week when you said you were a hundred and two." When he didn't laugh, she sobered and quickly pulled into the parking lot of their condo building. She shut the car off, and before he could reach for the door, she turned to him. "You're doing amazing, okay? You've made more progress than a lot of people, and that's saying something."

Blowing out a frustrated breath of air, he nodded because he knew she was right, and he knew she would never lie to him, because there was no point. Sarah had never wanted anything from him other than his company, and there were days he still struggled to believe this was real.

"I know."

"So trust me when I say that this will help. You won't use it all the time, just like you won't use your wheelchair all the time. But they're meant to make your life more accessible. Not less." She reached out and laid a hand to the crook of his neck, and he tried not to lean into it, but he was so fucking touch starved for affection—casual or intimate. "Try to remember that everyone here telling you what to do is doing it because they want you to be happy."

And that was certainly a concept, and he believed her.

"Come on," Sarah said, opening her door. "Let's get you shit, showered, and shaved."

Reaching between his legs, he unfolded his cane and carefully climbed out of the car while she took his coffee. "Why do you always say that? It's such a vulgar phrase."

"My brother used to say it after he went into basic," she said. She grabbed his bag out of the back, then walked around to the side of the car and locked the doors after him.

"Basic?"

"Army," she said. "They had a limited time in the bathroom, so they had to shit, shower, and shave in like five minutes. Maybe longer—I don't know. He's a chronic exaggerator."

Thierry followed her to the elevator and waited for her to push the button. The only thing he really knew about her family is that her brother had been injured while he was deployed overseas, and helping him recover was enough that she changed her degree and became a licensed therapist. He appreciated the rough, sarcastic relationship she had with him because it meant she hadn't handled Thierry like he was made of glass.

She wasn't afraid to laugh at him, or let him cry, or scream. She didn't let him spiral too far, but she also gave him room for bad days. She didn't tell him he'd hike mountains again, but she reminded him there were some mountains he could carefully walk up.

And that was enough.

Thierry dug his keys out of his bag, then opened the door and let her in. She walked right to the bathroom to start his shower, giving him time to breathe a little and check his messages. He had a little desk in the corner of his living room, and his laptop was open to the email he'd gotten about the interview.

The client who needed a chef was being booked through their PA—someone who required an NDA, which wasn't uncommon with the company he was working for now. He felt a little nervous walking into the situation without even an inkling of who they were, but most likely it was some millionaire CEO of a company who pretended to be green and friendly but still took bonuses while they cut ten percent of the staff at the end of the fiscal year.

But he wasn't going in this to do something moral. He was going into this to prove that he was ready to take this new life by the horns and decide the direction he was going in.

No more friends like Hervé.

No more jobs that put him at risk.

No more believing that his only worth was protecting others—even at the expense of himself.

And no fucking more putting his needs second.

"Shower's ready," Sarah called, interrupting his mental tirade.

Pushing back in his desk chair, he eased up to his feet and made his way into his bedroom, using the wall for balance.

Sarah was standing in the bathroom doorway wearing a big grin, waggling her eyebrows.

"What?" he asked, eyeing the suit that was lying on the bed for him to change into.

"I'm just trying to remember that phrase you taught me. *Cul comme…peach?*"

"*Pêche.*" Thierry rolled his eyes, blushing just slightly as he walked past her. "Are you going to watch me undress?"

"Dude, come on, don't prude out on me. I've seen way more than your pretty little peach," she said. "Besides, I want to use all those sexy French words tonight when I go out with Hailey. She's gonna help me get laid."

"Trust me, that phrase will not get you laid," he told her as he pulled his shirt over his head. His fingers automatically went to the knot of scars on his stomach where the bullet had exited his body. "Now…if you don't mind."

She threw up her hands and backed away. "Fine, fine. But if you need me, just yell. I'm going to go rearrange your kitchen."

"Don't—" he started to call after her, but she slammed the door in his face, and he sank onto the toilet to finish undressing.

It was a frustratingly slow process the way it always was after PT, but he eventually got his socks and sweats off and tossed into his laundry basket. He grabbed the handle on the shower and eased under the hot spray. He didn't mind how hard it beat down on his shoulders as he braced his hands against the tiles and let it soak him.

He could hear Sarah puttering around through the thin walls as he indulged just a few precious minutes before he had to get washing up. As the bubbles trickled down his back, he bent over as far as he could and scrubbed off his legs, then in between his toes.

Nothing about his life was particularly pretty, but he did

find a sort of elegance at how routine it had all become. And he really couldn't deny the little flickers of pride as he finished his shower, dried himself off, and got dressed without needing to call for help.

Just as he was finishing his buttons on the shirt, his bedroom door opened with a loud creak, and he turned his head to find Sarah there with a grin on her face.

She gave him a wink as he approached the bed, her finger on her chin as she stared at his suit. "Shouldn't you go with a chef's...whatever? You know, that fancy shirt and pants they wear?"

"Unless the person has a..." He closed his eyes, reaching for the word. He'd been speaking English since he was a child—having lived in Brighton until he was ten—but he often lost modern slang. "When someone is sexually aroused by one specific thing?"

She laughed. "A fetish?"

"*Ouais*. A fetish...unless the person has a fetish for chef's whites, I don't think it'll be necessary. And if they do, I'm not sure I want that job."

She laughed and ruffled his hair, making him groan. "Please, you know that would be hot as hell." She walked up behind him as he turned back to the mirror on his dresser and began to reorder his hair. "Oh, Chef, do it to me," she groaned like a bad porn. "Stuff me like a turkey."

He gently elbowed backward, sending her laughing and tumbling down onto his bed. "*Cochon!*"

"You love it," she said sweetly. She picked herself up, then walked over to the bathroom and wrinkled her nose. "Anyway, *you're* the piggy. Look at this mess!"

"Did you check the traffic?" he asked, ignoring her. "I don't think they're going to consider my resume if we're late. Even if the traffic is shit."

Pulling out her phone, she tapped on the screen for a few seconds. "We're good. No accidents," she turned from the doorway, a few stray locks of hair having escaped her bun. "Fuck, I can't wait for you to finish your driving classes though. You know I hate the freeway."

He felt only the smallest surge of guilt, tempered by the fact that she was the one who insisted on driving him everywhere. The last time he tried to call an Uber, she'd yelled at him for half an hour. The pizza-and-wine nights, the snuggles on his sofa with bad American '80s movies—she claimed those as payment, and he felt almost spoiled.

Sarah headed out to pull the car up to the front as Thierry loaded up his small carrying case with his knife set, some cooking spoons, and a single ceramic pan. He wasn't sure if his resume was going to be enough or if the client was going to want a demonstration. And he damn well knew he'd better come somewhat prepared.

A couple of the chefs at the agency told him to prepare a simple spice kit to take with him, and the clients usually handled the rest. But he was worried they were going to take one look at him and send him packing.

He half considered bringing his wheelchair because his legs were feeling weak. Fuck, Sarah was right, and he hated when she was right about stuff like that. But he knew he wasn't far from accepting his life as complete and whole exactly the way it was now. He just needed to make sure potential employers saw him as worthy of that.

He knew he deserved the chance, no matter how bad his past had been.

He was a little more morose when he made his way down to the curb, but she ignored his attitude as she stored his supplies and he got back into the car. It was likely she chalked it all up to nerves, and he was in no mood to correct her on that. She'd only give him a lecture about his worth as a person and how getting work might be hard but he could do it.

Blah fucking blah.

He'd heard it a thousand times from his parents, from his therapist, from himself when he gave his morning pep talks to the mirror.

None of that could stand in the face of the potential rejection he was heading into. And he didn't have the energy to explain it all to people who would never be in his shoes.

EXITING THE FREEWAY, Thierry was relieved to see they were ten minutes ahead of schedule, which meant he could take his time getting out of the car and double-checking the bag to make sure it was fully stocked. He only felt the smallest pulse of intimidation when they passed through the massive gates to the absurdly rich community of homes.

He'd never been up that way. The nicest place he'd ever visited was the house Hervé had been sharing with Pietro, and he was glad to know they were on the opposite side of the city from where that man lived.

Sarah came to a stop in front of one of the smaller houses on the street, though it was still a mini mansion. He shoved back his nerves and gave a sharp nod. "You'll wait here?"

"Not going anywhere. I've been saving up one of my webcomic updates for an afternoon just like this," she said with a wink.

He swallowed thickly, trying to muster a smile for her, but he couldn't. Instead, he put all of his focus into making sure his legs were steady, that his cane wasn't loose, and that his bag was properly packed and nothing had fallen out.

The biggest crime in the world would be losing his little sachet of salt and having to serve something bland. In that case, he'd deserve to be blackballed from the entire market.

Taking one last look behind him, Thierry squeezed the rubber grip and began the trek to the front door. The agency had made sure the client's house was accessible by chair if it ever became necessary, and he was grateful to see there was only a small slope upward from the driveway to the little covered patio.

The place didn't seem very lived-in. It was perfectly manicured in the front, but there were no homey touches. He missed that about France. Even in the poshest neighborhoods outside of the big city, there was always life in their homes.

Americans were so focused on how things looked, they forgot to pay attention to how they felt.

Rolling his shoulders a few times, he reached out and rang the bell. He could hear it beyond the door, a sort of hollow, pretentious gong that echoed off what he assumed were probably gaudy marble floors and columns. He gripped his cane tighter, annoyed that his hand was sweaty, and he tapped his fingers in an off-beat rhythm.

Maybe no one was home. Maybe someone was looking out the peephole and decided not to answer when they saw him. Maybe...

The door opened with an honest-to-God groan, like an old haunted house, and a man with thick eyebrows and a familiar face appeared. He gave Thierry a long once-over, then folded his tattooed arms over his chest. "Are you soliciting for charity?"

Thierry bit back a string of curses. "I'm here for an interview."

"*You're* the chef?" the guy asked.

"Last time I checked," Thierry shot back. He said a small prayer that this was not the man he would be working for.

"Well," the guy said after a beat, blowing out a puff of air, "you're certainly French enough. Come on in. Interview's being held in the kitchen."

"Are you the..." Thierry started as he stepped over the slight bump in the doorway and onto tiled floors. He lost his train of thought as he took in the immense room with the vaulted ceilings and bare walls.

"...upstairs, but he'll be down in a minute," the guy was saying. "Kitchen's this way, and I assume you got your NDA and all that shit signed."

"Ah, *oui*," Thierry said absently as he followed the tall man down a corridor and through a massive arch that led to a wide kitchen. There was a ton of counter space, but as predicted, it would be far too tall for him if he had to work in his wheelchair.

"Would you like something to drink?" the man asked.

Thierry stared at him. He'd missed most of the conversation, but he was pretty sure that man wasn't the owner of the house, and he sure as hell didn't look like a PA. At least, not if the ridiculously expensive Bulova watch on his wrist was anything to go by.

He was leaning on the counter with something like amusement in his gaze, waiting for Thierry to answer.

"*Non, merci.*"

The guy nodded. "So, like, how would you even work? Sorry for being an asshole, but you don't seem very steady on your feet."

Thierry took a breath to tell the man exactly where he could shove that question, but before he could, a voice sounded through the echoing corridor. "Scooter, are you being a dick down here? Because Kelly said this guy is the only one who answered the ad, and..."

Thierry froze because in spite of how much time had passed, he doubted he'd ever forget that voice. His blood turned to ice as a shadow appeared and then the last man in the world he ever wanted to see.

Pietro was smiling until he reached the doorway. His gaze fell on Thierry, and his eyes narrowed. "Oh, fuck me. Oh *hell* no. You can't fucking be in my kitchen right now."

The other man—Scooter, apparently—went wide-eyed. "Dude, you can't talk to a guy like that just because he's walking with a cane!"

"I don't give a fuck about his *cane*," Pietro hissed, taking two steps forward. His hands were balled into fists at his sides like he was going to start swinging, and Thierry's heart began to race with something bright.

Like anticipation.

Scooter let out a nervous laugh. "Dude, can you calm down? What the fuck is going on?"

"Oh, nothing. I guess I just didn't expect to see the guy who fucking told Hervé I was cheating on him, then knocked my front teeth out standing in my goddamn kitchen," Pietro spat. He seemed to reconsider the whole punching thing, and he crossed his arms over his chest. "James, meet Thierry. The reason everything in my life went to hell."

CHAPTER THREE

If you asked his brother, Gabriel would gladly tell anyone who was willing to listen that Pietro had always been a drama queen. He never passed up an opportunity to be the center of attention or to twist the narrative to make everything seem much worse than it already was.

Most of the time, that was true.

And as the words "everything in my life went to hell" passed his lips, he knew he was doing it again. But it was hard to help it when the last person in the world he expected to see in his kitchen was Thierry Bourget. It had taken everything in him not to clock him in the fucking eye and send him home without a job and a nice new shiner to nurse.

He wanted it to hurt for as much and as long as getting his teeth knocked out and capped had.

He would also be a liar if he said it wasn't the cane that stopped him. In a way, it was more surprised than it was anything else to see Thierry on his feet. He had deliberately not kept up on what happened to the man after the incident with the shooting, but the last he'd heard, Thierry was paralyzed.

Seeing him standing in Pietro's kitchen had shaken him more than he was willing to admit.

He couldn't deny his anger or his confusion at seeing the man there. He'd always known that Thierry had wanted to be a chef, but with everything between them, why had he decided to come apply for this job? And why the fuck was he in the States, let alone in Denver?

"Okay," James said, interrupting the tension in the room. "I think everyone needs a breath. This guy here's all red in the face."

Pietro's eyes widened when he saw that Thierry's chest was almost hitching with his breath. "Woah, okay, hey. What's going on?"

Thierry took several seconds before he answered. "I...my blood pressure's high. *Pardon.*" He gripped his cane and turned around, and Pietro stood on edge because it felt like there was something seriously wrong.

He glanced up at James, who mouthed, 'What is going on?'

Pietro shrugged and wondered if he was going to have to, like, call 9-1-1 or something. *Fuck.*

After a short forever, Thierry finally turned back around, and his face had lost some of the high, bright color. "Sorry. It happens sometimes. My body's still adjusting to my injury, and I thought..." He didn't finish his sentence, and Pietro wasn't brave enough to ask him to. "I didn't realize the interview was for you. I should go..."

"Wait," Pietro said. It was mostly desperation with maybe a little curiosity, but Thierry really was the only chef who had answered the ad, and things were getting dire and a bit tragic. "You're...a chef now?"

"I'm hardly much use as a bodyguard these days," Thierry said dryly, tapping his cane on the floor for emphasis.

If the situation hadn't been so fucked, Pietro might have

laughed. He actually did manage a smile though, and he leaned against the counter before glancing at James. "Can you go find something else to do?"

James looked between the both of them. "Are you two going to beat the shit out of each other?"

Pietro scoffed. "We're grown men..."

"One of whom already knocked teeth out," James pointed out.

Pietro dragged a hand down his face. "Will you please fuck off? I didn't even ask you to be here today."

Making a face, his friend strolled out of the room, and only when he was gone did Pietro see a line of tension leave Thierry's shoulders.

"I thought he might try to fight me for your honor," Thierry muttered after a beat.

Pietro laughed. "That dude won't fight for the honor of anything except soft pretzels and Idris Elba. Besides, not to be patronizing or anything, but I don't think anyone on any professional sports team is going to make a habit out of knocking out a guy walking with a cane. Do you want, like, a stool or something?"

Thierry's face darkened. "I...yes, thank you."

Grabbing a barstool, he walked it over to the man and deliberately didn't watch him ease himself down, but he was glad Thierry was finally sitting. Pietro could only imagine the headlines if Thierry really did collapse. Disabled man found unconscious in star MLB player's kitchen. It was all he'd need—the cherry on a shit-sundae of a year.

With a breath, he walked over to his little beer cooler and pulled two bottles out, turning back to the other man. "I have this or wine," he offered, "and I don't know about you, but I'm not sure I can get through this without a drink."

Thierry watched him for a long second, then shrugged. "I'll take the beer."

Cracking the tops off, he handed one over, then walked to one of the other barstools and sat. There was a complicated war of emotions in him, and part of him wanted to just cancel the afternoon because he had not signed up for this. But he also knew he couldn't just let an opportunity slip by him. The reality was the ad had been up for two months now, and he hadn't gotten a single call.

Things were getting desperate.

"Would you actually take a job if I offered you one?" he finally made himself ask.

Thierry took a long swallow of his beer before he answered. "Yes."

"Yes?" Pietro couldn't help his surprise. "Just like that?"

"Do you need more explanation?" the man fired back at him. "It's a job I'm interested in. I wouldn't have come all this way if it wasn't."

"Yeah, but..."

Thierry stared at him expectantly. "Are you having trouble with your English?"

Pietro scowled. "No, you asshole, but you fucking hate me. You literally destroyed my relationship. And then you punched me."

Thierry was quiet for a long time, and then he leaned forward over his thighs, the bottle hanging loosely from his fingers. "I do owe you an apology for that."

"I should fucking say so," Pietro couldn't help but snap. He took an angry drink and almost choked on it. "I wasn't goddamn cheating on him."

"No, but he was cheating on you."

The words were almost like a slap to the face, and Pietro hated that they hurt, even after this long. Even after coming to realize he had never really loved Hervé. He took a slow breath and shrugged. "I can't say I'm surprised. But it's kind of fucked-up you punched *me* instead of *him*."

Thierry closed his eyes in a slow blink, then leaned toward the counter and set his beer down. "I should leave. There's too much past between us."

"You need this job though," Pietro pointed out, hopping to his feet. "Am I right?"

There was pain in Thierry's face. "I'll figure something out. When your friend pointed out that cooking here would be... complicated for me, he was right. I don't always work on my feet. I need to use my wheelchair sometimes."

Pietro glanced around and realized that was more than true. The counters were tall even for him. But...Thierry had to have known that. He had to have known whatever job he was showing up to wasn't going to have a kitchen built for a man like him.

"If you want the job, it's yours," Pietro said.

Thierry looked at him, blinked, then shook his head. "No."

Unable to mask his surprise, Pietro took three steps closer before Thierry flinched, and he stopped. "What do you mean *no*?" he demanded. "You want a fucking job."

"You can't just offer it to me like this," Thierry shot back. "This was supposed to be a job interview. I don't want the offer out of pity."

Pietro's mouth opened and closed because...was that what he was doing? Was it pity? Desperation? Or was it a strange need to cling to something familiar? Thierry had already seen him at his worst—kneeling on the ground spitting blood and curses as his shitty ex laughed in his face. It couldn't get much worse than that. He didn't have to pretend to be some snob who was too good for cooking.

He could tell Thierry his brain was just a bag of wet, angry cats on a good day, and he was tired of surviving off takeout and the microwave.

Hell, if there was any pity to be passed around, it should be for him.

"Come back," Pietro said.

Thierry's brows furrowed. "*Putain*, I haven't actually left yet. I'm sitting right..."

"No," Pietro interrupted. "I mean, go home and figure out if you really can work for me without any of this shit from the past affecting you. And if you can work in my kitchen. Then come back, and do the damn interview. Make me...make me a fucking omelet or something. And if it sweeps me off my feet, you have the job. That's what I would have asked anyone else to do."

Thierry's face was unreadable, and then there was light in his eyes. It was so subtle, if Pietro hadn't been staring so hard, he might have missed it. "Promise you'll see other candidates too."

Pietro laughed—he couldn't help it. But when he saw the hurt on Thierry's face, he held up his hand. "I'm not laughing at you, man. Just...I've had this ad up forever, and you're the first person who answered it."

Thierry softened. "Ah."

Ah. The sound was short and probably not meant to be offensive, but it hurt Pietro's feelings which were just a little bit delicate lately. "Yeah. Ah. I can't even seem to fucking *throw* money at people these days. But look, if a better offer comes along for you..."

"I won't hesitate to take it," Thierry said. "Hervé was wrong—I was wrong about what happened before. But that doesn't mean I like you."

For whatever reason, that set the last of Pietro's nerves to rest, and he smiled wide enough that his cheeks hurt. "That's all I wanted to hear. Redo?"

"I'll be in touch" was all Thierry said, and then he gently climbed off the stool, steadied himself on his cane, grabbed his bag, and started toward the kitchen door. Pietro didn't mean to watch, but he couldn't help noticing the way Thierry moved now—slow, deliberate, careful. Nothing like the man who had quietly hovered in the shadows when he was guarding Hervé. Nothing like the man who had stormed across a club dance floor and clocked him in the face.

This was a man whose entire life had been shattered, and Pietro couldn't begin to know what that was like. His brother did, of course, but he knew if he called Gabriel for advice on how to feel about this, his brother would only make the ugly, dark emotion welling in his chest even worse.

He waited 'til he heard the front door slam, and he wasn't surprised when he heard James' footsteps a few minutes later.

"Damn, that was fast. Do you have a new chef or what?" James asked, walking into the room. He eyed the beer Thierry left behind, then grabbed it.

"You have no fucking shame," Pietro said as he dropped back down to the stool he'd vacated.

James rolled his eyes and finished off the last half of the bottle. "Shame would be letting this gorgeous microbrew go to waste." Swiping his mouth with the back of his hand, he tossed the bottle into recycling, then leaned on the counter in front of Pietro. "And you didn't answer my question."

"He's coming back," Pietro said, staring down at his hands. "He's going to, uh...he's going to go home and decide if he really wants to interview for this job. For me," he clarified. He let out a helpless laugh. "Then he'll, I don't know—what do personal chefs do? Audition? And I'll fucking hire the man who knocked my front teeth out because no one else is interested in the job."

"You're a fucking disaster, man." James slapped his hand on the counter lightly. "But that's why I love you." He went quiet for a moment. "Do you really think this is a good idea though? You and Hervé..."

"Hervé isn't involved anymore," Pietro quickly defended. He didn't know why he felt the need to come to Thierry's defense. Maybe because his ex had fucked them both over, and he knew what that pain was like. "He apologized."

"Yeah," James said from behind a breath. "You think he means it?"

Pietro stared past his friend, eyes going fuzzy like maybe he could almost—almost—see into the future. "I don't really know. But I think he at least knows I wasn't in the wrong."

He wasn't sure if that was enough, but it was at least a start.

CHAPTER FOUR

There was nothing like the roar of the crowd as Pietro stepped up to bat. His ankle had been giving him shit after rolling it on his last attempt to slide into third at the top of the seventh, but it was nothing an ice pack and a couple of hours on the massage table wouldn't fix when it was over. The game wasn't exactly a throwaway, but they were at the bottom of the ninth and up by six. The Huskies were fucking tired, and his team was already riding high on the edge of their assumed win.

He glanced down the line at Coulter, who had the fucking audacity to wink at him, tossing the ball into the air and rolling his wrist. Pietro gathered spit into his cheek, then shot it between his teeth as he approached the plate and spread his legs. He grimaced at the twinge in his foot and looked over at the empty first base, then down the line where Scooter was perched between second and third.

The Huskies' outfield was at their peak that night, which meant he could either try for a home run, which didn't feel likely, or keep the ball low and aim for O'Connell on third, who looked like he was nursing his elbow. The injury was about as subtle as his ankle, but Pietro had always had an eye for shit like that.

He knew wasn't batting well enough for a home run, but he could get Scooter home.

He spit again and tapped his helmet once, twice, a third time. He heard Brandt mutter something behind him, but Pietro had long since learned to tune out the catcher. That was a little league habit that was cooked out of him after several fights and four suspensions.

He tested the balance of the bat, the weight of his own body as he bent his knees. He flexed his toes and grimaced at the pain shooting up his calf. He was fucked if he couldn't get the ball past O'Connell.

The first ball flew past him, and he took a step back.

"Strike one!"

He spit, then rolled his neck. Coulter winked again, and Pietro fought the urge to blow a kiss at the fucker just to see what he'd do. He'd hit on Pietro more than once during the off-season, but Coulter just wasn't his type. Pitchers were always fucking weird and touchy, and Pietro had enough of that shit in his life from his brother.

The bat hovered over his shoulder, and he gently circled it as he waited. He saw Coulter's body twist in the way he always did right before he threw a submarine pitch his way. Not everyone could hit them—but Pietro could.

He dropped his stance and swung.

The crack was more than satisfying as the ball went sailing past O'Connell. As predicted, he reached with his glove, then pulled back just enough because he was hurt. Pietro took enough time to make sure Scooter was hauling ass, and began his run.

The ball had made it to first long before his foot touched

the plate, and Jackie gave him a frown as he tapped him with the back of his glove. "You good, man?"

Pietro shook his head with a grin. "You know how it is." He wasn't going to give himself away, but Jackie was a good dude, and he wasn't about to tell the man to go fuck himself, either. He tried not to hobble as he made his way back to the box, and he could see his manager staring at him with narrowed eyes.

"You wanna tell me what the fuck that was?" Weber demanded as Pietro finally gave in to the pain and hobbled the few steps down.

He could feel Weber behind him as he flopped onto the bench and leaned his head back. "Ankle's busted."

Just then, James came stomping down the steps and shoved Pietro to the side as he flopped next to him. "Is it broken?"

"You knew?" Weber demanded.

"You didn't see that shit?" James fired back, leaning forward.

Pietro laid his hand on his friend's arm. "I rolled it sliding into third. I don't think it's broken."

"Get your ass out of here," Weber said. He pulled out his phone and began to talk at a rapid-fire pace as he exited the box.

"Just go. Get that shit wrapped up," James told him, giving him a shove. "You need a hand up, grandpa?"

Pietro flipped him off and quietly tried to exit without making too much of a stir. There was no doubt it would be noticed and blasted all over radio and TV, but he'd have answers by then. They were midway through the season, and there was no fucking way he was letting a little twisted ankle throw him off like some Victorian debutante.

It wasn't long before he was sitting on the table with his ankle wrapped and the fattest fucking ice pack he'd ever seen strapped to it. The X-ray had already been ordered which meant there was no chance of him going right home and slipping immediately into his bath, which had been the original plan.

He tried not to feel disappointed, especially because he'd found a nice queue of porn he hadn't seen yet, and there was nothing better than rubbing one out after a good win, then soaking to his neck in lavender Epsom salt bubbles.

"Quit staring at me like I'm about to put your dog down," Carson said as he finished tucking in the loose end of the bandage. The man had worked as an EMT for years before going back to school for sports medicine, and he was practically team family at this point.

Mostly because he knew all the deep dark secrets of everyone on the Vikings, and they wanted to keep his lips tight shut and happy.

"I don't think it's broken," Carson went on as he propped a stray yoga block under Pietro's leg.

People tended to treat Pietro with kid gloves when it came to injuries. They all assumed he was paranoid because he'd seen what happened to his brother firsthand. They assumed he'd have a phobia of losing it all.

Of course, he couldn't lie and say that injuries didn't keep him up at night, but he was also well aware that life went on. That life didn't turn into a pit of fucking despair just because one thing ended. And maybe he was a little more touchy a few years before Gabriel had met Ezra, but since the pair had fallen in love, everything had changed.

"I'm not worried about it," he said, flopping back onto the table. The paper beneath him crinkled and made him think about when he and Gabe were kids, trying to hide behind the exam table to avoid getting shots. It never worked, and they always left a crying mess that no lollipop could soothe.

It had been years since he'd given a single shit about a needle stick.

"What's got your panties all twisted?" Carson asked him, rolling around the table on his little stool. "Or is it constipation. I know how you fucking eat."

Carson hit the nail on the head. Not the constipation part, but he didn't care about his damn ankle. He cared that it had been over a week and he hadn't heard a word from Thierry. He thought they'd had an understanding. He had Kelly call the company that was handling Thierry's employment, and they said he hadn't accepted another job, so now Pietro was just... left in limbo.

He felt a little foolish for getting so worked up about it. He really, really shouldn't want that man working for him.

"I'm trying to hire a personal chef," Pietro finally admitted. "My brother got me all spoiled on his boyfriend's food, and we all know I'm never going to master cooking."

Carson sighed. "If you need your dosage upped to help you concentrate better..."

"I don't," he said, his voice a little tense. He'd adjusted to the low dose of Kapvay alright. He wasn't getting headaches or dizzy spells anymore, and he wasn't in the mood to start the cycle all over again. Especially not now.

He had the World Series in his sights this year, and he wasn't going to let anything get in the way.

"What's the point of being ridiculously rich if I can't spend my money on luxury things like personal chefs?" he shot back.

Carson lifted his hands in surrender. "You want me to call a car for you? I just got a message that said they're ready at the lab."

He wished the fucking game was over so Scooter could drive him, but he knew he couldn't wait around that long. "Yeah. I'm gonna send Allie for my car later too, so tell

Weber to leave my shit at the front desk so she can grab my keys."

Carson offered a hand, and Pietro scooted to the end of the table and hopped down as the other man disappeared into the little supply closet and came out with a set of crutches. Pietro glowered at them, but he knew better than to fight. At least he was heading to the lab in a car instead of an ambulance.

At the very least, it took his mind off the looming question of whether or not Thierry was done with him and if the whole thing had just made him look like an even bigger, more pathetic ass.

CHAPTER FIVE

Thierry had never been a big dancer. He had hit his growth spurt early on in his childhood. When his parents moved back to Paris, he was the tallest kid in his class, and it took until he was sixteen to realize that was going to be his reality for the rest of his life.

He didn't mind it so much, but there were times he wondered what life would be like if he possessed the grace of men smaller than him. Thierry didn't mind being a protector. It was in his nature—it was like breathing. But sometimes it would have been nice to have someone take care of him for a change.

He relegated himself to the shadows—to dark corners where only the bravest people ventured. It led to a lot of dark closet and bathroom stall hookups, but those were not how romances were made. His heart grew cold as it grew lonely, but he knew better than to hope for a change.

He felt the same now—and maybe even worse—as they stepped into the Platinum Cat. Chris had his hand wrapped around Thierry's free arm, and they carefully made their way through the thick crowd.

Getting in hadn't been a problem, but the moment Thierry got a good look around, he knew this place wasn't for him. He could barely maintain a steady gait let alone join the crowd even though he was free to dance. It meant curling up in a booth with a single drink, watching the world turn around him.

Just like always.

"I'm going to go order," Chris yelled in his ear. "Can you find us a place to sit?"

They had VIP access thanks to Chris' cousin, so he made his way to the platform where all the booths sat. He flashed the little bracelet at the bouncer letting people past the rope, and he managed to find a nice table shaped like a C, facing the crowd. He folded up his cane and tucked it beside him as he sank into the plush faux leather. He fixed his eyes on the crowd and watched them—almost mesmerized—as they moved almost like a single thought to the thrumming beat.

He lost himself in it until Chris appeared with two drinks in his hand. They were short glasses, a single sphere of ice in the center of a dark amber liquid. He had no doubt the drinks were expensive, and no doubt the drinks were *good*.

Curling his hand around it, he took a sip and let himself savor the burn. "Do you want to dance?" he asked after a beat.

Chris looked at him with wide eyes. "You want to get out there?"

Thierry couldn't help his laugh. "*Mais non*! I'm going to sit here and rest my back. But you go. Have fun."

Chris' face darkened. "I came to hang out with you..."

"And you can. But go dance first. What's the point of paying all this money?" Thierry insisted. And he meant it. It didn't matter that being alone would sting. It helped knowing his friend was having a good time.

Chris hesitated until Thierry threatened to hit him with his cane, so he wandered off with a promise to be back soon. Thierry wasn't going to hold him to it. No, he was just going to sip this top-shelf whiskey and deliberately not think about how fucked his day had been and the decision he was being asked to make.

"Seat taken?"

Thierry hadn't realized how much time had passed until he heard a voice speak from his left. He glanced down at his glass first, which was empty, then to the stranger who wasn't a stranger at all. He was the man from the interview. Scooter...or, James, he supposed.

"Are you here to punch me for Pietro's honor?" he asked.

James threw his head back and laughed. "Should I? I mean, I heard his side of the story."

Being a man of manners, Thierry gestured to the seat across from him, and James took it with a happy grin on his face. "It's probably the same as my story. I was his ex's bodyguard. Hervé told me to punch him...so I did."

"And you told Hervé that Petey was cheating on him?" James pointed out.

Petey. The name almost made him want to smile, it was so wrong and so absurd. "I told him it was likely."

"Why?" James didn't sound angry—just curious. He leaned his elbow on the table, then reached out and snatched Thierry's empty glass up and drank what was left of the whiskey dredges and melted ice. "Gross."

"So says the man who drinks from a stranger's glass," Thierry pointed out.

James smiled again, shrugged, then lifted his hand and

signaled for more service. "So, are you denying my accusation?"

"Is that what it was?" Thierry asked. He fell silent when a server approached, and he didn't put up a fight when James ordered two more of the same drink, though he doubted he could afford to drink like that all night. "I'm not denying anything," Thierry said when they were finally alone.

James sighed, though Thierry couldn't hear it, but he saw the man's shoulders rise and fall. "That was fucked-up, you know, but I can't really be angry at you. I mean, I can for the whole punching thing. But Hervé was fucking toxic, and it seems like he was a massive dick-weasel to you too."

Thierry licked his lips and nodded because he knew. He'd dedicated his entire professional life—sacrificed everything personal—all to be dismissed after saving Hervé from an untimely death. He'd been permanently disabled and discarded, and the truth of his reality was so bitter, it clung to his throat.

"Why did you do it?" James asked. His voice was so soft, Thierry mostly had to read his lips.

He hesitated before he shrugged and decided honesty was the best policy. "I was an asshole back then. I'm trying to be better now."

James stared, then laughed, his smile only getting wider as the drinks were delivered. "Thanks, Holls. Keep 'em coming, yeah?"

"Wait," Thierry said as James tipped his drink back. The man looked at him with raised brows. "I can't afford to keep drinking like this."

James' smile was toothy and almost terrifying. "I own this place. We can drink however the fuck we want."

"Is Pietro here tonight?"

James looked almost concerned for a second. "Nah. Fucker

busted his ankle pretty bad at the game tonight, so he's at home sleeping it off."

Thierry didn't know what to make of the little twisted feeling in his stomach. "I hope he's okay."

"He'll be fine. He's a giant, dramatic baby when it comes to getting injured."

Thierry very much doubted that. The man had taken the punch like he was born to do it—like he'd done it too many times. "Tell him—if you see him..."

"You tell him," James interrupted. He glanced over his shoulder at the sound of a shout, then sighed. "Look, drinks are on me, okay? But only if you promise you're going to show up for this job. He..." James stopped, then licked his lips and shook his head. "He's probably my best friend, and I'm not even sure he knows that because he doesn't feel like he deserves people who care about him. And I hate that for him because he's a fucking good guy. He needs more than a chef."

"I can't be more," Thierry said, his voice thick and bitter.

James shrugged. "You may surprise yourself. But if it helps at all, take the job because you're not going to find a man who gives a shit more than Petey Bassani."

With that, James gave the table a pat and left before Thierry could say another word. The conversation settled on his bones, heavy like they held the weight of the world, and it didn't take him long to finish his drink and decide he had better things to do with his night than sit around and wish for all the rest he couldn't have.

***

THIERRY MANAGED to convince Chris to leave early, and he was back in his place, wearing sweats instead of the too-tight jeans, nursing a cup of tea well before midnight. He felt a little ridiculous and a lot old, but he didn't mind it so much. He hadn't really planned on trying to meet anyone, and even if he had, James' words were bouncing around his skull the moment he was on his own.

There was a tinge of guilt that rippled through him shortly after because he really had been avoiding Pietro. He'd promised to go home and think about what the job would really mean to him, and then he'd promptly spent the last week avoiding anything to do with the baseball player. At least, anything except stealing glances of him on ESPN every time he could catch highlights of the game.

But that wasn't fair to either of them. Pietro needed a chef, and Thierry needed a job, and he wanted to believe he could be the bigger man and move past all the shit that was left in the past.

He was finally settling into bed, dealing with that small existential crisis when his phone started to buzz with a series of texts. His heart jumped a little in his chest, because what if it was Pietro? What if he was letting him know the position was filled?

What if he wanted an answer now?

It took him a full three minutes to be brave enough to check, and when he did, his veins turned to ice.

Hervé: I'm at the airport. Can I come see you?

Thierry stared at the screen in a numb sort of shock, not quite sure what he was reading wasn't some moment of broken sanity. The last he'd seen of Hervé's face was just before he hit the club floor. He hadn't shown up to the hospital during his recovery, he hadn't called, he hadn't sent any messages.

Thierry's former boss, Marcel, let him know that Hervé

terminated his contract with the company a week after Thierry woke up from his second surgery, and that was that.

Thierry had laid eyes on him just once more, through a photograph that was circulating through the media. Hervé was leaning on the railing of a yacht off the coast of Nice, a drink in his hand, a petit man on his arm. It was business as usual.

Hervé had almost been murdered, Thierry's life had been turned upside down, and the only evidence was the wheelchair waiting for Thierry to accept it, almost as necessary as a new limb.

Thierry: What do you want?

Hervé: To say sorry to your face. Not over text. Marcel told me you were living here now.

Tapping his fingers on the side of the phone, he contemplated telling the man to go fuck himself. Hervé had always been a selfish bastard. It was evident from a young age when Hervé realized that Thierry really would stick by him no matter what. He turned their friendship into a glorified man for hire, sending Thierry to torment and beat the shit out of all the boys who had once bullied the smaller man.

Hervé would spend hours crying with his head buried in Thierry's lap. "No one will ever love me. I always come second. I'm never important enough."

Thierry had never been the sort of man who wore his heart on his sleeve, but a small part of him believed that he could love Hervé through it. That if he just stuck by him long enough, if he proved himself loyal enough, Hervé would believe that he was worthy.

He hadn't realized how conditional it all was.

How easily Thierry would be discarded—when all was said and done. He wasn't quite sure Hervé deserved his moment to apologize.

Hervé: I know I've been a bastard. Please. I won't stay long.

Thierry: Fine. You can have ten minutes.

Hervé: I'll be there in an hour at most.

Thierry was a fool, but he had embraced that about himself long ago. He sent Hervé the address, then tried not to work himself into a small panic attack. When he stood up from the bed, his legs felt instantly like wet noodles, so he shuffled over to his wheelchair and sat.

He debated about calling Sarah to see if she was home, but instead, he just gripped his wheels and rolled through his little condo until an hour had gone by, and the buzzer to his front door was ringing.

He wiped sweaty palms on his jeans, then rolled to the door and opened it.

It wasn't often that anyone got to see Hervé looking the way he did as he stood in Thierry's doorway. His hair was flat and oily, his eyes heavy-lidded and surrounded by dark circles, his lips chapped. He was wearing expensive tight jeans and a thick sweater, the sleeves pulled over his hands, which meant he was nervous. Thierry wanted to take pleasure in seeing Hervé looking so low, but oddly, he couldn't.

"Well?" Thierry demanded.

Hervé looked over his shoulder and huffed. "Are you going to invite me inside?"

Thierry took his time debating, though he already knew he

was going to let the man in. He rolled back slowly, Hervé staring so hard his gaze felt like a physical touch, and he slammed the door hard enough to make the smaller man jump.

He felt a little good about that. He didn't want the man to get too comfortable.

"Do you want something to drink? I don't have any of your usual brands, but I have some beer and water," he started, rolling toward the kitchen.

"No." Hervé cleared his throat, glancing around as Thierry looked over his shoulder at him. "Marcel said you were walking again. He said you...that you had recovered."

"I can walk," he said, making his way to the kitchen. "But I'm still paralyzed, and on bad days, I use my chair."

"Thierry," Hervé breathed. He sounded different, though it wasn't enough for Thierry to trust him. "I'm..." He waited, and eventually Hervé let out a sigh. "Do you like it here? In this little...apartment?"

Thierry shrugged. Hearing his native tongue spoken so easily was almost like a taste of home, but hearing it in Hervé's voice was enough to ruin that small joy. "It was the first open place they could find that I didn't need to modify." He aborted his trip to the kitchen and instead rolled toward the window, gesturing to the sofa, though he wasn't sure he wanted Hervé to sit. "It's for elderly people, but it works for me."

Hervé's nose wrinkled. "Surely you can find somewhere else a bit nicer? More modern?"

"I don't have the money," Thierry snapped. "My parents have paid all of their savings for my private therapy, and the pathetic settlement I got after being shot is almost gone. You, of course, were not held liable, so I was just let go from my job."

Thierry still wasn't sure whether he blamed the man for

the incident or not. Hervé had been picking a fight with the stranger who shot at him, but Thierry was also doing his job when he'd taken the bullet. It was the risk—the inevitable fallout that every single one of the agents that worked with Thierry had accepted.

But it was hard not to be bitter when everyone else had gone back to their old lives except him.

Hervé stared down at his hands, taking a long, slow breath. "I haven't been able to sleep much since that night."

Thierry let out a small, bitter laugh. "Is that so? Well, you're not alone. Except it's usually the pain that keeps me up."

"I know you blame me for what happened…"

Thierry made a frustrated noise in the back of his throat. "I don't blame you for that. I blame the piece of pig shit that shot me in the stomach. I blame you for not showing up after. For firing me instead of seeing if I was going to live. You…you just… got on a yacht and went on a *vacation*," he spat.

Hervé made a small sound, almost like a sob, and Thierry was quickly losing patience for him. He was not going to let Hervé make this about him. Not this time. "I didn't know how to deal with it. You're my oldest friend in the world, and you took that bullet for me."

"I took it because it was my job," Thierry said. Once upon a time, he believed he would have taken it simply because he cared about his friend, but now, he wasn't so sure that was ever true. "Please don't think it was some self-sacrifice. I just thought…" He stopped and let out a long, slow breath. He was surprised at how quiet his anger was—how tepid. He wished he was in a rage instead of this dull resignation that Hervé was who he was. "Never mind what I thought. It didn't matter back then, and it certainly doesn't matter now."

Apathy, he decided, was oddly painful.

"I should have come to see you. I know that's unforgivable," Hervé said.

Thierry passed a hand down his face and then realized he didn't care about making Hervé suffer because he didn't really care much about him at all. "I've had a long while to come to terms with this new reality," he finally said, and he didn't back down when Hervé flinched. "My therapy is going slow, but it's helping."

At that, Hervé perked up and shifted to the edge of his seat. "Does that mean you'll go back to..."

"No," Thierry said. "No, I'll never go back to that life. I might be able to walk, but I'm still injured. For the rest of my life. It is what it is. And I'm learning to be happy."

"With *that*?" Hervé asked, gesturing at his wheelchair.

And now his temper rose. Thierry gripped his wheels, unlocked the brakes, and rolled forward. "Yes. With no help from you. And I don't really know what you want from me, Hervé. You can't just stroll back into my life after this long and expect me to absolve you of your guilt."

Hervé's jaw trembled, but for the first time since he'd met him, Thierry felt nothing. "I understand."

"Do you?" He sighed, then sat back. "Right before all this happened, we were here."

Hervé blinked. "Here?"

"In this city. You fucked one of the room service men who delivered you cheesecake, and the next night you had me punch your boyfriend in the face because you believed he was being unfaithful." Thierry knew he was leaving out the part where he'd been the one who got Hervé all worked up about Pietro cheating. It was not his finest moment. In fact, it was maybe one of his worst. "You weren't sorry when you found out that you were the only one in the relationship who was unfaithful."

"I believed *you*," Hervé said quietly. "When you lied and told me he was sleeping with other people."

Thierry nodded, staring down at his hands which were resting in his lap. "I know."

"Why did you say it?" Hervé asked. "I know you don't really believe it was true."

Thierry shook his head. "I don't know. Maybe because it was important to me that he was just as bad as you. Maybe the thought of him being just as big a bastard as you made it easier to stomach protecting your lies. Hiding all of your sins."

Hervé licked his lips. "I'm not a bad person."

At that, Thierry laughed, though he didn't mean to. He wasn't trying to be cruel. "You have never been a good one, either."

Hervé's cheeks pinked. "I'm trying! *Putain*! I don't know what else you want from me."

"Nothing," Thierry said, and his surprise was obvious in his tone. "I didn't ask you to come here. I didn't track you down when I realized you were just going to let me rot away at some hospital like the last fifteen years I spent at your side meant nothing."

Hervé swallowed thickly, his Adam's apple bobbing. "They were not nothing."

"But they were easily discarded to protect your feelings, and that's how it's always been. That's how it always will be." Thierry unclenched his hands and rolled back, gesturing for Hervé to stand up. "You should go."

Hervé didn't argue, but his steps toward the door were slow and hesitant. "I'm staying in town."

Thierry shook his head. "Don't..."

"I'm not a bad person," Hervé said. "I want to prove that, but I can't do it if I'm across the ocean."

Thierry pinched the bridge of his nose and let out a small sigh. "I don't have time for you."

"Make some," Hervé said, his tone more determined now—and that was terrifying, because more than anyone else, Thierry knew exactly how stubborn Hervé was capable of being. "I'll work around your schedule, and I'll prove to you that I understand what I did was a mistake. And that our friendship always meant something to me."

Thierry didn't believe him, but he was also too tired to argue anymore. "Do what you will," he finally said, laying his hand on the door. "Just keep your expectations low."

Hervé gave him a smile after that and a small wink as he took a few steps away from the door. "*Mon coeur*, if I did that, I wouldn't be where I am today."

Thierry quickly shut the door behind him, and though he knew he had a life to start, the frustration in his chest and the old ache of a failing friendship quickly eclipsed any hope of moving forward.

CHAPTER SIX

Thierry did what he always did when things got a bit too much. He shut down. He managed the walk from his living room into his bathroom to take care of his nightly routine—washing up, having a piss, brushing his teeth.

When he was done, he spread down pads on his mattress because his bladder control was still shaky. It was yet another reminder that miracles were nothing more than fairy stories people told themselves to feel better with their circumstances. They had helped, in the beginning. When he wanted to scream and cry and rage and give up. They were a light at the end of the tunnel that didn't really exist.

Anger came after that.

He was still working his way toward true acceptance, but seeing Hervé—oddly—had helped.

A small part of him had wondered what he'd do if he ran into the man some years down the road. Would he yell? Punch him the way he had done to Pietro? Would he have just ignored him like he meant nothing?

He wasn't quite sure he was proud of himself for the way

he handled the visit, because Hervé was still in town and Thierry hadn't shut him out entirely, but there was some relief in knowing the first part was over.

It was easier after that, to curl up under his weighted blanket and put the TV on. He didn't question himself this time when he turned on Sports Center and waited for the game highlights, because as much as his mind was still on Hervé, it was on Pietro too.

Seeing Hervé had momentarily distracted him from his decision at hand, but it had also lit a fire because his ex-boss and ex-friend was nothing more than a reminder he was ready to move on. He wasn't exactly sure Pietro would take him now that a week had passed with total silence, but he was pretty sure he was going to try.

Hell, he was damn sure of it.

He whispered a prayer into the universe as he pressed the phone to his ear, and when it rang until it reached voicemail, he allowed defeat to settle in his bones. Leaning back against his pillows, he stared at the TV which was on silent but playing highlights of the game. He had no idea what they were talking about, but he was sure they were discussing Pietro's apparent injury. All the clips were of him at the start, and then somewhere after the seventh inning, something happened.

Thierry stared at his face as the camera zoomed in on a close-up. His cheeks were a ruddy olive, glowing with sweat. His eyes were narrow, determined, focused. In short, he was almost like perfection.

He was rugged and raw—unlike all of the men Thierry had known while working for Hervé. Even in his off time when he was with Hervé, Pietro had never been fussy. He never spent more than five minutes in the bathroom, and yet he always managed to look like a classical demigod.

Maybe that's what had gotten under Thierry's skin.

Maybe he'd spent all those years resenting him because he...

Putain. He had *feelings*.

It couldn't be right. Reaching onto the nightstand, he grabbed the remote and turned the TV off before he shuffled back as far as his body would allow.

Bzzt!

Thierry almost cried out when his phone vibrated against the desk, the sound painfully loud. He snatched it up with trembling fingers, then hit the screen, and his eyes widened when he saw Pietro's number waiting with a text.

Pietro: Ça va?

Thierry smiled to himself even as a war of emotions collided in his chest. He'd been worked up and determined just minutes ago, ready to plead for another chance at this job. But now, facing the reality of asking for it—and the inevitable explanation as to why he'd taken his time, well...

Pietro: Missed your call. I've been at this hospital for a hundred years waiting for an X-ray right now. Can't talk.

Thierry: I know. I ran into your friend James tonight, and he told me you were injured. Sorry to hear it. I also wanted to apologize for not calling sooner.

Pietro: Is that your weird way of asking if the job is still open?

Thierry: Peut être.

Pietro: Don't tell me. I remember that one. Because?

Thierry: Maybe.

Pietro: Did anyone ever tell you that playing hard to get with a JOB is not the way to go? But if you must know, yes, it's still open. Still no line around the block trying to cook for me.

Thierry: Are you free this week?

Pietro: Looks like it. Fucked up my ankle real nice so I won't be playing until next week.

Thierry: I'm sure your team will miss you.

He very nearly typed out that he'd been watching the highlights, but he quickly managed to backspace and recover. That was something Pietro didn't need to know. It was something he never needed to know.

Thierry: Do you still want an omelet?

Pietro: LMAO, bro. I don't care. I've been eating Lean Cuisine. Just...surprise me.

Thierry had to do a quick Google search to find out what Lean Cuisine was, and what he found horrified him. The man was a professional sports player. What the hell was he doing? He quickly ran through his internal recipe index. He knew that Pietro was from an Italian family—the sort that passed down sauce recipes and all knew how to hand-roll gnocchi.

He also knew that Pietro couldn't cook any of that long before the man had admitted to being a disaster in the kitchen. Thierry had half expected the man to cook for Hervé in an attempt to impress him. Instead, they survived on delivery and five-star reservations at all the local spots that only celebrities like Pietro could get into.

Pietro: Did I scare you off?

Thierry: I'm coming up with a menu. I can be there on Thursday. That will give me time to pick up my supplies.

Pietro: Then I guess I'll see you soon.

Thierry: À bientôt.

Typing bubbles appeared on the screen, then disappeared, then appeared again. But when no text came through, Thierry turned his phone on silent and set it on the nightstand. He had PT the next day, which meant he could pick Chris' brain for what else he suggested to help him with the new job.

After that, he could figure out the rest.

He knew Pietro would give him the job, even if he served up bitter slop. Part of it was pity, but part of it was something else Thierry just hadn't quite figured out yet. He'd once thought the dark look in Pietro's eyes was from Hervé, but now...now, he wasn't so sure.

Closing his eyes, he felt a small well of satisfaction warming the cold void that had appeared since Hervé showed up at his door. He wasn't sure what would happen with his past still haunting his doorstep, but he wasn't ready to give up on a future, either.

CHAPTER SEVEN

"What time is he going to be here?"

Pietro turned and lifted his brows at Ezra, who was wandering around his kitchen, arranging and rearranging everything. Pietro had enlisted Ezra's help once Thierry had agreed to come back, just to make sure he had everything Thierry might need for the job.

Assuming he took it.

"He said he'd be here after four. He's getting a ride from someone," Pietro muttered as he watched Ezra shift the little dish holding the serving spoons for the fifteenth time. "Fuck's sake, just leave it!"

Ezra's hand snapped back, and when he spun around, his cheeks were pink. "Don't be a dick."

Pietro put his hands up in surrender. His brother didn't talk about all the starts and stops he had with Ezra much, but he knew that Gabriel had been an ass, and Ezra was still a little tender when it came to raised voices.

"Sorry. I'm just..."

"Nervous?" Ezra offered.

Pietro sank onto a barstool and buried his face in his hands. "Confused. Like why hasn't anyone else answered my ad, for one? But also, why did it have to be Thierry? I want to hug him and punch him, but the hugging part is because I feel fucking bad for him, and I know he'd hate that."

"You probably shouldn't punch him, either," Ezra pointed out. He grabbed the bottle of wine from the counter and poured two glasses, pushing one toward Pietro. "And not just because he was shot."

Pietro swung his annoying walking boot alongside the leg of the stool, snatching his glass up and taking a long drink. "He punched me first."

"It sounds to me like the whole situation was one, big, fucked-up mess," Ezra pointed out. Rightly, though that was also irritating. "And for what it's worth, your teeth barely look fake."

"Oh," Pietro said, giving him a wide, grimacing smile, "thanks."

Ezra snorted, and then his face brightened, which meant Gabriel had appeared behind Pietro. The younger man turned his body, opening himself up for the embrace that came shortly after, and Pietro looked away. He was more than happy for his brother, but it only served as a reminder that he was painfully alone and probably always would be.

Hookups were getting old, but all his friends said he needed to date within his world, and dating celebrities never worked out. Most of the guys on his team were on their third and fourth marriages.

He wanted something different—something soft and careful. His parents, who were overwhelmed with the sheer volume of children they had produced, still found time to love the shit out of each other even after this many years.

"That's plenty of PDA," Pietro grumbled.

Gabriel snorted, then reached over and plucked Ezra's glass from the counter, taking a small drink. "Is there anything else you need?"

Pietro blew out a puff of air and shrugged. "I don't know, man. I mean, I feel like I should hire someone to come in and tell me what to do."

"It can't possibly be that complicated," Gabriel said with a frown.

Pietro shrugged. "I don't actually know. I mean, he didn't tell me much besides sometimes he uses a wheelchair which he'd be SOL in this fucking kitchen on those days."

Ezra lifted a brow. "I think the only thing someone would advise you on is a kitchen remodel."

"What kind of kitchen remodel?" he asked at the same time as Gabriel said, "That's a lot of work for someone you haven't officially hired yet."

Pietro ignored him as Ezra cut in. "So, I was watching HGTV the other day," he said, and Gabriel groaned over him. He gave his boyfriend a gentle smack. "Fuck you, it's entertaining. Anyway, there was this guy who was like...fuck, I don't remember. He was injured during a deployment or something, so they came in and put his kitchen on like..." His nose scrunched up, and he lifted his hand and raised it up and down. "You know, like a lever or something that can raise and lower all the counters and the oven and shit."

Pietro's brows rose. "Really?"

Gabriel leaned against the counter. "As I said, for a man who you haven't even hired yet..."

"Yeah, but we both know I'm going to since Ezra doesn't want to quit teaching, and no one else has responded to my request," Pietro mumbled. He took another drink of wine before making himself stop because he didn't want to be even remotely tipsy for Thierry's interview. God only knew what he'd say. "I feel like I'm cursed."

Pity flooded Ezra's face, and Pietro hated it. "You're not cursed."

"You are," Gabriel said primly. "It's a family thing. You have to find your true love to break it." He hitched Ezra close and smiled.

"Oh my God," Pietro said, and he hobbled to his feet, his walking boot making a loud thump on the floor. "Get the fuck out of my house, you disgusting assholes."

Ezra laughed, but he walked over and hugged Pietro anyway. "I'm sorry it's shitty, but I have a good feeling about this."

Pietro nodded and accepted the hug and the glare from his brother since he'd once attempted to flirt with Ezra knowing full well Gabriel was into him. And Pietro couldn't deny that if things were different—if Gabriel hadn't been interested—he really might have considered going after Ezra. He was as gorgeous as he was kind.

But Pietro also knew that Ezra didn't deserve the chaos that came with his life.

"Thanks for your help," he said, drawing back. He met his brother's gaze, hoping Gabriel understood how sincerely he meant those words.

Gabriel softened. "Let me know how it goes." He raised his arm and gathered Ezra close, and Pietro decided to spare himself the last bit of pain by not walking them to the door.

The clock mocked him with the hours it would take before Thierry arrived, and Pietro decided he'd do everything he could to keep himself busy so he didn't have to think about the strange sensation now living in his gut.

THE DOORBELL RANG JUST as Pietro was done wasting a row of zombies from the little fruit-throwing game his nieces had gotten him addicted to two summers ago. He let out a small, annoyed growl until he remembered why the doorbell was ringing, and he shot to his feet. He turned off the TV as he bolted toward the door, then forced himself to slow down and breathe before he reached for the handle.

His heart was still pounding, but he hoped he looked somewhat composed as he opened it. As expected, Thierry was there, leaning on his cane and looking at him with a familiar, expressionless stare. He raised a brow when Pietro continued to stand there and stare at him.

Then there was the sound of someone clearing their throat, and Pietro looked up to realize Thierry hadn't come alone.

The woman was holding on to what he was pretty sure was a walker—though it was a far cry from the rickety metal one his nonni used in the last few years she was mobile. This one was sleek and black with rubber-gripped handles and a bench in the center, and the woman gave it a slight push forward.

"So, can we come in, or...?" she asked, and Pietro stared at her another second. Was she Thierry's girlfriend? *Fuck.* "Is this a bad time?"

Thierry snorted. "Don't worry, just give him a second. He does this sometimes."

Pietro wanted to slap himself in the face, or maybe slap Thierry for thinking it was fucking funny. Even with all the meds in the world, he still got lost in his rambling train of thoughts and memories that tended to congeal into one big mental mess.

It was why people used to laugh at him as a kid. It was why half the guys on the team called him a dumbass whenever he'd zone out during games and miss that he was up to bat.

Pietro cleared his throat and took a step back, gesturing for them to enter. "Sorry. Uh. Thanks for coming by again."

"You're the one doing me the favor," Thierry reminded him, though Pietro didn't think that was strictly true. They were kind of helping each other at this point, but he didn't think drawing attention to that was going to make the situation any less awkward. "Do you mind if Sarah comes into the kitchen with us for a minute?"

"I'm not here to crash the interview," she said, looking back over her shoulder and smiling.

She was very attractive, which sat a little heavy in Pietro's gut. She was petite, but her arms were ripped, and she had an air about her like she could probably lift a fucking car under the right circumstances.

In short, she was probably perfect for Thierry.

Not that he should care. He sure as shit wasn't ever going to be interested in the man who had created the drama between him and Hervé—no matter how much he apologized for it or how readily Pietro had forgiven him.

He was just sick of seeing love everywhere he turned.

"You can stay if you want," Pietro finally said, finding his voice. He followed the pair into the kitchen and shoved his hands into his pockets as Thierry looked around. "I don't think this is supposed to be like a normal interview."

Sarah shook her head, a lock of hair falling over her forehead. She brushed it away and gave him a smile that set him at ease. "Nah, it's fine. I never get up to this side of town, and you know that little coffee cart on Base Ave?"

Pietro's eyes widened, because yes, he did. It was a Turkish place called Mud Coffee, and he would have gone broke if he let himself go there as often as he wanted. "Ugh, yes, okay. Have one for me."

"Why don't I bring you something?" Sarah said. She pushed the walker over to where Thierry was leaning against the counter. "You want something too?"

"Mm," Thierry said, grunting as he abandoned the cane and grabbed the handles of the walker. Even bent over slightly, the man was ridiculously tall. "Maybe if they have pistachio baklava."

She gave his cheek a pat, then turned on her heel, staring at Pietro expectantly.

It took him far too long to catch on. "Oh. Shit. Uh...just a mud coffee."

She winked, then headed for the front, and he didn't really breathe properly until door slammed shut. Leaning against the counter, he shook his head.

"She's..."

"I know." Thierry chuckled very quietly as he turned around and settled on the walker's sitting bench. He sat a lot higher that way, which gave him more access to the counters, and Pietro felt a little less stressed about how Thierry was going to work in his kitchen. "I've known her since I got here, and being her friend is a lot sometimes." Thierry was smiling, which was an odd look on him. "But I appreciate it."

Pietro's eyes widened. "Oh, damn. Is she a chef too?"

Thierry's brow lifted. "No. She's my neighbor. She's also a therapist."

And shit, Pietro hadn't considered that he'd need one, which was ridiculous. He damn well knew you didn't get shot and permanently injured without needing at least a little help to get through it. "Sorry."

Thierry waved him off. "It's kind of nice you'd assume chef. Most people see us together and think she's someone who follows me around and wipes my ass. But they taught me how to do that at the hospital myself, so I don't have to pay for the extra expense."

Pietro's cheeks flamed as he winced because something like that—paying for a caregiver—wouldn't have even been a consideration if the situation had been reversed. And while he could tell from Thierry's expression that although he was telling the truth, he was also being blunt to get a rise out of him. Which he probably deserved.

"Anyway, uh," he said slowly, rubbing fingers through his hair. "I invited my brother's boyfriend over to help set things up. I wasn't sure what else you might need. I guess I'm mostly worried about the counter height if you need to use your…um."

Thierry raised a brow. "Wheelchair? You know the word doesn't bother me, right?"

Pietro blushed again, and he wished he was better at shit like this. "Yeah. Wheelchair."

"This is all fine for now," Thierry said. "And it might be a problem in the future, but your kitchen has a lot of room for me to work in. It's surprisingly well equipped, which is interesting for a man who doesn't know how to use it."

Pietro forced a laugh, dragging his hand through his hair before wrapping his arms around his middle. "It's not…that simple."

Thierry's brows furrowed. "Oh?"

"I'm not some spoiled asshole who just doesn't feel like cooking, okay?"

Thierry regarded him for a long moment, then shook his head. "I never thought that about you."

Pietro couldn't help a small, bitter chuckle. "Nah. You just thought I was some philandering dickhead who got off by cheating on his boyfriend."

Thierry said nothing, and Pietro realized that maybe this was a mistake. Maybe the shit between them—no matter how brief it had been—was too heavy to make this work.

"Sorry. Sorry, I..."

"I deserve it," Thierry replied, his voice quieter than Pietro had ever heard it. "I still don't know why I..." He let out a soft *ha* sound and rubbed a hand over his face. "I wanted you to be as horrible as him. It...I think it made me..." He trailed off like he was searching for the words, and Pietro debated about letting him go through all this, but maybe he needed to. And maybe Pietro needed to hear it. "I protected him for so long, and it made it easier to keep my mouth shut about him believing you were doing the same thing."

"I wasn't," Pietro started to defend, but he went quiet when Thierry raised a hand.

"Ah, *je sais*. I know," he clarified in English, though Pietro could understand his little sprinkles of French just fine. "I think I also knew back then. It made me angry. It made me realize I was choosing the wrong side, and I didn't..." He went quiet again, staring down at his feet. "Sometimes I wonder if I deserve..."

"Don't. Please, fuck," Pietro said in a rush. It brought back all the ugly feelings—all the ugly conversations—he and Gabriel had when his brother was first hurt. "I don't believe disability is some sort of karma or punishment. I don't know what you're going through, but I watched my brother deal with it when he was first hurt, and I've already had this conversation with him. Being a dick to me—punching me in the face—doesn't mean you have to pay. Not like that."

"Maybe not, but Hervé abandoning me? I deserved that," Thierry said.

Pietro shoved his thumbnail between his teeth and scraped at the corner of it. The last thing in the world he wanted to do was talk about all of this, but it wasn't like he had much choice.

"Did he ever explain why he just disappeared?" Pietro asked.

Thierry let out a breath, shook his head, and gave a two-word answer. "Not really." Silence settled between them again, and then Thierry clapped his hands together. "Alright, I have a small meal in mind for you, but if it's all the same, I'd like you to leave the kitchen."

Pietro's eyes widened at the abrupt, sharp change of subject. But it was fair. They'd flayed themselves open enough for one afternoon. "Aren't I supposed to be watching you?"

"Unless you think I'm going to call for takeaway and try to pass it off as my own cooking," Thierry said, a hint of warning in his deep, rumbling voice, "then I'd say you can let me do my work and judge whether or not I'm worthy of the job by how it tastes."

"Is it going to be an omelet?" Pietro pressed.

Thierry's eyes narrowed. "No. *Vas t'en.*"

Pietro knew that phrase well. He threw up his hands, backing up, his boot clunking hard on the wall as he misjudged his steps and almost crashed. Thierry started to lean forward like he was going to try and catch him before pulling back.

As Pietro righted himself, he watched just a flicker of something like heartbreak flash in the man's eyes. "Yeah, yeah. I'm still a fucking disaster. Nothing much has changed."

Thierry's face softened. "I'm glad your foot will be okay. Your season needs you."

My season, Pietro thought with a small, internal grin. Not his team, but the season. It was oddly poetic, and he liked it. "I'll be in the other room. Just yell for me when you're done."

"I'm not a heathen," Thierry snapped. "I'll fetch you when the food is prepared."

Pietro took that as the final dismissal, then turned and carefully made his way back to the now very unsatisfying zombie game.

CHAPTER EIGHT

Pietro told himself to keep away, but half an hour into the game he was losing badly, he was drawn by the smell. It gave him a sudden burst of nostalgia—maybe not exactly like his childhood, but it lacked the acrid scent of to-go boxes from even the most high-end dining places.

And knowing that there wasn't a microwave in use was enough for him to crack, tiptoe down the hall, and peer around the kitchen wall.

Thierry was seated at the stove on a barstool rather than his walker, which he was holding off to the side for balance. His other arm was occupied by constant stirring, and it was only the slightest twitch in his elbow that told Pietro he'd given himself away.

"*Me-tu fixe?*" Thierry asked after a beat, and Pietro didn't know that phrase, but he could infer he'd been caught staring. "You might as well come in."

Pietro sighed and put his hands behind his back like a scolded child. "Sorry. It just smells amazing."

Glancing over his shoulder, Thierry rolled his eyes, but his cheeks were flushed, and his mouth was turned up in the corners. "I perfected this recipe years ago. Risotto," he clarified.

Pietro couldn't help his groan. It was one of his most favorite things, and his mouth began to water in earnest as he saw a bowl of bacon, mushrooms, and green onions all cooked and sitting off to the side. There was a bottle of white wine uncorked, perched near Thierry's elbow, and Pietro's hand darted out to grab it.

"Ah, *putain*! Are you trying to ruin the dinner?" Thierry demanded, letting go of the walker so he could give Pietro a shove away.

Pietro laughed as he stumbled, catching the counter as he brought the bottle to his lips and took a small drink. "How could I possibly ruin the food? It's already perfect."

Thierry scoffed quietly as he reached for a small ladle and added something from a simmering sauce pot. "If anyone could do it, you could."

Pietro took another sip of the wine, then set it on the counter and used his hands to heave himself up. He perched on the edge and gently swung his legs from side to side, listening to the heavy thud as his walking boot caught on the edge of the cabinet door.

He ignored Thierry's tisk, grinning at the man. "Is it hate or habit?"

Thierry looked at him, his face a mask of confusion. "I don't understand."

"Do you hate me still, or is it just habit to insult me?"

At that, Thierry looked away, but Pietro was sure he caught guilt on his face. "I never hated you. I didn't understand your relationship with Hervé, but it wasn't hate."

"And yet you thought it was a good idea to make sure we split up. I mean, even if you thought I was a massive piece of shit like him, wouldn't that have been a good thing?" The words burned a little as he said them, but Pietro couldn't seem to stop himself. "Keeping him off the market and away from all the good men who don't deserve them?"

Thierry gave the risotto one more stir, then dropped the spoon and turned it off before swiveling to face him. Pietro's heart began to thud in his chest because he knew he'd at least approached the line between them, if he hadn't crossed it already.

"I don't think this is a good match."

"Wait..."

"I love cooking, and I'm eager to get my life started again, but if we can't move past what was..."

Pietro held up both of his hands. "Okay. Okay...I'm being a dick. I get that. You apologized and that's fine, but it doesn't erase that you punched me in the face. With your fist."

Thierry's eyes widened. "You would have preferred I use something else? Like my knee."

"Fuck's sake, dude," Pietro said. He hopped down as Thierry pulled himself up off the stool and gripped the handles of the walker like he was using it to help his balance. "I had to get *veneers*."

"Yes. The tragedy of a man so rich he can afford to get whatever work done he needs," Thierry sneered, the sound of his voice telling Pietro he'd touched a nerve.

"I wouldn't have needed it if you hadn't *punched me in the face*," Pietro stressed.

"As I said," Thierry murmured quietly, "we can't work like this if neither one of us can move on."

He started to move away, but Pietro caught him by the sleeve and held tight. Their gazes locked for a long moment, and Pietro swore he could cut the tension between them with a knife.

"I guess you were kind of right. I wasn't a great boyfriend," he finally said.

Thierry swallowed thickly. "You weren't like him."

"No. But I was definitely an asshole at the best of times. I…" Pietro let out a small laugh because he hadn't admitted this out loud to anyone before. Not even his therapist. "I felt justified because Hervé wasn't a nice guy, either. Like, I told myself it was okay to be a shitty boyfriend because he was someone who deserved it. I was in a bad place, and I just wanted someone to hurt as badly as I was hurting. And that…" He blew out a puff of air and slowly removed his hand from Thierry's sleeve. "That means I probably did earn a little bit of what you dished out."

Maybe he didn't deserve to get clocked in the face by Hervé's hired guy, but he couldn't exactly stand as the moral poster child of good relationships. He and Hervé had been toxic, and he was done trying to pretend he was totally innocent.

"How do we move on?" Pietro asked.

Thierry took a breath and carefully turned back to the stove. Pietro tried not to stare at his shuffling steps, instead fixing his gaze on the back of the man's head as he tipped the bowl of mushrooms, bacon, and onions back into the cooked rice. He added a handful of cheese after, stirring for so long, Pietro wondered if that was it.

The conversation was just…over.

Then Thierry looked over his shoulder again. "If you'd like to get bowls? I forgot to grab them when I was setting everything out."

Pietro leapt at the chance for something to do, and he pulled his cheapest, ugliest bamboo bowls from the cupboard. "You're having some too, right?"

"Normally I'd say no," Thierry said, "but we should probably talk this out. So, if you don't mind..."

"*Fuck* no. It makes me feel way less of a giant loser if you eat with me," Pietro told him. He pushed them close to the edge of the stove, then waited for Thierry to fill them up. As he was pulling sprigs of parsley from a bushel as a garnish, Pietro stepped back. "We can, uh, eat at the table?"

Thierry said nothing, but he offered a terse nod, so Pietro grabbed the bowls. As he took a step to the side, his boot caught on the edge of Thierry's walker, and he almost hit the ground face-first.

"Shit," he gasped as he barely managed to catch himself and save the dinner.

Thierry covered a laugh with his hand. "Do you need some help?"

Glowering, Pietro righted himself and marched toward the table to set the food down. "Laugh all you want. I'm as fucking graceful as a gazelle out there on the field, and that's the only time it matters."

"If you say so," Thierry said with a small smirk. Pietro grabbed forks, and Thierry joined him a second later with a bottle of white wine and two glasses tucked in between his fingers. "So we can be a bit more civilized than drinking right from the bottle."

"Don't knock it. Bottles of wine remind me of my college glory days," Pietro told him, giving each glass a generous pour as Thierry got settled. He took a drink, then eased back into his seat and stared at the food. "If I cry, promise you won't judge me."

"Only if they're happy tears," Thierry said. There was tension in his voice, and Pietro realized he was nervous.

To end the anticipation, he shoved his fork into the cheesy rice and scooped a massive bite into his mouth. It was hot, but it was perfectly cooked, and his eyes really did water—entirely with happiness. "Real food," he groaned.

Thierry shook his head, but he was grinning. "Is that all you need to be satisfied?"

Pietro rolled his eyes and grinned. "You want compliments? Fine. This is the best risotto I have ever eaten. It's so good I'd actually tell my aunt that and risk being disowned by my entire family."

Thierry burst into a small laugh and shook his head before taking his own bite. He smiled around his fork and nodded. "I think it was a very good effort on my part."

"So, can I offer you the job now?" Pietro asked.

At that, Thierry sobered a little. Pietro watched his face move through several expressions, and he couldn't tell if any of them were good or bad. It was probably what made him such a fucking good bodyguard for all the years he'd worked for Hervé, but Pietro was starting to have doubts that it would work here. In his home.

"I don't want you to resent me for the past," Thierry finally said. "And it's clear it still bothers you."

Pietro sighed and leaned back, rubbing at his mouth with the tips of his fingers. "It does. The whole situation with Hervé really fucked with my head. It...hell, it went on for so long, you know? And I feel like I only know half the shit that he got up to. Knowing he was worse doesn't excuse my behavior, but..."

"I understand," Thierry said quietly. "He leaves a trail of destruction wherever he goes. And now I know what it feels like to be on that end of it." Thierry's gaze darted away, which told Pietro enough. "I don't want him to be the ghost that follows me around until I die."

Pietro hadn't expected him to say that. "Has he tried to talk to you about...what happened?"

Thierry shook his head, but there was something in his

gaze that told Pietro he wasn't being entirely honest. "Whatever he has to say, it's not important anymore. I've moved on."

Pietro knew how those words—as honest as Thierry wanted them to be—probably tasted like a lie. He and Hervé had never really been in love, but he still felt wrecked as he watched the man walk away, knowing in his heart it would be for the last time. He couldn't imagine what Thierry was going through.

"It wasn't the same for you though," Pietro finally said, then shoved another bite into his mouth and spoke thickly through cheesy rice. "You two were, like, forever."

"Not forever, but I gave up so much of my future for him," Thierry muttered. "The day I met him, I had just moved to France. I was eight. My parents...they'd been living and working in England for almost ten years."

Pietro went completely still. Hervé rarely talked about his past, and only when he was drunk, so the details were always so muddled. From everything his ex had said, Pietro had assumed Thierry and Hervé had known each other since they were in diapers.

Thierry looked like someone had cracked him in half with a cleaver. "He was miserable—constantly bullied—and I thought I was doing something good for him when I started protecting him. I thought... maybe it would matter. In the end."

Pietro blew out a long breath of air, then found the courage to ask, "Were you in love with him?"

Thierry looked up and gave a breathy laugh through his nose. "Everyone assumes—but no. It was never like that. I saw who he was when the cameras weren't watching. He was too..."

"Cruel," Pietro finished for him, because he was. Hervé wasn't just selfish. He delighted in holding the threat of pain over the people in his life. Pietro had fed that drama for a while because it let him forget that being still and quiet hurt just as much, but in the end, it hadn't been worth it.

"I became cruel for a while too," Thierry went on. "It was impossible not to be when it surrounded me at every turn. Being shot, I think..." He shook his head, then shrugged and laid his hands on the table. "It saved me. There are days I want my life back. I want to walk without pain or falling over. I want to believe I'll run again—or that I'll regain control over my weaknesses. But I also know that if things hadn't happened this way, it might have taken another decade—maybe longer—to realize I was drowning in Hervé's world."

Pietro swallowed thickly, and as much as he didn't want to pity the guy, he couldn't help it. It wasn't just his injury. It was knowing how it felt to be swept up in Hervé's storm and held there without hope that he would ever set him free.

For Pietro, it had taken getting punched in the face and his teeth knocked out. But he also hadn't served more than half his life under Hervé's thumb.

"Is this what you want to do?" Pietro finally asked, waving his hand toward his kitchen. "Cook for people like me?"

"I need a job," Thierry admitted. "I can't go work in a professional kitchen, and no matter how many times I drag myself across the floor at my physical therapy, I'm never going to get my old body back. This isn't all I want, but it is a start."

Pietro had heard that before—from a person he loved more than life itself. Those words had tripped past Gabriel's lips during one of their bigger fights just after his brother accepted the job at the high school. Pietro was angry because he wanted Gabriel to keep fighting—to keep working—to keep believing that there was some miracle that would give him his life back.

But he'd come to realize that was selfish because he wanted it for him so he could stop feeling so fucking guilty that he got everything, and Gabriel had been left with the next best thing.

Pietro's own blind spot had been not realizing the next best thing could also be the one thing that made his brother feel whole. And it was only now, after seeing him with Ezra—after seeing Gabriel smile again and laugh again—that he realized the truth.

Gabriel didn't need his old life to be happy, and maybe Thierry didn't, either.

"The pay will be good," Pietro finally said.

Thierry blinked at him in surprise. "The...pay?"

"Working for me. I don't expect you to be here morning, noon, and night to cook. I was thinking maybe you could whip stuff up for my breakfasts and lunches that I could heat up? Then maybe you could do dinners Monday through Friday. I can handle weekends. My nutritionist will be so fucking happy I'm eating normal food during the week, he'll definitely give me weekends off."

Thierry's lips twitched. "I think I can make that work."

Pietro looked at him a long moment. "And," he went on when Thierry's face started to fall, "if you're happy and I'm happy, I want to renegotiate outside of that employment service company. They don't need to be taking a percentage of your wages."

Thierry bit his lip. "I don't know. If it doesn't work out down the road, I can't..." He let out a frustrated growl. "I don't remember the fucking phrase. Set the bridge on fire?"

"Burn the bridge?" Pietro asked with a small grin.

Thierry rolled his eyes. "*Ouais.* Burn the bridge. If we don't work out—if you decide you don't want to look at the man who hurt you the way I did—I need to be able to find another job. I can't go back home to live with my parents."

"If I decide I can't stand your face," Pietro vowed, knowing damn sure that would never be a problem because he'd never had an issue with the man's *face*, "I swear I won't terminate our agreement until you have something else lined up. I'll put that in writing and make sure my lawyer gets it all nice and legal so you don't get fucked. But I'm going to be firm on this, okay? I'm not paying a company for your services."

Thierry hesitated. "I need health benefits."

"Done," Pietro said. Of course, he didn't know what that would take, but he had people who could figure it out. "Insurance, vacation time—shit, Christmas bonuses. Whatever you need."

Thierry licked his lips, then finally nodded. Before he could say anything else, the horrible bong sound of the doorbell Pietro desperately needed to change rippled through the room. They both jolted, and Pietro groaned.

"If that's fucking Scooter right now..."

"Sarah," Thierry said quietly.

Right. Sarah. Pietro had all but forgotten about her. Pretty, sweet, badass Sarah, who knew Thierry like most people never would. Jealousy was not a good look for him though, not in this situation. He didn't want Thierry, anyway. He just felt... connected, he supposed, to the man that was also ripped apart by Hervé.

"I'll get it. Then we can chat hours and shit before you go."

Thierry nodded and said nothing as Pietro hobbled to the door on his awkward boot, wondering if he was making the right decision or the wrong one.

CHAPTER NINE

"Sensation check?" Chris made his hands into something like claws, then moved his fingers like he was squeezing a fruit.

It only took Thierry a second to realize what he was implying. "You don't even fuck men. Why are you so desperate to grope my ass?"

"Because I'm secure enough in my sexuality to admit that it's a goddamn work of art," he said with a wink.

Thierry let out a quiet groan of relief as Chris let his legs go. It was never pleasant, lying flat on his back on the floor. His nerve pain was almost unbearable like this, and his toes felt like they were on fire.

But it was a relief to be done with his PT for the day. He hadn't worked out too hard. Chris had modified their schedule since Thierry would be starting work soon and would be on his feet more than he had been in the last year.

Thierry didn't need Chris to tell him he was worried about it, either. It was written all over his face. During his recovery, he used to scream anytime someone wanted to treat him like glass, but the reality was, it was necessary.

It was a bitter pill to swallow, and worse, Pietro's job offer might be the only real viable way for him to follow the dream he had once let go at Hervé's request.

"You're distracted," Chris said. He slapped his palms gently down Thierry's calves, sending a fresh wave of tingles to the soles of his feet, then crouched to the side and offered his hands to help Thierry sit up. "Do you want to talk about it? Or is this more of a Sarah problem?"

Thierry didn't really know. Sarah wasn't his official therapist. She was more of a *get wine drunk and talk about how much boys suck* sort of best friend therapist. But sometimes, that's who he needed.

"I think I need to go shopping" was what he said instead.

Chris' brows rose. "*Shopping.*"

Thierry gently rolled onto all fours, then rocked himself up to kneel and slowly climbed to his feet. His balance was always shaky after these long sessions, but Chris was waiting with his cane and a dry towel so Thierry could mop the sweat from his brow and the back of his neck.

"I need to look professional," Thierry said as he made his way over to the water table.

"So this guy...this super-secret celebrity guy who wants you to cook for him, also wants you to change your wardrobe?" Chris asked.

Thierry turned slightly and stared at him over the length of the water bottle as he gulped enough down that the liquid started sloshing around in his stomach. The NDA had prevented him from telling anyone but Sarah—and even that was technically a breach, but he didn't think Pietro much cared.

He didn't know how to tell Chris the truth without giving

Pietro's identity away. "All I own are sweats."

"All the better to ruin with your fancy sauces," Chris pointed out.

Thierry turned on his heel and walked as fast as he could manage, ready to leave the rest of the day behind him. He wasn't annoyed that Chris followed, either, but a small part of him wanted to be alone. "I need this job. I need to be taken seriously." He needed to draw a line in the sand and make sure whatever happened at Pietro's stayed firmly professional.

He had a crush, which was expected. Pietro was a good man, and he was funny and good-looking and strong. Thierry would get over it. He always got over it when his heart started to warm into actual feelings. That wasn't the problem.

The problem was Pietro was obviously too prone to making things personal. He could see it in the man's eyes. He was lonely and a little lost, and he was…something else Thierry hadn't quite figured out just yet.

And he wasn't sure he wanted to.

But his financial situation was looming over his head like the goddamn Sword of Damocles, and he wouldn't survive the wound if it fell. He'd have to go home. Back to his parents. Back to square one. Back to giving up his dream to do something he hated—a compromise because his body would no longer let him have this one thing.

"Hey."

Thierry froze when Chris' voice carried across the tiled walls of the changing room. He bowed his head, staring down at his socked feet—the white very stark next to the pitch-black cane tip. He wriggled his toes and smiled because they didn't hurt.

"Listen, man. I know I was coming down on you a little hard," Chris began.

Thierry shook his head, turning to glance over his shoulder

at his therapist who was also very much his friend. "What was it you said the other night? Shit got real?"

Chris snorted a laugh. "Yeah."

Thierry rubbed a hand down his face, then slowly backed up until he could ease down on the changing bench. His back still ached, but it was nice to be off his feet for a minute. "It happened. Shit...got real. Hervé showed up at my home."

Chris' entire body went stiff. "Bro. You need me to deal with this fucker? Because I am down..."

"To what? Lose your job? Because believe me, he will make your life difficult, and he's not worth it," Thierry said. His heart felt warm. "Anyway, he didn't do anything. He came to my apartment and tried to...apologize, I suppose. He told me he wasn't leaving until he made it right. But he hasn't tried to contact me since then, so I'm assuming he got bored."

Chris scoffed and straddled the far end of the bench, ducking his head until he caught Thierry's gaze properly. "First of all, fuck that guy. Second of all, you can't let him get in your head."

"He's been in my head this whole time," Thierry said. He licked his lips and glanced away. "I want to prove to myself I can do this, but it's complicated."

Chris was silent for so long, Thierry finally looked over and saw the man staring at him with determined eyes. "Fine. Then let's shop."

"No, I didn't mean," Thierry started, but Chris waved him off.

"Nah, bro. We're going shopping. I'm gonna make you look fly as fuck—like that kitchen should be yours. And who the fuck knows, right? Maybe it will be one of these days."

Chris was one of the most optimistic people Thierry had ever met, and he just didn't have the heart to tell him that with the way his luck had always run, that would never be the case.

CHAPTER TEN

*C**rack!*
 Crack!
Crack!

"Slow it down before you fuckin' hurt something."

Pietro hit the button on the little remote just before another ball came whizzing past his face, and he turned his head to see James leaning against the fence. He hobbled away from the plate, letting the bat drop loosely to his side.

"Is there a reason you want to interrupt the one fucking thing I get to do right now?" he demanded.

James shrugged and pushed away from the chain link, taking a few steps closer. "Working some shit out?"

Pietro nodded, his jaw a little tense from how he kept clenching his teeth every time he thought about Thierry.

James let out a melodical little whistle, then gently reached for the bat and hip-checked Pietro out of the way. With a sigh, he put some distance between him and James, adjusted the timer on the machine, and let the first ball fly.

James made contact, sending the ball flying into the net.

"I saw your boy the other night."

Pietro almost dropped the remote. "You...my boy? What fuckin' boy?"

"French chef." James hit another ball, then another before he turned, and Pietro quickly turned off the machine before it sent one flying into the side of his friend's head. "He came to the club."

Pietro blinked in surprise. As far as he knew, Thierry hadn't really been much of a club guy, even before his injury. Whenever Hervé would go out, Thierry would stand in the shadows with his arms crossed, like he wanted to be anywhere else but there.

And Pietro had a feeling it wasn't just because he was on the job. He'd seen a couple of pap shots online where Thierry was clearly not on duty, but he never looked happy.

"What did he want?"

James walked over to the little rack and dropped the bat in before he jerked his head toward the field. His ankle was hurting like a bitch, but he felt better as they began to round the bases at a more sedate pace than he had ever walked the field.

"I can't decide if you hiring him is the best decision or the worst decision of your life," James said instead of answering Pietro's question.

Pietro folded his arms as his boot gently touched the edge of first base. "How is it any of your fuckin' business to begin with?"

James snorted a laugh. "I've made all your bullshit my business for years, man. Don't act like you don't want me rifling around in your shit."

Pietro bit the inside of his cheek and said nothing.

After another long silence, James sighed harder. "It feels

like everything's on the edge of big change, you know? Did you get the email Weber sent?"

He had. It was some urgent team meeting, but he didn't really think twice about it. Everything Weber sent was fucking urgent. The last time they'd been rushed into one of the corporate board rooms, it had been because they were changing the blue in their team logo to a slightly different shade.

"Do you know something I don't?" Pietro asked him.

James shrugged, his gaze fixed on the wooden fence. Pietro had knocked more balls than he could count far past that point—but it had been a damn long while since he'd done it, and he was starting to feel his age in his bones. "I think it's gotta do with Tomas."

Tomas Singer. He'd been traded three years back from the Huskies, but he'd never quite settled. Then, during spring training in Arizona, he'd taken a nasty fall down the stairs as they were heading to their hotel lobby, and he hadn't been back since.

As cruel as it sounded, Tomas had never really mattered to the team. His stats were good, and he had potential, but there was something holding him back. But James had gotten close to him, so Pietro wanted to be supportive.

"Did he say something to you?"

"He was just real fucking cagey the last time I dropped by there," James said. "You know I goddamn hate change."

Pietro had always found that funny about his friend considering that was part of the business. Neither one of them had been traded. Up to this point, they were too goddamn good to lose. But he understood what James was saying.

They were getting old. They were all getting old. That's when management started getting twitchy. The more they lost, the further the World Series slipped away, the more they felt like a fresh start would make a difference.

He'd been in the business too long not to see it.

"Whatever Tomas has going on is his own fuckin' business," Pietro said. He shoved one hand into his pocket as they rounded third, and he stopped when James did. "And I've got a sprained ankle, man. It's not the end of the world. I'm not gonna lose the damn thing."

James gave him a pained look. "What are the chances that we just stay here until we're too goddamn old to lift a bat, and they throw us into the furry costumes?"

That startled a laugh out of Pietro, who grabbed his friend by both shoulders and shook him. "Calm down."

James smiled, but it didn't quite reach his eyes. "You're my family, you know? You're pretty much all I got here, and I don't know why this chef thing is throwing me off."

"Me taking control of shit that has been a mess for, what, ten years? That's a *good* change," Pietro reminded him. "Antonio is going to cry happy tears when he realizes I'm not eating frozen meals."

James laughed softly and shrugged Pietro's hands off him before heading into the outfield. Pietro followed, his feet sinking into the grass that was going to need a mow in the next few hours.

"Look, man, not to be a dick," Pietro said quietly, "but this is making me feel like there's something else going on that has nothing to do with my future chef hanging out at your club."

James said nothing, but the look on his face gave it away. "They tell you how much time you got left in boot jail?"

Pietro sighed, but he knew better than to push. "Not too long. It's a little sore, but I think that's because I'm not using it and it's getting stiff. These old bones," he added.

That, at least, got James to roll his eyes and elbow him. "Come out with me tonight?"

Pietro knew he should say no. He had shit to do, even if he

couldn't work out. But at the sad puppy look on his friend's face, he knew he didn't have a choice.

GOING out with James was always a damn adventure. His current club was the fourth business venture he'd gotten into. He started off buying his way into things like restaurants and cafés, but he realized clubs were going to earn him prestige in the celebrity world.

Pietro had never been interested in rubbing elbows with actors or the new wave of obscenely rich YouTubers that were flooding the scene. He knew the word "influencer," but he didn't know what the fuck it meant, and he didn't want to know.

James was in his element though. He was constantly on social media and was constantly drawing in people and their entourages from all across the country.

Pietro was happy for him, but it was yet another reminder it just wasn't his thing. It was far too like the chaos of dating Hervé. It was a constant flashback to the darkest place he'd ever been in. A place so awful he still hadn't discussed it with his therapist, and she knew about the time he'd eaten a whole pan of pot brownies and literally shit his bed.

It was easy to duck out of James' line of sight though. He was distracted by some young women Pietro was pretty sure had been on a fashion reality TV show, and he escaped to the little VIP lounge where he sank into a booth, ordered a gin and tonic, and hunkered down to count the minutes until he could sneak out without hurting his best friend's feelings.

Sipping his drink, Pietro laid his head back against the booth and felt the beat of the bass through the leather as it thrummed up the back of his neck. Nights like these weren't good for his performance on the field, but he supposed that didn't matter. Not while he was injured. It had just been a long time since he'd let himself take advantage of off time.

The last time he'd let loose in a bar, it had ended with him on his knees, blood running down his chin, and his ex sneering at him as he turned his back and walked away.

"Is this seat taken?"

Pietro snorted and shook his head at the sound of his best friend's voice. "Don't you have mingling to do?"

"Not when you're up here sulking. I asked you out so you could unwind," James told him. Pietro didn't look over, but he felt the booth jostle as the man shoved his bulky body between the cushion and the table. "We can go anywhere else if it would help."

"It won't help," Pietro said. He felt something in his chest —fragile, threatening to crack. "I'm unhappy."

"And water is wet," James shot back. It was one of Pietro's favorite sayings, and it was rough to be on the other end of it now. He knew he was obvious, but there wasn't a solution to his problem.

"I envy my brother, and that makes me the world's biggest asshole because I didn't think Gabriel's life would ever be..." He shrugged, chasing the words with a long drink as he finally sat up and opened his eyes. "Life worth living?"

"You and I both know you don't buy into that," James told him, leaning in close so he could be heard over the music. "This shit is temporary."

Pietro nodded, but he wasn't really sure he believed that for all the times he'd said it. Beauty was fading, talent was short-lived, skill eventually died. All facts, but Pietro had never been able to see a life beyond all this. It was some abstract idea —a blob of colors and shapes—and he figured he'd have time to figure it out.

And, he supposed, he did.

He was still young enough and spry enough. He might not hit a homer every game the way he used to when he was twenty-two, but he wasn't being put out to pasture yet.

So why did it feel like he'd swallowed boulders?

"Look, I won't ask you out here again if it's making you this miserable," James told him, reaching over to lay a hand on his arm. "But just come dance with me for a bit. If you still feel bad, I'll call a fucking limo to cart your ass home."

"Make it a Bentley with heated seats," Pietro said, but he could already feel himself giving in. He didn't put up any kind of fight as James' fingers dragged down to his own, then eased him from the booth and toward the dance floor.

Pietro let himself wallow in guilt as he moved with the beat, because he really wasn't miserable. He was just lost, and confused, and very lonely. It was easier to let his friends think he was having some kind of existential crisis about his future rather than the truth: that he was pretty sure he was too much of an asshole to ever really be loved.

That was a bitter pill to swallow, but it wasn't going to consume his life.

It was just making the idea of a future uncomfortable because it meant he'd have to admit he'd be alone. He'd sit there and watch all his friends and family find their forevers. And shit, he'd be happy for them.

Because he loved them.

But he wasn't sure he was strong enough to be around it.

Finishing the last of his drink as he and James moved further into the crowd, he passed the empty glass to a wandering server, then dragged his fingers through the product in his hair, leaving it thoroughly mussed. He grinned when James rolled his eyes, and laughed hard when his friend gave him a shove into a small group of men in mesh shirts looking unsurprisingly delicious.

They were probably some sort of low-grade celebrity with the way they were commanding the room, but Pietro didn't care. If he couldn't find his soul mate—not that he believed in shit like that—he could at least have a good time.

And god*damn* if it hadn't been a while since he'd been touched.

When the smallest one of the group dragged a hand from his sternum to his belt, Pietro fought back a groan and surged closer. He never really had a thing for twinks. Like most of their relationship, Hervé had been the exception to Pietro's rules. But the guy looking up at him was gorgeous, and the small laugh lines around his eyes settled Pietro's momentary fear that he was too young to be getting handsy.

"Come here often?" he asked, leaning down into the man's space.

The guy laughed and shrugged. "*Je ne comprends pas.*"

It took him a moment to register that the man was telling him he didn't understand in French. Then he was hit with two warring emotions: irritation and want. The melodic words still reminded him of Hervé, but they also now made him think of Thierry and the unwanted desire for that man to be here.

He wasn't sure what it would be like if Thierry had come, of course. They wouldn't be on the dance floor, that's for damn sure. Pietro wouldn't be putting his big hands on Thierry's hips and urging him to sway a little closer like he was doing with this stranger.

He wouldn't be leaning in to smell his neck.

He wouldn't be grinding up against his ass.

No, if he was with Thierry, he would be at the man's mercy. Injured or not, he was still massive and commanding and...and fucking perfect. Pietro would be a liar if he hadn't thought about the man just once or twice when he was with Hervé. A quiet, unspoken fantasy about what would happen if Thierry's stoic resolve cracked and he put his hand around Pietro's neck, backed him into a wall and...

God.

Anything. He would have taken anything if it meant he could feel small and held and protected for just once.

The stranger murmured something else Pietro couldn't hear over the music, but before he could ask him to repeat himself, he was gone, and another body took his place.

Pietro was ready to smile at the newcomer until the lights flashed brighter. Until his gaze settled on a face he never thought he'd see again. A face he never wanted to see again.

Hervé had just enough time to put his hands on Pietro's waist before he shoved him away. "What the fuck?"

"Pietro..."

He didn't waste time waiting to hear him. Pietro spun on his heel and all but ran for the back exit. He felt like he had the devil himself on his heels as he kicked at the metal door, and he breathed in deep when the cold Colorado night air hit him full in the face.

He hadn't realized he was gasping for breath until his lungs opened up again, and he had only a second of reprieve before that voice called his name again.

"Pietro! Why are you running? Fuck's sake, don't be a child..."

Pietro turned around, and he could only hope it was his glower that had Hervé stopping in his tracks, putting hands up in surrender. "Why are you here?" He meant to sound angry. He meant to sound furious. Instead, the words came out with all the exhaustion now settling into his bones as he set his eyes on Hervé for the first time in so long.

And yet, it wasn't long enough.

"I'm here for work," Hervé said after a beat. He folded his arms over his middle, taking a step back. He looked small and vulnerable, and once upon a time, that would have worked on Pietro. It was a tactic he used time and time again to diffuse his anger.

But Pietro didn't see a man who needed saving anymore. He saw a cold, calculating narcissist who was an expert at reading people—at manipulating them into giving themselves until there was nothing left.

Until they showed up—a shell of a man—on Pietro's doorstep, asking for a job.

He blinked and saw Thierry's face, and bile rose up in his throat, filled with the taste of his anger.

"You're lying," he said.

Hervé's eyes went wide. "How would you know?"

"Because unfortunately I haven't forgotten what you sound like when you're talking through a mouthful of bullshit," Pietro told him.

Hervé's eyes dropped, the sad creature morphing into something full of hot anger. "Is that so? Are you still following my schedule, *mon âme*?"

Pietro's eyes narrowed at the old pet name he now knew had always been bullshit. "No. In fact, the only time I've thought of you at all in the last year and a half was when I learned you abandoned your so-called best friend in the hospital after he was injured saving your life."

At that, Hervé's face crumpled in a way Pietro had rarely seen before. Hervé had always been good at faking emotions, but he had always been terrible at hiding it when something truly affected him. Pietro had only ever seen it once or twice, and never directed at him.

"How do you know what happened with Thierry?"

"That's not your business," Pietro shot back. He took

another step away and prepared to say something else, but the door crashed open, and James appeared with a couple of his bouncers.

"I want this fucker banned," James said in a low voice.

Hervé's face went back to the way it always was—a casual, devil-may-care sort of arrogance. "You think you have the power just because you can hit a ball with a stick?"

James' smile turned into a smirk. "I have the power when I own the fuckin' club. I have the power when I'm good friends with most of the club owners in the city. And I can't believe you had the audacity to show your face here again after what you did."

"I wasn't the one who—" Hervé began, but Pietro lifted a brow at him, hoping Hervé would read the expression for what it was: proof that he knew everything. After a beat, Hervé spat on the ground, swore in French, then threw up his hands and walked toward the street and disappeared around the corner.

It wasn't until Pietro was certain he was gone that his knees felt weak, and James was at his side a second later. "Woah, hey. You should probably sit."

"It's just the adrenaline," he said, though he was pretty sure he was just trying to convince himself because he didn't want Hervé to affect him like this.

He fucking hated that a man he had no feelings for could still get him all twisted up inside. Of course, he knew why. It wasn't some lingering emotion he hadn't dealt with. Hervé was just a sort of glowing beacon of proof that the only sort of companionship Pietro would ever be able to find were men like that.

Selfish.

Cruel.

Loveless.

He passed a hand down his face, then straightened up and rolled his shoulders back. "I need to take off."

"I know. I already called you a car," James said. He squeezed the back of Pietro's neck gently, giving him a shake. "I didn't know he was in town. I didn't think he'd ever show up again, otherwise I would have banned him a year ago."

Pietro waved him off as he shoved one hand into his pocket, curling his fingers around his phone. "I didn't, either. And I don't know what the fuck he's really doing here, and I'm not sure I want to."

"Want me to get someone on it?" James asked quietly.

"Nah." Pietro started toward the mouth of the alley, and when he saw the street was empty and Hervé was long gone, he let out a small breath of relief. In the distance, there were headlights on a car that started to slow as it approached the club, and he knew it was the ride James had called. "Talk tomorrow?"

"Weber says you're back at practice, right?" James said.

Pietro nodded, and he was grateful for it, because keeping busy would prevent him from overthinking. He just had to get through the night. "Pick me up on your way to the field," he said.

James clicked his tongue and gave Pietro a salute with two fingers flicked off his forehead before he started back toward the club doors. There was a moment of still, quiet silence on the street, and then the driver got out and opened the door for him, and he eased up onto the soft leather.

"Home, sir?" the man asked.

Pietro drummed his fingers on his thigh, then pulled his phone out. "Give me a sec." His thumb hovered over Thierry's contact, debating about calling the guy to warn him that Hervé was in town, but he knew he didn't have the strength for it right then.

Instead, he hit his brother's number and held his breath as it started to ring.

"Emergency?" Gabriel sounded tired but not like he was in the middle of anything.

Pietro swallowed thickly. "Got a couch I can crash on?"

Another voice popped up in the background. "Tell that fucker he knows he's got a bed here."

Pietro laughed through the ache in his chest. "Yeah?"

"Yes," Gabriel said. "I'll leave the door open for you."

The call ended, and he flopped back against the seat before giving the driver Gabriel's address. He felt ridiculous, and small, and weak. But knowing he had somewhere to go also made all the difference.

CHAPTER ELEVEN

"Shit! Fuck! *Shitfuckshit!*" For someone who ran for a living, Pietro never got any enjoyment out of it and actively tried to avoid it when he wasn't training or on the field. But now he felt like he had the devil on his heels as he scrambled from the end of his street to his driveway.

Behind him, his car sat dead, a call to his roadside assistance left hung up because halfway through bitching about his dead battery—or whatever the fuck was wrong with it—he realized that it was Thierry's first day.

And the man was waiting for him at his door, if the text he'd gotten was anything to go by.

Pietro's calves were burning from his dress shoe he was forced to wear at the fucking obnoxious ESPN interview his agent had set up for him, and his boot thumped heavily on the pavement as he tried to haul his ass across the distance.

As he finally made it, his blurry eyes caught sight of Thierry leaning against one of the columns near his front door, his face drawn but almost amused. Pietro forced himself to slow to a hobble as he pushed a lock of sweaty hair from his forehead, and he tried for a smile but failed with his gasping breath.

"Out of shape already?" Thierry asked.

Pietro flipped him off as he reached a trembling hand out and punched the door code in to unlock the damn thing. "God, why did I run? I could have just texted you the code to get in," he said, mostly to himself, feeling like a giant moron as he stepped inside.

Thierry snorted a laugh behind him as he followed. "It's what I thought you would do. Is everything okay? You don't look like you're out for a run?"

Pietro glanced behind him as he listened to the quiet clink of Thierry's cane keeping pace with his steps. "My fucking car died at the end of the street. I didn't realize you were going to be here already."

They made it to the kitchen, and Pietro leaned heavily on the fridge door as he reached in for a bottle of water. He snagged two by the tops and offered one out to Thierry, who shook his head.

"Your email, it said nine thirty, yes?" Thierry asked with a frown.

Pietro's eyes cut to the microwave with the little glowing green numbers telling him it was almost ten. "Fuck my life. Fuck my..." He spun and looked at the man, who didn't seem that bothered. "I'm so fucking sorry. My PA told me I had a last-minute interview, and I completely..." He trailed off because somehow, telling this man he forgot about Thierry's first day there felt worse than telling a lie.

"It's fine," Thierry said mildly.

Pietro waved him off as he finished the water, then tossed it into his little recycling bin. "It's super not, but I appreciate you not being a dick about it." He wiped a hand down his face, then glanced around. "Can I...is there anything I need to do?"

Thierry shook his head. "Not right now. You look like maybe you need a shower though?"

Pietro let out a tense laugh, rubbing the back of his neck, which was gross with sweat. "Yeah. I...okay. And you're...?"

"I'm going to cook. Then you can eat, and we can discuss the menu for the week," Thierry said primly.

Pietro swallowed thickly and felt the weight of his run-in with Hervé resting even heavier on his shoulders. It seemed unfair not to tell the man, but he also didn't want to put that on Thierry if Hervé was no longer around. James said he had a friend who could track where Hervé was staying and what he was doing, but in the last forty-eight hours, Pietro hadn't heard a word.

There was no sense in worrying his new employee over something that wasn't going to be a problem.

He threw Thierry one last, tense smile before hurrying up the stairs, his boot clunking all the way up. It caught on the last step, and he fell, managing to catch himself on his hands. He squeezed his eyes shut, bracing for pain, but it never came.

"*Tout va bien?*" Thierry called up after him. "Did you kill yourself?"

"Fuck off," Pietro grumbled to himself as he clambered back to his feet. "I'm fine. I...meant to do that."

He heard Thierry snicker, and to save what little of his pride he had left, he took the rest of his steps slowly. He managed to close his bedroom door without slamming it because the last thing that man needed to think was that Pietro was some child throwing a tantrum, and then he walked over to the bed and flopped over face-first.

Pietro had always been kind of a disaster. He really was very graceful on the field, but his brain and his body never quite seemed to connect outside of it. His mind moved faster than the rest of him, and it left him fumbling and stumbling around like a jackass.

And being that he was now closer to forty than he was twenty, he wasn't sure he was even allowed to blame it on his ADHD. Even if he had been diagnosed late.

Everything just felt messy right then, and a small lump formed in his throat. Of course, Pietro hadn't cried in years, and he wasn't about to start now, so he pushed himself up and quickly pulled the boot off before limping toward his bathroom.

Starting the water, he turned it up as hot as he knew he could stand it, then dropped down onto the toilet and pulled his phone out of his pocket. There was a missed call from his PA, and he quickly hit the button to call her back.

"Is there a reason you hung up with the car people?" Allie demanded.

He sighed. "Yeah. I just had to run—in my fucking boot—because I left Thierry at my front door for like forty minutes."

She was quiet for a long time. "You didn't give him the code to…"

"I didn't think about it," he snapped, then sighed because it wasn't her fault his brain was just a bunch of goblins on too much caffeine. He began to bounce his leg, and the sensation started to calm him. "Anyway, they know where the car is, and they can unlock it remotely. I need to hop in the shower, then I'm due back at the field in like two hours, so can you…"

"Yes," she interrupted. "Whatever you need, you know I can. Do you want me to put together a little welcome packet for Mr. Bourget with all the codes and everything?"

"Oh my God, don't call him *that*," Pietro groaned.

Allie scoffed. "Just forward me his email address, and I'll get it all set up. And don't forget you have your meeting about the charity Little League game tomorrow at six."

He reached up and pinched his eyes shut with his thumb and fingers. "Yep. Right. I haven't forgotten." A lie. He had absolutely forgotten. It was why he rarely did shit like that, but it was why he was constantly criticized in the media for not doing enough with his celebrity status. "Send me a reminder text?"

"I always do," she said. "Now, go enjoy your shower, and I hope to fucking Christ you're alone, because if you called me with some naked guy next to you..."

"Bye," he said in a rush. He hung up, then stripped his suit off and left it in a pile by the door before stepping under the hot spray.

The heat stung his skin, but it felt good over his sore shoulders and aching back. He tested the pressure on his ankle as he soaped up his hair, and he was relieved to find it didn't hurt much at all. It only occurred to him to be terrified his little running jaunt would set him back now, but he didn't feel any weird popping or pulling in his tendon.

He was going to be good, of course, he thought as he rinsed off. He wasn't going to go without the boot until he was given his official okay, but he could already taste the crisp fall air of his next night game.

Toweling off, he threw on a pair of joggers and a T-shirt, fitting his boot over his sock, then trying to find his running shoe with the thickest sole. He ran a comb through his hair, then stared at his face, but there was almost no growth along his cheeks and chin, so he left it alone and swiped the screen of his phone on as he carefully made his way back down to the ground floor.

Staring at Allie's text updates, he came to a skidding halt when the smell of food—actual food, with spices and flavor and everything—surrounded him. He took a deep breath and kind of felt like a cartoon character floating through the air propelled by a scent stream as he made his way into the kitchen.

Thierry was at the far counter, sitting on one of the barstools, and Pietro felt another small surge of guilt because his kitchen really wasn't great for the man. He wondered if Thierry avoided bringing a wheelchair because the counters were so fucking tall.

Before Thierry sensed his presence, Pietro sent a text off to Allie asking her to look into a company that could do kitchen remodels for disabled people. Shoving his phone into his pocket, he cleared his throat, and his heart thrummed a little harder when Thierry looked over his shoulder and smiled.

The fucker had no right to be so good-looking.

Not after their past.

"Feeling better?"

Pietro shrugged, then looked over at the table and saw it was already set with a plate, a glass of juice, and a carafe he assumed was filled with coffee.

"I had to assume you didn't get much for breakfast," Thierry said, turning back to whatever he was doing. "I have everything almost ready if you want to sit."

"Dude, you're the chef, not the server," Pietro told him.

Thierry scoffed. "I'm the chef, and it's important for me to set the plate right. I don't know why you Americans are always so obsessed with breakfast, but I still know how to do it better than most of you."

"Your humility kills me," Pietro mumbled as he made his way to the table. He chose the seat in the stream of sun, stretching a bit like a cat in the warm rays. His face erupted into a blush when he realized Thierry was watching him, but he didn't apologize. He was allowed to do whatever the fuck he wanted in his own house.

"There's no need for me to be humble about my talents."

Thierry carefully slid off the stool, then balanced the plate in one hand as he leaned heavily on his cane. His pace was slow, but it was enough time for Pietro to get a good look at what he was holding.

A frittata—or something like it. It was definitely eggs, and there were green things throughout, and he was pretty sure there were little rolls of smoked salmon on the top.

His mouth watered as Thierry set it down in front of him, then reached over and grabbed what looked like a miniature gravy boat. He drizzled a small stream of something thick and white, which gave Pietro all the inappropriate thoughts unrelated to food.

Before it could become a problem though, Thierry freed his hands and clapped them together. "*Bon.* You eat, and then you can tell me how happy you are that you hired me."

Pietro rolled his eyes, but he picked up his fork as he gestured to the empty seat across from him. "Join me?"

Thierry hesitated, then turned on his heel and reached over to the counter, where he swiped a plain black folder from the edge. "I'm not going to eat."

Pietro froze with the fork halfway to his mouth. "Dude. You can eat my food..."

"It's not that," Thierry said as he lowered himself down, and when Pietro fixed him with a flat look, he sighed. "I promise. I never did enjoy eating in the morning."

"How the fuck did you keep so fit?" Pietro asked, then finally stuffed the bite into his mouth. The noise he made wasn't quite pornographic, but it definitely wasn't PG, either. He blushed again, but he didn't care, especially not when Thierry looked at him with actual joy on his face. "Seriously, how do you not eat all your food all the time?"

"I enjoy cooking more than eating," Thierry said. "Working

for Hervé..." He stopped and shook his head. "Most of my life, things were done out of necessity."

"So why cooking?" Pietro asked. He cut into another piece and savored the sauce and the salmon on his tongue.

"I like to be creative. I was never good at." He mumbled something in French, then shrugged. "Painting, drawing, writing—none of that ever came easy to me. My parents were very creative. My sisters—" He shrugged with a small laugh. "—they went into music, into art. Cooking was the only thing that made sense to me, but I was too mean for it."

"I don't know how it works in France," Pietro said, finishing the last of his plate before reaching for the coffee carafe to fill his empty mug, "but I've seen reality TV, and those chefs are fucking brutal."

Thierry scoffed. "For money. To make people watch. But people didn't look at me"—he ran his left hand over his right bicep—"and think I should do anything other than hurt people. Threaten them."

There was actual pain in his voice that crawled under Pietro's skin, and he hated it. Mostly because he made the same assumption about the man when Hervé first showed up with him. He assumed Thierry was nothing more than muscle—a human robot who was good for nothing more than taking orders and beating the shit out of anyone who got too close to Hervé.

He never thought about Thierry as a person—not until everything had come to a head. Not until Hervé had abandoned him.

"I'm glad you're doing it now," he said quietly.

Thierry said nothing for a long while, then cleared his throat and opened up his folder. In the crease was a very slim ink pen, and he tucked that behind his ear before spreading out the few pieces of paper he had. "I'd like to discuss likes, dislikes, allergies," he said. "I'm hoping you might let me get creative, but I also want to provide you with things you know you enjoy."

Pietro bit the inside of his cheek and began to bounce his leg again. "Hey, man, you're the expert."

"And you're my boss," Thierry pointed out.

The words weren't spoken with any kind of cruelty or resentment, but Pietro very nearly flinched anyway. He didn't know why. It was the absolute truth, and there was no shame in it. But something about that still bothered him.

"Look," he said. He paused to take a drink of the coffee, which was still piping hot and surprisingly not bitter without sugar and cream, "I get this is a weird situation, and I'm sure there are plenty of assholes out there who are like, *oh I'm not picky*, and then turn into a raging dick because they are and you couldn't read their minds."

Thierry's lips thinned, but only because he was very clearly trying to hold back a smile. He didn't say anything, but he gave a little grunt of acknowledgement, which made Pietro grin.

"I really am that guy who isn't picky. I mean, you've seen my freezer."

Thierry scoffed. "*Ouais*."

"So you know I've been living off literal garbage and the goodwill of my brother's boyfriend, who invites me over for dinner sometimes," he said, spreading his hands in a shrug. "I want you to feel like you have the space here to be as creative as you want."

Thierry was quiet for another long while, and then he pulled the pen from behind his ear and tapped it on the paper before twisting it to deploy the nib. "*D'accord*." He looked up at Pietro. "I think I remember you having some allergy to cashews."

It was such a random, obscure fact, and Pietro was almost

floored that he remembered. He didn't know how Thierry had even come by that information. "How…"

"Hervé tried to feed you cashew milk ice cream," Thierry said quietly.

Shit, he'd forgotten that. It had been such a nothing moment—just a random fucking blip on a date when Hervé had spotted the little vegan ice cream parlor. He didn't know what that said about him that he didn't remember, but it definitely highlighted that Thierry had deserved so fucking much better from everyone around him.

"That's…yeah. Okay. I'm allergic to cashews and macadamia nuts. And my stomach gets a little funky with almonds sometimes, but it's not a big thing."

"I don't need to cook with any of those," Thierry said, making a note. His lips parted, and his tongue rested in the corner of his mouth—a totally absent gesture that was giving Pietro ideas. Bad, *bad* ideas. "Is there anything else?"

Pietro blinked before he shook his head. "Uh. No?"

Thierry raised a brow. "Is that a question?"

"No?" Pietro repeated, then grabbed his coffee and gulped it down because unlike most of the known world, the caffeine tended to calm him. "Sorry. Actually, I hate raw onions unless they're pickled."

Thierry's face gave away nothing, but he made another note. After staring at the sparse few words he'd written on the page, he dropped the pen, then snapped the folder closed. "I think we're done here."

Pietro felt a small pang in his gut. "Oh. Yes, right. Yes."

Thierry pushed his chair back, but he didn't stand. "I'm going to shop, then cook for your breakfasts and lunches starting tomorrow. I just need to call for a car…"

"Whoa," Pietro said, hopping to his feet. "Do you not have a car?"

"I do," Thierry said slowly, and there was something in his eyes Pietro couldn't quite read. "I'm learning how to drive it. They had to install special controls because my legs don't always move fast enough...if I need to react."

"Right. Shit. Right, okay," Pietro said.

Thierry smiled just a little. "It's fine. I'm almost finished. It was just...expensive."

Once again, Pietro felt like a dick because it wasn't something he'd ever have to worry about. "Can I..."

"No," Thierry snapped, then softened. "No. It's already taken care of. I just need a little more time to learn."

"Fine. But I'm going to send a car for you, okay? Consider it part of the employment package," he added when it became obvious Thierry was going to argue with him.

Thierry swallowed thickly and nodded. "Fine, but only because it's something you would have done for any other employee." The statement almost sounded like a challenge, and it was fair, because Pietro probably wouldn't have.

At least, not so damn readily.

He walked over to where he'd thrown his wallet and keys, then extracted a credit card from the fold. Turning around, he held it out between two fingers. "This is for the weekly budget. I don't care what you spend. I just want stuff that's not going to give me a heart attack before I turn forty, but I also want it to, you know, not taste like garbage."

Thierry didn't move for a second, and then he carefully pushed himself up to stand and took a couple of steps, holding the edge of the counter as he plucked the thing from Pietro's grasp. "I can do that."

Pietro grinned. "Also, shop for kitchen supplies if you need any. This place kind of came prefurnished, and my designer outfitted the kitchen, but I have no idea if any of it's good."

Thierry looked like he wanted to say more, but instead, he tucked the card into his wallet and nodded. "*Merci.*"

Pietro bit his lip, but before he could decide whether or not he wanted to respond to that quiet thanks, his phone buzzed and he saw Allie's name on the screen. Which meant he had to get back to reality. "I, uh…"

"Go," Thierry said.

"I'm going to have her call you a car. Just get comfy. They usually take a while," Pietro ordered, and he answered the phone but said nothing until Thierry settled back in his seat.

It was strange—it was an upset to his living situation that had been working mostly fine for him for a while now. And yet, he couldn't help but feel like he was on the verge of something great.

CHAPTER TWELVE

"I like to think he takes us out because he understands he's blessed by our company."

The words were the first things that drew Thierry out of his thoughts in, well, far too long. He hadn't realized how far he'd drifted until he turned his head to see Sarah smirking at him, and he let out a small sigh.

"Sorry."

She reached out and gave his head a little pet like he was a puppy. "There, there."

He batted her hand away and scowled. "I can't believe people pay you for their mental health."

She laughed and nudged him which considering he was in his wheelchair and far less movable than her, she bounced herself right into Chris' fiancée, Hailey, who caught her with a short laugh. "I'll have you know I'm the paradigm of excellent when it comes to therapy. But I am not on the clock, and I don't need to perform for any of you assholes."

Chris winked at Hailey, then smiled at Sarah, and Thierry

felt something both warm and jealous behind his ribs at the way it was just so easy for the three of them. How Hailey, Chris, and Sarah could exist together as friends without jealousy or resentment or any of the ugly things which Thierry had only ever known as friendship.

"Okay, so we're in this horrible store," Sarah said, glancing around. The aisles were mostly too narrow for Thierry's chair, but after working in Pietro's kitchen, then having a rough PT session, walking was out of the question. But the trip was necessary.

Pietro's kitchen was well equipped, but the designer must have known Pietro was never going to use that room because they were all very cheap, and he knew they were going to break down after a few months.

Plus, the man didn't own a cast-iron pan, which should have been considered a goddamn crime.

That was the first thing he spotted, and he managed to roll his chair through the little displays until they came to the wall full of every brand imaginable. Thierry gripped the wheels, and his gaze began to roam.

"Get the most expensive one," Hailey said, running her hand over a couple of the hanging tags. "Your boy's rich as fuck."

"I'm going by functionality, not price," Thierry said absently. Of course, functionality usually came with the price, and it was both relaxing and painful to be able to shop without restrictions.

And the feeling of comfort was getting worse the more time he spent in Pietro's presence.

The way the man had all but melted over a simple frittata —the way he stared at the food almost like he didn't deserve it —Thierry wasn't quite sure what to do with the emotions growing in his chest.

With a sigh, he leaned forward and took the cast-iron pan from the shelf and tested the weight in his grip. Working with anything heavy would be tricky. It would put strain on his body in ways he now had to consider where he never did before. It angered him, and yet, it was worth it.

"Babe?"

Thierry looked over to his right at Sarah, who was frowning at him. "This one."

"Okay, but..." She took the pan and passed it off to Chris, who added it to their cart. "Is everything okay?"

Thierry nodded, but he wasn't quite sure he believed himself. He didn't want to lie to his friends, but he also didn't know what the truth was, either. "I need better knives."

Chris chuckled. "What is it with chefs and their knives? My sister got really into this show where these people were competing to open up a restaurant, and the fuckin' *knives*, man..."

"A chef is only as good as the equipment he works with," Thierry said, grinning around the bullshit on his tongue.

Hailey laughed. "Really? So *Chopped*?"

"Oh hell no," Chris said as he led the way to the massive section of knife sets that were displayed on lower racks so Thierry wouldn't have to stand to reach them. "Fuck that show, man. Hay and I almost broke up after a weekend marathon."

Hailey laughed and elbowed him. "Shut up."

"I don't know what that is," Thierry muttered as he heard Sarah smack Chris' arm with the back of her hand in Hailey's defense. He rolled toward a very elegant, very expensive Miyabi Kaizen set. It wasn't the most expensive on the market, but it had always been beyond his budget.

He ran his fingers over the edge of the box, only half listening to his friends.

"...naw, naw, naw, he had to make dinner out of pig eyes or some shit," Chris was saying. "And the dessert round had some kind of fuckin' *cactus*? I don't care who you are—there ain't no way you're gonna wow me with *cactus* ice cream."

Sarah laughed, but the sound trailed off, and he felt the gentle press of her hand on his shoulder. "Ooh. Fancy."

Thierry cleared his throat and attempted to roll back, but he found his path blocked by Chris. "It's too much for this budget," Thierry tried to argue.

"You said you didn't have a budget," Sarah argued. "You have his platinum card."

Thierry rolled his eyes. "For food—for equipment. This would be for...for me. And I don't need anything of this quality working in someone's personal kitchen."

He tried to back away again, but Chris shoved his foot behind his wheel, then leaned over his shoulder. "If that man was here right now, what would he say to you?"

Pietro wouldn't even ask. He'd just throw the damn set into the cart and be done with it. Then Thierry would choke on his resentment because he would love it, but he would always know he only had it because of Pietro's good graces—or his lack of care about money.

"*Putain*, just let me back up," he growled.

Chris immediately stepped out of his way and shoved the cart back so Thierry had room to move to the midrange sets. "Hey, look..."

Thierry quickly spun the chair and fixed both of his friends with a sharp look. "This isn't easy for me, okay? And it doesn't matter if he can afford it or if he wouldn't mind. That's...it's not about that."

"I get it," Chris told him.

Thierry scoffed. "*C'est vrai?*" He couldn't help his sarcasm, and he appreciated that only because Chris spoke no French, but his tone must have told the man everything.

"Alright, that's fair. I don't understand where you at right now. Both my parents had good jobs. I got out of college with no debt, just like my sisters did." Chris softened. "But that don't mean I don't get where you're coming from. My field, man? I had to fight my way in. And I will be doing that until the day I die."

Thierry knew Chris meant an entirely different fight. The fight of being a black man in spaces where a lot of the old white men didn't want him.

"Sorry," he murmured, because Chris was right. The only reason he was alone on his little island was because he was shutting everyone out.

Chris shook his head. "Don't apologize. Get those knives when you're ready to get them."

Thierry hated himself a little for killing the mood. At least, he hated himself until Sarah and Hailey came back around the corner, Sarah holding a pepper grinder with a huge grin on her face.

"Do you think everyone looks at this and sees a giant dick? Or am I the only pervert in this store?"

Thierry rolled his eyes.

Then he bought the pepper grinder along with everything else.

TUESDAY MORNING FOUND Thierry letting himself into Pietro's house just after seven. He had no idea what the man's schedule was like or if he would be around. Right after his shopping trip, he'd come home to find an email from Pietro's assistant detailing out all the codes he'd need to access the house and that he should stop and pick up an employee swipe card from the gate attendant so he could get in and out without needing Pietro to put his name in every morning.

The Uber driver was a little annoyed at the stop, but Thierry didn't let the man's attitude get to him as he got the card, then directed him around the corner and into Pietro's driveway. There were no cars parked there, but the garage was shut, so he assumed the man was either home or at the field early for practice.

His fingers were steady when he reached for the keypad on the door, and he took that as a good sign as he stepped inside the foyer, dragging his little rolling cart behind him. It made an obnoxious whine, the metal straining under all of his supplies, and he cringed as he tried to hurry toward the kitchen.

His legs, of course, weren't going to cooperate. His steps were a slow shuffle, so he murmured a prayer to any god listening that he wouldn't wake Pietro. The house was massive, so there was every chance he'd gone undetected.

Pausing in the doorway, he didn't hear movement, so he continued into the kitchen and took a deep breath. It smelled very clean, and he highly doubted that was Pietro's doing. But maybe it was. He had a sudden, unbidden image of Pietro wearing yellow dish gloves and scrubbing the counters and…

God. That should *not* be sexy.

If his hands hadn't been full, he would have smacked himself in the face.

Pulling himself together, Thierry carefully unpacked the cart until everything was laid out on the counter. He'd started the season on the cast-iron pan, but it would be a little while before he could properly use it. Which was fine—he wasn't planning anything complicated for Pietro in the first week.

He set that aside along with his new knives, then began to

unpack the groceries he'd purchased to tide him over for the next two days. The rest were coming through a delivery service that Thierry had found, and he had an alert on his phone so he could make sure to be at the house when they arrived.

For now, he'd prepare a few days' worth of breakfasts and lunches, and then he'd get to work on dinner. The man said he wasn't picky, but Thierry only took that as a challenge to wow him.

No. To *ruin* him for anyone else who might ever step into this role.

Perhaps it was cruel, but it was the only power move he had. Maybe one day he'd find enough success to open up his own restaurant. He'd never be a full-time chef there, but he didn't need to be. He could still create. He could control the menu and hire only the best, and maybe it wouldn't be his hands preparing the food, but the tastes would belong to him.

That little bit of hope fizzled in his chest like a firework just before it went off, and he rubbed his sternum before he got to work. Meal prep hadn't ever been high on his list of things to learn. He always assumed the meals he cooked would be served fresh and warm, right from the oven to the table.

He'd spent most of the night on Google looking up meal prep for breakfast, and the thought of it was...concerning. There was so much use of the microwave, and it would leave everything so dry and overcooked and...*putain*! If he was braver, he'd ask Pietro to just let him stay over during the week so he could do his job properly.

But he wasn't brave. Not really.

And he wasn't about to cross that line.

He gathered up all the recipes he could—mini frittatas made in muffin tins that Pietro could heat up, overnight oats, parfaits, tofu scrambled burritos—everything that even a man like Pietro couldn't ruin with a quick heat, and then he set himself to work.

It wasn't anything like the last two meals he'd prepared for the man. His job officially wasn't hinging on whether or not he could get his risotto to the exact perfect consistency, or finish plating a dish without one or both of them bringing up Hervé and the punch.

This was official. This was the start.

His back began to ache, and his legs weakened, so he pulled the stool over. It wasn't much help. It was unforgiving on his damaged spine, and he knew it wasn't a long-term solution, but he wanted to be comfortable first. He wanted Pietro to look at him as a man capable before he started asking for things.

He pushed those thoughts aside as he carefully slid the muffin tin into the oven, and as he straightened up, there was movement in his periphery.

Ever the bodyguard, he spun and caught himself before he lost his balance. His hand reflexively went to his waist for a weapon he hadn't worn in too long, and shame burned through him as he watched Pietro's eyes follow the movements.

"I didn't mean to startle you," Pietro said. His tone was flat, mild, and obviously trying to play it off like what just happened was nothing.

But Thierry had never been the kind of man who could just let it go. "I'm not used to it yet."

Pietro swallowed thickly, then nodded. He had a faint sheen of sweat on his forehead, which he swiped away with the back of his hand, and he moved to the cupboard for a glass, filling it with water from the fridge door. "I get that. I mean, I don't. But I know what you mean."

"You don't always have to explain that," Thierry said. He was irritable now, and it wasn't Pietro's fault, but he knew his mood was going to sink further if he wasn't careful. "I don't think you're trying to claim you understand my experience."

Pietro drained the glass, then set it on the counter. He looked like maybe he wanted to say more, but after a beat, he shrugged. "Did you happen to start any coffee?"

Thierry shook his head. "It's on my list. I'll make sure I start it earlier...next time." He almost said tomorrow before remembering his normal shifts would only be dinners unless he was cooking for the week.

"You don't need to—" Pietro began, but Thierry snapped and turned to face him again.

"I do. It's my job. It's what you hired me for."

"To cook. Not to fucking serve me," Pietro shot back. He reached past Thierry, giving him a defiant glower, as he shoved a coffee mug under the little spout and hit the single-cup button.

"That's part of the job, and you know it," Thierry said, trying to keep his tone even. "It's the job of any personal chef."

Pietro threw his hands up, then spun toward the fridge to get the cream from the door. "You're such a stubborn asshole, you know that." He slammed it on the counter, then folded his arms over his chest. "I guess I shouldn't be surprised, considering you..."

"Punched you in the face?" Thierry parroted meanly.

Pietro blinked, and then his eyes went hard. "Took orders from Hervé for most of your life."

The words hit harder than Thierry expected them to—enough to steal any possible response. He stood there and watched as the first tendrils of regret hit Pietro's face before he turned because he wasn't ready to see what was going to come after.

"I'll have your breakfast done soon."

"I didn't mean—" Pietro began, but Thierry didn't want to

hear he didn't mean it, because that was a lie. He did mean it, because it was true. Thierry had been mean, strong, and stubborn. But he also had no backbone when it came to being his own person.

"Yes, you did. You're welcome to have a seat. These will be done soon, and the rest can go in the fridge or freezer for the rest of the week. I...also have oats."

Pietro said nothing, but Thierry wasn't surprised when he heard the clunk of his walking boot hit the floor as he left the room.

***

The only thing that surprised Thierry about the morning was the fact that a car showed up when he was finished cooking and everything was put away. Pietro didn't come back down to eat, and his coffee cup remained full and tepid under the little spout.

Thierry wasn't even sure the man was still there when he finally gathered up his things and headed for the driveway. He hadn't heard him leave, but he'd also been lost in his own thoughts as he finished up the last of the oats and then set out to make a handful of lunches for Pietro that could either be heated at home or taken down to the field for when he was at practice.

He was partway through a simple stir-fry when he realized they needed another talk about his diet plan and probably the number to his nutritionist. But the tension in the house, whether or not Pietro was even still in it, was too heavy to cross a line.

It was easier to leave and consider how to approach being in the same room with a man who was determined to treat Thierry more like a friend than an employee.

And maybe that's what was bothering him. It wasn't the small embers of feeling he had toward the man—it was the fact that Pietro didn't know how to draw a fucking line. He wasn't and never would be as cruel as Hervé, but at least Hervé could separate the two.

Thierry just hadn't realized how badly he needed the definition.

Squeezing his eyes shut, he shook his head, then leaned forward to get his driver's attention. "Sorry, can you take me to a new address? It's not too far?"

The man didn't mind when Thierry gave him the name of his favorite restaurant. It was a little hole-in-the-wall Moroccan place that always had a table for him at the very back against the wall. The benches there were all covered in fluffy cushions, which made it easier to tolerate his pain on bad days, and the family that ran the place knew to bring his food and let him be.

It was one of the few places in public he felt like he could get some peace.

Stepping out of the car, Thierry hitched his bag on his shoulder, then planted his cane firmly as he tested his legs. Bad, but not terrible. His feet dragged a little as he made his way toward the doors, but a little more rest and then a taxi home would take care of it. It would give him enough reprieve before he had to be back at Pietro's to prepare his dinner—assuming the man still wanted it.

Stepping inside, the young woman at the host stand gave him a smile as she beckoned him through the door, and she brought him to his spot, which was away from the few patrons who had crept in early to avoid the lunch rush.

He was only half an hour before the place would start to get crowded, but it was enough time to order and settle in. The cushions felt good against his back, and he didn't even bother looking at the menu as he ordered the mint tea and the vegetarian bastilla.

It would take some time, so he closed his eyes and leaned his head back, just enjoying the quiet sounds of the kitchen's hustle and bustle, and the low, melodic sounds of their unique Arabic peppered with enough French that he understood, and it made him smile.

"That's a new expression for you."

The voice was only vaguely familiar, and he winced at the way the sudden tension in his body made his back and legs twinge. Opening his eyes, Thierry looked to his left and saw the man from the club there. Scooter—James. Whatever.

"Don't tell me you own this place too," he said.

James' eyes went bright with a silent laugh, his shoulders shaking. "Nah. I'm just an addict. You too?"

"I don't know if I'd say that," Thierry said, though he didn't think that was entirely the truth, either. "They know me. It's…a comfortable place to sit."

James' gaze darted lower, then back up again, and there was understanding and pity in his eyes. Thierry wanted to be annoyed, but he didn't know this man, and strangers always pitied him. It was nothing new. "What did you get?"

"Do you really want to talk to me about food?" Thierry asked, reaching for his tea. The honey was barely there, just a touch of sweetness on the edges of his tongue as he took a sip and let the mint soothe his throat.

James shrugged and curled his hand around his water glass. "We can talk about why Pietro showed up at the field this morning and broke a bat, but…"

Thierry choked on his second sip of tea. "He did what?"

"I figured there was trouble in paradise. That's why I decided to go out for lunch," James said with a quiet laugh.

Thierry wasn't sure if he was supposed to feel guilty for that or not. "He's not a very good employer."

James' eyes went brighter—not quite angry, but on the cusp of it. "How's that now?"

His tone was dangerous, and Thierry immediately liked him for that. "He won't let me do my job. He..." Words were starting form—things he didn't realize he had been feeling until he'd been given permission to give them a voice. "He prevents me from doing things like he thinks it's shameful. Like part of my job is...like I should be ashamed to do them."

James settled back down into his seat and breathed out a small sigh. "That's not you. You know that, right? I mean, it's not personal."

Thierry lifted a brow. "It feels personal. He hired me, and he thinks it's something I should be embarrassed about?"

James made a small noise, then shifted over on his bench until he was at the very edge of his table. Thierry didn't love the way the man had pushed into his space, but it was easier to hear him that way. "Pietro grew up with a certain way of looking at the world. He had expectations about what the future would be like. Then it was all shattered when his brother was injured."

Thierry knew a little bit about the brother—older by a year, maybe less—and every bit as talented as Pietro. And then he'd been hit by a car and his career in baseball was over. Pietro never spoke about it though, not even when he was drunk out of his mind and crying all over Hervé about never being loved enough.

"He's just starting to understand that you can lose something and not..." James shrugged like he was struggling to find the word. "That living beyond that isn't a compromise."

And ah, *well*. Thierry could understand that because he was still trying to accept that about himself. He'd said as much to

Pietro. He just hadn't realized it had affected the man so much. "I told him this job was a compromise."

James' eyes went wider. "Oh. Well, fuck, dude."

That startled a laugh out of Thierry. "I didn't mean working for him was a compromise. It has nothing to do with him. But being a personal chef was not in my plan."

"Yeah. He…he'll be able to get it. He just doesn't—" James stopped, and there was that same look in his eyes he'd seen in Pietro's. The look that said there was something they weren't saying. "It takes him a little bit longer to put things in order."

Thierry let out a breath, but whatever words were coming next were interrupted by the arrival of his food. The server smiled at him and passed him a napkin, which he draped over his shoulder, and he waited until she wandered off.

"Sorry. I should let you get to your food," James said.

Thierry bowed his head, then looked over at him. "Working for him isn't a compromise. Living in this body is. Just like the last fifteen years of my life were a compromise." He used both hands to break apart the bastilla so the steam could escape. He stared down at the bright squash and layers of pastry, then licked his lips and glanced over at James. "He saved me with this job."

James said nothing, but there was a profound understanding in his eyes. "Do you want me to say anything to him?"

Thierry smiled very softly, then tore a piece of the pastry off and laid it on his tongue. It was perfect—buttery and crisp and full of the flavors he had wanted to create for himself for all these years. And maybe with Pietro, he'd get his chance.

"No," he finally answered. "It's probably something he needs to come to terms with on his own. I don't want him to feel like he has to live up to it."

"Yeah. I get it," James said. A second later, another server appeared with a small plastic bag holding to-go containers. He passed over a wad of cash before he eased up from the bench and looked down at Thierry. "For what it's worth, you gave him something too. He also just needs time to realize that."

Thierry had nothing to say to that, so he didn't bother trying as he watched James make his way out the door.

CHAPTER THIRTEEN

Pietro was drunk, which was not good. His boot was off, and they'd won the game, and James had said they needed to celebrate. Pietro had no real intention of going so far overboard, but his emotions had been raging, and Thierry was waiting for him at the house with dinner, which was still so damn confusing.

So, he had beer. Then a couple of shots. Then more beer. Then things got a little...fuzzy.

"Oh, buddy. Oh, this is bad."

The words sounded like the person was speaking through water, and the thought of James or Luke or Orion shoving their face into a fish tank popped into his head, and he couldn't stop laughing. Of course, it was made worse by the fact that he was drunk which, in hindsight, was a terrible idea. But the beer had been free-flowing, and they'd won the game, and he couldn't play anyway, so...

"My head hurts," he said, still laughing.

A warm hand landed on the back of his neck. "I called you a car."

The man had a slight accent, which meant it wasn't James, unless... "Scooter, are you doing your Rosetta Stone?"

There was a quiet scoff, and then the hand at his neck squeezed harder, and Pietro glanced over to see the very soft curls on Orion's head.

"Ace," Pietro murmured, reaching up to give the man's cheek a pat.

Orion laughed and carefully eased Pietro to his feet. "Petey, what the fuck have you done to yourself?"

He scoffed, looking down at his shoes which...did he always have four feet? No...no. No just two. He could run so much better with four though. He wriggled his toes, then realized something was missing. "My boot!" He started to lunge forward, but Orion caught him by the back of his T-shirt and hauled him against his chest. Orion wasn't as tall as him, but he was just as strong. Stronger, even. Maybe. At least his left arm because he was a lefty.

"Lefty loosey," he sang.

Orion smacked him upside the back of his head, which made the world swim. "What the fuck has gotten into you?"

Pietro sniffed, feeling heavy and sad all of a sudden, and he'd almost forgotten why. Then he remembered because it was the whole fucking reason he'd started drinking anyway. He missed Thierry's dinner. "I'm bad. Bad, bad man."

"Drunk, drunk man," Orion said. He looped his arm around Pietro's waist and began to walk him toward the back doors where none of the press could catch a glimpse of him sloppy and pathetic. "You wanna talk about it?"

"No," he said, then sniffed again. He wasn't going to cry or anything. He was just sad. He wondered if Gabriel would yell at him if he went to his house instead. "I hurt his feelings."

He glanced down to see Orion staring at him with a brow raised. His eyebrows were so blond. He traced one with his finger, and Orion batted him away. "You sound a little lovesick there, bud. You have a breakup?"

Pietro laughed. "No. Can't break up. He punched me."

At that, Orion went stiff all over. "Pietro. Petey...you know that if your partner hits you, that's abuse, right? Like, I know you're a big dude, but that's not okay."

Pietro's cheeks hurt from how wide he was smiling. Orion was such a sweet man. He patted his cheek to let him know. "I'm...he's not my boyfriend."

Orion's brows furrowed. "Okay. Buddy, you're not making much sense, and you don't look hurt..."

"I twishted my ankle," he reminded him primly.

Orion snorted and let Pietro's arm go just long enough to hit the little automatic door button. It swung wide and Pietro sighed in relief at the sight of a car waiting for him. God, he wanted to sit. He fumbled with the handle, then felt a little bit like his bones were made of liquid as he slid onto the seat. Orion was kind, though, and helped him get upright and buckled in.

"I won't throw up," Pietro vowed solemnly, but he thought maybe he was lying about that.

"If you do, they'll just bill you," Orion reminded him.

"Yeah. Because I'm rich," he reminded himself, and then the pain was back again because that was part of the problem, wasn't it? Thierry wasn't rich, and Pietro was. And Thierry was working in his kitchen because Pietro's brain was a big dumb dummy mess that couldn't even boil water without getting distracted and ruining the pan and leaving him hungry and...

"Bud."

Pietro blinked, and he realized his eyes were kind of hot. "I'm drunk."

Orion laughed. "Yeah. You are. Maybe I should go with you and make sure you get in okay."

The driver spun around suddenly and passed back a bottle of water. It was very cold, and Pietro let out a happy hum as he fumbled with the cap, then took several long drinks. "I'll be okay," he said after a beat.

A small voice in the back of his head was telling him he was going to be mortified come morning. His team wouldn't let him hear the end of it. He could only hope that Orion had been the only one there to hear the really embarrassing shit.

"What do you do when you fuck up?" Pietro asked.

Orion blinked at him. "What do you mean?"

"When your life is just a reminder to someone else that theirs is…wrong?" No, that wasn't the right word. "Broken?" No, that wasn't it, either. He squeezed his eyes shut and hated how the beer made everything so damn foggy. He just wanted to think. He took another long swallow of the water, until the bottle was empty. "I need to go home."

"Yeah." Orion gave his cheek a pat, then backed up and shut the door. Pietro kept his eyes shut, but he heard Orion lean in toward the driver and speak too softly for him to understand the words. But it was probably something about letting him know if Pietro got sick, or made a fool of himself, or something bad happened.

Orion was sweet like that.

It was too bad Pietro couldn't fall for a man like him. Life would be so much easier that way.

His baby face was fuckin' wasted on all these pretty-boy dickheads who were always so unkind. And the one time he decided to go and fall for someone else, they were too good for him. Far too good.

The car started down the street, and instead of making him sick, it just put him into a slight doze.

He woke with a start sometime later with a hand shaking his shoulder, and Pietro tried to bat the person away until he remembered he was in a hired car and the poor driver had to get home. He opened his eyes, and the world swam, but instead of a stranger helping to keep him upright, it was Thierry.

He blinked. It was so fucking late. What was he doing here...

"I'm not strong enough to lift you, so you're going to have to do most of the work," Thierry said.

Pietro stared owlishly at him. "Your accent is so fucking pretty. It's so much prettier than...than. *His*," he finally said. He couldn't bring himself to say Hervé's name.

Thierry just laughed and offered out his massive hand as he leaned heavily on his cane. Fuck, Pietro was such a goddamn mess. He steadied himself on the sidewalk, then turned to the driver, who was watching with an amused smirk.

"Pay?" he said, struggling for words. He was slightly more sober, but not enough.

The driver waved him off. "Got your account. Have a good night, sir."

"He called me sir," Pietro whispered—or, at least, he thought he whispered, but he wasn't so sure when his voice echoed off the pillars near his porch.

Thierry laughed again, quietly, as he held Pietro's hand, guiding him to the door. He let go only to open it, then helped the man inside. "Would you like water? Or something to eat? I saved your dinner."

"Dinner," Pietro said, then sniffed harder, swallowing against the lump of guilt in his throat. "I missed dinner." His voice cracked a little.

"I wasn't expecting you. You were at a game," Thierry said.

Pietro was far too drunk to read his tone, so he wasn't sure if Thierry was offended or not. His gaze darted between the direction of the kitchen and the massive stairs. "I can't."

Thierry lifted a brow. "Can't what?"

"Stairs," he said and gestured at them. "Too tall. Gonna fall down."

Thierry sighed, then bodily turned Pietro and walked him through the archway and into his sitting room—the one with his Xbox and the comfy couches instead of the monstrosity his designer had picked out which gave him a backache and a headache every time he heard the word "formal."

"Like this couch," he said, falling onto his side. He nuzzled his face into the cushion as he felt the couch dip with Thierry's weight. "So soft."

A hand brushed his hair off his forehead. "Do you need me to stay?"

Pietro squeezed his eyes shut, then wriggled around until he was on his back. He couldn't quite bring himself to look at Thierry, but he could see him in his periphery as he fixed his gaze on the ceiling fan. The blades were spinning, making the room spin with it, but it felt oddly strange, like being rocked.

"I'm a dick."

Thierry laughed. "*Ouais*, but we knew that."

Pietro tried to kick at him, but he couldn't make his legs work anymore. His limbs were sleepy and heavy and finally comfortable. "I left you alone. With dinner."

"There are worse places to be, and the food will keep." Thierry started to stand, and with a speed and strength Pietro didn't realize he possessed in that moment, his hand reached out and grabbed the man tightly.

Thierry froze, staring at him, one hand gripping his cane so tight, his knuckles were white against the rest of his tanned skin.

"I'm a dick," he repeated.

Thierry softened. "Are you looking for..." He muttered a word in French, then shook his head. "Absolution."

Pietro's lips quirked. "M'parents are *so* Catholic."

Thierry bowed his head. "Mine are something like that."

Lifting his hand off Thierry's wrist, Pietro dragged a touch over Thierry's broad forehead. He didn't have permission to do it—he knew that. He also wouldn't normally have had the courage, so maybe that alcohol was good for something. Thierry didn't pull away at any rate, and Pietro felt himself get bolder as his fingers moved down toward the man's jaw.

"Always liked your face."

Thierry snorted a laugh and reached up to curl his fingers around Pietro's wrist, gently pulling his arm down. "You're very drunk."

"I don't lie when I'm drunk," Pietro pouted. He stretched his legs out and winced. He vaguely remembered being let out of the boot, but he was sore from not having used his foot in a while. "I can play again."

"*Ah, bon,*" Thierry said.

Pietro tried to reach up and touch his lips. He loved the shapes they made when Thierry spoke French. He spoke it like he loved the language—not like other people Pietro had known who spoke it like the language owed him beauty and grace.

"You need to sleep," Thierry said, firmly setting Pietro's hand on his stomach.

"If we'd never...if Hervé had never..." Pietro licked his lips. Sleep was tugging at his edges, as much as he wanted to avoid it. He wasn't ready for this moment to be over.

"We don't need to do this now," Thierry said.

Pietro shook his head, closing his eyes again, because he knew he'd never have the courage after this. "Would you still have hated me?"

The silence was almost his answer. It would have been if

Thierry hadn't eventually spoken. "I never hated you. I've told you this."

"But you..."

"I envied you. Beautiful and kind and charming, and you didn't let it turn you ugly."

Pietro opened his eyes and found Thierry was looking down at his hands. "I'm not good."

"You are. Too many people have told you otherwise—convinced you—and that's wrong." Thierry finally turned his head to look at him. "You deserved better from me, from him. From a lot of people." He reached out and brushed Pietro's hair back, and in spite of being drunk and near to unconscious, Pietro was profoundly aware that he hadn't been touched like this—a simple, casual touch of affection, in so long. Long enough to make his chest burn. "I'm not ashamed to be working for you. I'm honored."

Pietro tried to make his mouth work, but his eyes were falling shut, and the words were wrapping around him like the only thing he'd ever need to comfort himself. He was vaguely aware, sometime later, that Thierry had draped a blanket over him.

His heart was totally and entirely fucked. And there was nothing he could do about it.

THE EASIEST THING in the world to do was pretend like that night had never happened. Pietro wasn't sure what kind of person that made him, but the next time he saw Thierry, which was on his Thursday night off when he was free to have a hot meal, Thierry's demeanor was exactly the same as it had always been.

Part of it stung, but he liked to believe Thierry was just

allowing him to save face, and he'd take that. They smiled tentatively at each other and didn't bring up Pietro's drinking or Hervé or the punch. And Pietro got to eat properly and bring good meals with him for his lunches and postgame fuel.

He got a few weird looks from Orion, and he had a vague, foggy memory of the pitcher having been the one to load him up in the car, but he couldn't remember what the hell he'd said. Part of him wanted to ask, but another part of him was just happy to get back to the damn game and let his terrible choices fall by the wayside.

He couldn't deny how oddly domestic it felt later that week, though, as he sat at his table with a very French-style roasted chicken sitting on his plate, Thierry at the sink washing up. The only thing that would have made it better was if Pietro could have invited Thierry to join him.

But he knew better than that now.

"Hey," he said after clearing half his plate.

Thierry was wiping out his cast-iron pan with a small cloth, and he turned his head, lifting a brow.

Pietro cleared his throat, then chased the sound with a sip of tepid water. "Uh."

Thierry's lip's twitched into a small grin. "Are you trying to find a way to tell me you don't like this dish?"

Pietro's eyes went wide. The reality was, he'd lost his train of thought—just like he always did. Only this time it wasn't from chasing a dozen other thoughts. This time was getting lost in the way the cords of Thierry's neck moved when he was scrubbing the pan.

"Uh. No. Sorry." He passed a hand down his face. "I was going to tell you that things are going to get a little hectic with the playoffs getting closer. Oh, I have this, um. This charity thing?" He bit the inside of his cheek because he loved doing charity, but all the fancy bells and whistles that came with it like thousand-dollar-a-plate dinners and shit—it just felt like pandering to the superrich. "Anyway, it's this little league thing for kids with, um. With disabilities."

Thierry set the cloth and pan down and gently swiveled on his stool. "That's something important to you?"

"I've been kind of the head, I guess, for a while," Pietro said absently, picking at his cuticle. He realized what he was doing when his finger began to sting, and he dropped his hand into his lap. "Anyway, I just…I mean to say that we should probably change the schedule a bit because I won't be here a lot. And when I am, I'm going to be watching tape and sleeping."

Thierry's eyes narrowed. "You still need to eat."

Pietro let out a small groan, though he was smiling through it. "Yes, thank you, Mom. I'm just saying I'm not going to have a lot of time to eat fresh meals. We're definitely going to make it to the World Series this year, and that takes up most of my attention."

Thierry's mouth softened a bit, and after a beat, he nodded. "I hope you do. I don't watch a lot of sports, but I catch your games when I can. I like baseball."

It was maybe the last thing in the world Pietro expected him to say, and he perked up. "*Shit*. Yeah? You do?"

Thierry held his hands up in surrender. "Not enough to talk about it. I don't know all the terms and slang."

Pietro waved him off. "I don't give a fuck about that. I just… you know. If you ever want to come to a game, you know a guy who could get you some sweet-ass tickets."

That seemed to almost force a laugh out of Thierry, who shook his head, but he didn't seem like he was saying no. "Do you think…it might be complicated for me? The steps. I would probably need to use my wheelchair since working here takes up most of my walking time."

Pietro's mouth opened, but no sound came out. "You

know," he said when he regained his composure, "you can use that here. Your wheelchair."

Thierry gave him a small, almost sad grin. "No, I can't."

"I'm not going to judge you if you…"

"*Bordel!*" Thierry said, dragging a hand down his face. "I don't think you're judging me. Your counters come to my nose if I'm sitting down."

Pietro sank back because he knew that. It was why he still had his assistant looking into the reno where he could have moving counters for the man. His face flamed hot, and he really just wanted to tell Thierry why his brain was the way it was, but he couldn't make the words come. "I just don't want you to be miserable all the time because you're working here and can't walk around after."

"Using my wheelchair doesn't make me miserable," Thierry told him quietly. "It's a relief most nights. I appreciate what I can do without it because I was told that would never happen, but using it means less pain for me." He went silent for a long second. "I'd like to be able to enjoy your game…if I can."

"You totally can," Pietro said. "There's plenty of disabled seating."

Thierry hesitated, then shrugged. "If you think it won't be a hassle."

Pietro wasn't sure, but he could easily put a call in to make sure it wouldn't be. "Look, let me put your name at the box office, and I'll make some calls to make sure there won't be any issues. You can bring a friend. Bring Sarah."

Thierry laughed quietly and threw the rag into the sink, then carefully eased off the stool and walked over to the table. Pietro's breath caught in his chest and then stayed there when Thierry actually lowered himself to a chair and sat.

"May I also bring others?"

A hot wave of jealousy hit Pietro, but he shoved it down as hard and fast as he could. "Yeah. Yeah, of course. Your boyfriend, or...?"

Thierry's eyes, he swore to God, were twinkling. "No. My friend Chris and his fiancée I think would like to come."

Pietro didn't even bother to pretend like he wasn't relieved. "As many people as you want."

Thierry lowered his eyes, but he didn't look demure or shy. He just looked tired, and maybe a little bit happy, and Pietro could live with that. "*Merci*."

"*Rien*," Pietro said back, only to make the man smile wider.

CHAPTER FOURTEEN

Circling his hips, Pietro's gaze was focused on Luke, who was up to bat. There were days when he felt old—like he was getting ready to be retired against his will. But it never lasted.

Then he'd see Luke, with his grey hair and soft wrinkles in the corners of his eyes, come up to bat. He'd knock one out of the park. He'd wink at the crowd as he rounded the bases like he had nowhere else better to be.

Luke was a veteran—traded a lot early on in his career, but he'd settled with the Vikings about six years before Pietro had come on, and though the man was slowing, he was still hot.

His breath held still in his chest as he watched Luke adjust his stance, then nod to the pitcher. He was one of the Hawk's rookies that year—drafted out of high school, four years on his college team, then right onto the field—and not just to have a cup of coffee in the majors.

The Hawks weren't going to make it to the Series that year, but they were close, and they'd done it with the kid on the mound.

Pietro remembered what it was like to be that young and that full of fire. He remembered the first time he'd faced his brother, their greenest season ever, and the first time they ever played against each other. He remembered the look of determination in Gabriel's eyes, and the feeling in Pietro's chest that he was going to prove himself.

The Vikings had lost that game, but in the two years Gabriel got to play, Pietro had enough of his own victories against his brother to feel like he'd earned something.

He missed all those years of facing Gabriel down though—almost like missing a limb. He was bitter and angry because a small part of him had fantasized about how one day Gabriel would be traded, and they'd be on the same team again, and it would have been...

Fuck.

It would have been something so damn good.

Crack!

Pietro was unsurprised to see the ball fly over the field, high above raised gloves, and into the outfield with no hope of reaching home before Orion crossed the plate. The crowd lost their damn minds, and he laughed as Luke pointed and winked at the poor rookie, who looked like he wanted to put his fist through Luke's face.

There was nothing to be done now.

It was top of the ninth, and they were up by eight. Even if Pietro struck out, they were taking this. They were one step closer.

"Your boy watching?"

Pietro spit on the ground instead of cursing in James' face because fuck that guy, God damn it. Pietro had been so good all night not thinking about the fact that Thierry was there with his friends, somewhere near the owner's box.

Watching him.

"I hate you, Scooter," he mumbled as he swung the bat a little too close to James' face.

The pitcher, who was very obviously pretending to warm up his arm, just laughed. "Come on. You know you're gonna knock one out for him."

"No fucking pressure," Pietro hissed.

"Since when has it ever been pressure for you?"

At that, Pietro felt hot resentment climb up his throat because he was sick to death of so many people assuming he didn't work his ass off for everything he accomplished. Yes, he ran faster than a lot of them. He had broken records and won awards, and he'd seen his team to the World Series more than once. He had three rings sitting in a little case at home.

But it didn't come from nothing. There was *always* pressure to perform, because the moment he started to fail would be the moment people started to pay attention.

"Hey," James started, but Orion was already running toward him with a grin on his face, so Pietro leapt at the distraction and gave Orion's shoulder a gentle tap before grabbing his helmet and stepping up to the plate.

Everything around him became white noise. The pitcher in front of him was nothing more than a shape. All the voices had morphed into nothing but sounds. Words didn't exist. Not now. His gaze was focused ahead of him, and though he could feel hundreds of eyes boring into him—they didn't matter.

He blinked against the low glow of the setting sun and pulled his helmet down a little tighter before spitting on the ground, then tapping the edge of his shoe with his bat once, then twice. His bones settled as his knees bent.

He checked the pressure on his ankle, then the line between left and center. They were waiting for him, studying his posture, trying to anticipate him. He glanced over at Luke, who had made it to second—and the fucker winked at him.

His tongue dragged over his lip, and then he nodded.

The ball flew past him.

Strike one.

He rolled his shoulders, taking a single step back before adjusting his stance. He was learning this kid too—absorbing what he could give. He didn't have the unnatural talent James did, and he didn't hold a candle to the pitcher Gabriel had been, but he was good.

Just...not good enough. Not yet.

Pietro closed his eyes and couldn't help the image he'd conjured of Thierry watching him. He breathed in, and then the ball came flying.

Crack!

He didn't look. He didn't dare hope as he began to run like hellhounds were nipping at the backs of his feet. He ran until he saw the right outfielder drop his glove, and then he knew. It had gone over the fence.

He circled third, then began a slow trot home, grinning at the quiet insults Garcia shot at him. He fought the urge to finger-gun the crowd, and the only reason he didn't was because his gaze caught a glimpse of a man, way up in the stands, gripping the railing.

He was too far away to make out the details, other than a lock of dark hair over his forehead and a broad smile on full lips.

"Don't tell me that wasn't for your boy," James murmured in his ear as he skated down the steps and dropped onto the bench. He shoved his shoulder against Pietro's, almost knocking him over. "Or I will fucking hit you."

Pietro didn't do much more than laugh, but his friend was right. There was no denying it, and frankly, he didn't want to.

CHAPTER FIFTEEN

Pietro: Wait for me.

Thierry didn't really know what the hell do to do with that text other than wait, but it also felt a little bit like taking orders, and he wasn't sure he loved that. Still, he followed directions this time because it was that or take off with Sarah, Hailey, and Chris, who would have given him endless shit for the rest of the night.

After all, how many people got texts from an MLB star who hit a home run to secure their win?

It didn't help that watching Pietro in his element—even from high above the field—was erotic in ways Thierry had never considered before. It was one thing watching him on TV, but it was quite another to lean over the railing and watch the way his eyes narrowed and the sheer competence of his movements as he knocked the ball over the fence and casually made his way to home plate.

He wasn't as cocky as the player before him, but that was also part of his charm.

Thierry was in deep, and it was starting to become a fucking problem.

Pietro had sent a second text, giving Thierry directions to a little out-of-the-way set of double doors he could access with a code. It was meant to lead him to a lounge where friends and family hung out, and he let out a sharp breath of relief when he got there and found the place almost empty.

The only other occupant was a man in a suit speaking in rapid Spanish, who didn't bother even glancing over at Thierry as he wheeled up to a set of chairs and parked himself. He wasn't quite sure what to do or how long to wait, and his stomach was starting to squirm.

Luckily, he wasn't tortured for long. A door at the far end of the hall swung open, and a beat later, Pietro appeared. He was wearing a T-shirt and jeans, his team baseball cap pulled low over his brow, and there were stress lines by his eyes, but he was smiling the moment their gazes met.

"Where are your friends?" he demanded as he dropped into the chair nearest to Thierry.

"Left." When Pietro raised his brows, Thierry shook his head. "Trust me, it's for the best."

Pietro shrugged, then stretched his legs out with a heavy groan that, if Thierry didn't know better, might have been suggestive. "Are you hungry?"

Thierry laughed. "No. I compromised all my morals and ate stadium food. Chris bought me a hot dog."

Pietro twisted in the chair, his back arched in a way that had to be painful, but he hooked his chin over the cushion and grinned. "I love the way you say that. *'ot dog.*"

Thierry rolled his eyes at Pietro's shitty attempt at a French accent. "I hate the way you Americans make them."

"Why? Should they be stuffed with escargot?"

A laugh burst from his chest, and Thierry leaned forward over his legs. "Keep it up and you'll know what I'll be serving you at your next dinner."

Pietro pulled a face. "I'm not eating snails. I tried one on a dare once and never again."

Thierry waved him off. "Because no one has ever made them right for you. You need a lot of butter, and some garlic…"

"And a lot of red wine," Pietro said, "to chase that shit down. And speaking of…want to grab a nightcap at my place?"

Thierry wasn't quite sure what to say. They hadn't really defined their relationship as employer and employee, but they also hadn't quite defined themselves as friends, either. Thierry wouldn't have even thought it was possible, except Pietro was looking at him like he really wanted him to say yes.

"I don't have anywhere to be," he finally said.

Pietro grinned. "Thank fuck. I have to be up at the crack of dawn tomorrow, but I'm too wound up to sleep right now." He hopped up from the chair and kicked gently at Thierry's wheel. "Tell me you saw that shit though."

Thierry hummed as he unset his brake and began to push after him. "Saw what?"

"Don't fuck with me. Do not even pretend like you weren't screaming when I knocked the ball out of the park," Pietro said, pushing a door open and letting Thierry move ahead of him.

Thierry debated about messing with him for longer. He didn't want to think too hard about what it meant when he realized he liked seeing the man flustered. "Chris kept making me drink lemonade. I had to piss a lot."

"If you missed my fucking home run tonight…" Pietro started to whine.

Thierry eventually laughed as they went through a second

door and into a parking garage. "I didn't miss your very nice hit."

"*Very nice hit*," Pietro mimicked, another bad rendition of Thierry's accent. "Fucking blasphemy."

Thierry laughed again as he followed the man all the way to the end of the row, stopping by a very small, very sleek sports car. He hesitated then, knowing he could fit his chair in, but it would be tough. And it would probably scratch the leather.

"Maybe I should call a car," he started.

Pietro took a step back. "Shit. Shit...will that...I could probably squeeze it in the trunk. It folds, right? And uh..."

Thierry held up a hand. "The wheels come off. It fits, but it might nick your seats."

Pietro's shoulders sagged. "Jesus, dude. I don't give a shit about my *seats*." Thierry opened his mouth to argue because Pietro should, considering he drove something so nice, but the man didn't give him a chance. "If you want to take a car home, I'll call one. But I swear to God, I don't care."

The small curl of resentment made itself known again because what Thierry wouldn't give to be able to drive his own car—which was, frankly, a piece of shit. And he didn't want to hate Pietro for being able to have whatever nice thing he wanted, but it wasn't easy.

Easing himself up to stand, he waited for Pietro to unlock the doors, and then he sat and carefully began to disassemble his chair. He could feel Pietro's eyes on him, but he didn't hurry, trying his best to be careful. When it was safely stowed, he sat back in the too-comfortable seats and did up his buckle.

"You good?"

Thierry nodded.

The car started up with a roar, then settled into a gentle purr as Pietro backed out and headed for the exit. The tension in the car was palpable, but before Thierry could bring it up, Pietro glanced over at him.

"You know, we don't always have to hang at my place. If you ever want to just stay at home...I mean. I don't mind if we go to yours."

Thierry shook his head. "It's a shithole."

Pietro winced. "I seriously doubt it's that bad, but I also don't care. I mean all of this—" He waved his hand as he rolled to a stop and used a little card to swipe at the gate. The arm lifted, and Pietro pulled out. After a second, he shook his head and blinked, like he was coming out of a fog. "Sorry. What was I saying?"

"About how you like to mingle with the plebs," Thierry said, using one of Sarah's favorite phrases.

Pietro choked a little. "Oh my God, where did you even learn that word?"

Thierry scoffed. "I went to school. Not just beat, maim, kill bodyguard school, either."

At that, Pietro laughed so hard he swerved a bit. "Fuck, dude. Why didn't you tell me you were funny?"

"I've always been funny. You just never listened."

The mood sobered instantly because anything to do with their past would always be sharp and bitter. But it didn't last.

"Like I was saying," Pietro stressed after a beat, "I care so much more about the company than where we're hanging out."

Thierry thought it was a nice sentiment, but he wasn't entirely sure he believed Pietro was telling the truth. The man was kind—almost painfully so—and Thierry had no doubt he would have made himself uncomfortable for the sake of others. Without question.

"I like your place," Thierry said after a short moment. "And you have all the good wine."

Pietro laughed again, and the tension started to fade. "Okay. That's fair. Just don't let me get too wasted. The last time I drank..."

He trailed off, and Thierry swallowed thickly because the last time Pietro drank, he'd poured the man onto his sofa and tucked him in. And there had been a moment Thierry still thought about, even now. A moment he hadn't wanted to let go, but he knew it was for the best.

It was dangerous to go there again.

It was easy to slip into silence after that though. Pietro rambled on about the game, about his season, about their chances of making it to the World Series. Thierry understood almost none of it, but the sound of Pietro's voice was soothing, and he loved how much passion was in his tone. It made Thierry want to learn, want to understand all the subtle nuances of this game that made up a good piece of who Pietro was.

And the man didn't slow down until they neared his driveway, and then he stopped himself with a laugh. "Oh my God, why did you let me ramble on like that?"

Thierry smiled at him and shook his head. "I like listening to you talk."

Pietro's laugh was slightly self-deprecating. "Yeah, right."

"You think I'd lie to you?"

"I think you're nice," Pietro fired back, and that was a surprise because Thierry wasn't sure when the hell he'd ever given *that* impression. "I think you don't want to hurt my feelings. I just..." He shrugged, and the car rolled to a stop as the garage opened. Rubbing the back of his neck, he turned his slightly pinked face toward Thierry. "I can kind of go off on tangents sometimes. You can absolutely stop me."

"I don't want to stop you," Thierry told him, and he hoped his honesty was obvious in his tone, because he meant it.

Pietro said nothing, but a new sort of tension flooded the car, and Thierry was grateful when the engine died, and he was able to get out. He debated about getting his chair, but his legs felt stable, and it wasn't like he and Pietro were going for a run, so he shut the door.

"Do you need help?" Pietro asked.

Thierry shook his head and gestured toward the door. "I'll leave it for now."

Pietro looked like he wanted to argue for a minute, and then he seemed to change his mind and turned, leading the way inside. Thierry had never used the garage door before, and he hadn't realized it opened right into the kitchen. It felt odd being there now without work to do, and he let his fingers trail on the counter as he slowly made his way inside.

"This is weird, right?" Pietro asked.

Thierry laughed. "I was thinking something like that. It's not weird. I just never expected to be here with you like this."

Pietro bit his lower lip, then let out a slow breath and grabbed glasses from the cupboard.

"You don't want to be like a college student?" Thierry asked.

Pietro frowned before his eyes went wide. "Oh, fuck you. That was a joke." He grabbed the wine, then rummaged through one of the drawers for a wine key. "I stand by it though."

"I'm French. If you think I haven't spent too many nights with only a bottle of wine and a day-old baguette, you don't understand us very well," Thierry shot back as Pietro led the way into his sitting room.

Glancing over his shoulder, Pietro shrugged. "I think it's safe to say after getting to know you, I definitely don't understand the French at all. Though...do you even count? I know your secrets now, Mr. England."

"I count enough," Thierry said, then flipped him off while he lowered himself onto the far cushion of the couch. "I lived in Paris longer than I didn't."

Pietro laughed as he carefully measured out two very large pours, then handed the glass over and settled back, hitching one foot up on the coffee table and turning to face Thierry.

"Yeah, yeah." He took a long drink, then sighed. "Was it hard? Being in a new country and everything?"

Thierry took a sip, and he waved his hand dismissively as he swallowed it down. "Not really. My French was poor, but my parents spoke enough of it at home that it didn't take me long to catch up with everyone else. They never wanted me to feel English, so they treated us moving back to Paris like it was coming home. I never did think I'd leave again."

"And now you're here," Pietro said quietly.

Thierry inclined his head, a single nod, then took another drink. "It didn't feel very much like home anymore...in the end. After I was released from the hospital, and the doctors weren't sure how...what...my recovery would be like, I started to realize it wasn't a very friendly city to be disabled."

Pietro grimaced, but Thierry could tell the expression wasn't pity. "That's rough, man."

"It is what it is," Thierry offered back, because it was. There was no point in lamenting over his city—which was once an ancient Roman City before it was ever called French—was not modern or accommodating. He knew better than to hope the world would change for people like him. "I will go back and visit, of course. There's still a place for me. Just...in a different way."

Pietro was nearly finished with his glass, and Thierry realized how quickly he'd been drinking his own. It was dangerous, and yet, he couldn't help but lean forward when the other man offered to top him off. "I guess that's why I love baseball, you know?"

Thierry frowned and shook his head. "I don't understand."

Pietro drank and waved his hand through the air. "It's different. I mean, it can still be shitty. Before players started coming out left and right, I was kind of terrified to go pro. My parents took the queer thing pretty well, but I think that's because Gabriel and I were the youngest of so fucking many, they just stopped worrying about who was going to bring home grandbabies."

Thierry pulled a face, which made Pietro laugh. "You want kids?"

Pietro choked a little on his swallow. "Oh God. I, uh...I don't know? Right now, that's a firm hell no, and I don't see that changing. So many guys on the team have kids and like, shit, they love them, right? But they never get to see them. And I know how much it sucks to have part-time parents."

Thierry couldn't quite relate to that, either. The American way of parenting was foreign to him—but maybe it was also just that his parents loved in a different way.

"Sorry. I'm being way too melancholy for wine night," Pietro said. He leaned back a little further, then stretched his long arm out for the bottle when he winced.

"You're hurt?" Thierry asked.

Pietro scoffed. "Nah. Just sore after the game. Normally, I soak my happy ass in a nice Epsom salt bath."

Thierry's eyes went wide. "I can call a ride if you..."

"No," Pietro barked, then flushed and shook his head. "Sorry, just...no. I wanted the company. I wanted *your* company," he amended, like the difference was important.

And hell, maybe it was, which made Thierry's stomach twist into a knot. The tension hit him suddenly, and his legs began to tremble a little. He immediately felt it when Pietro's gaze locked on his thighs, but before he could say anything, the man was sitting up further, setting his wineglass down and making grabby motions with his hands.

Thierry froze. "What..."

"Massage time."

Thierry started to shake his head. "Ah, *non, je suis*..." His words died off at the flat look Pietro gave him.

"You're not going to put me off by speaking French. And hey, look, I won't if you really don't want me to, okay? If it won't help."

It would help, which was the problem. It wasn't just for the tremors but for the lack of touch that wasn't clinical. Sarah, Hailey, and Chris were free with their affections, but when Thierry wasn't in PT, people tended to avoid him like even the most subtle hugs would shatter his carefully put-together façade.

Pietro was offering him something he'd been craving since well before his accident, and the words to resist him were getting caught in his throat.

"Did I overstep?"

Thierry licked his lips, then shook his head and tried to shift in his seat. His legs were being uncooperative, but Pietro wasn't deterred. He grabbed them by the edge of Thierry's jeans and hauled them up, over his thighs, feet pressed against the cushion behind Pietro's back.

Scooting further into the V of Thierry's calves, Pietro laid his hands down on his knees. "Just tell me if I hurt you."

Thierry nodded, still unable to unstick his tongue, so he quickly gulped down the rest of his wine. The buzz settled quietly in his blood, making his face warm and his head a little fuzzy, but it was nice. It was made even nicer when Pietro began a firm stroke from ankle to thigh, the pressure just hard enough that he could feel it properly.

"It's not the same," he found himself saying.

Pietro didn't look up, but he hummed quietly to show he was listening.

"I can walk. I can move them without much thought, but it's...it's not the same. I don't feel it the same." English was getting harder, the way it always did when he started drinking. He wanted to sink further into that feeling, so he reached for the bottle and just managed to snag it without tipping it over. He stared at his glass, then set it down and took a swig from the opening, grinning when Pietro laughed.

"That's what the fuck I'm talking about. Gimme," he said.

Thierry passed it over and followed the line of Pietro's bobbing Adam's apple as he took several gulps. The bottle was more than half-gone now, and Thierry knew they were encroaching on dangerous territory. But he didn't care.

How could he, when Pietro was so...

Perfect?

"Okay, get comfy," Pietro ordered when he passed the wine back.

Thierry did his best, though he wasn't even sure what comfortable meant for him anymore. His legs were still trembling, his muscles alternately seizing and relaxing, but it was hard to care when he was gently buzzing from the wine and losing himself to the sensations of Pietro running impossibly strong hands over his body.

"Good?"

Thierry blinked, then came back to himself a bit more as Pietro laughed. "*Desolé.*"

Pietro laughed again, leaning further up onto his knees as he kneaded harder along the tops of Thierry's thighs. "You apologize way too much."

"I'm..."

Pietro squeezed harder and gave him a glower, and Thierry's jaw snapped shut. "That's better." He eased up a bit, dragging his hands down before settling into the other side of the sofa and taking both of Thierry's feet into his lap. "I never told my brother this, but I took three months of massage classes after his injury. When he was first in the hospital, his PT tech told us that one of the best ways for him to start regaining range of motion was keeping his muscles limber."

Thierry bit his lower lip as Pietro hit a particularly sensitive spot along the arches of his feet. He fought back a groan, but tendrils of pleasure were racing through his limbs. "Did it help?"

"He wouldn't let me touch him," Pietro said quietly. "Which...I mean, I get it. Our relationship got a little weird after he was hurt, and he still thinks I'm an asshole."

"Are you?" Thierry asked. His head flopped to the side and his eyes closed against his will. He was almost floating, and he never wanted to come down. It had been so long—*God*, it had been so long.

Pietro snorted softly. "I can be. It was worse with him because I didn't know what to do with all these fuckin' feelings, you know? I was angry at him for being in the wrong place at the wrong time, and I was angry at the person who hit him. I was angry at myself for being okay and for wanting to, you know, still be good at the game." Pietro went quiet for a long moment, then he sighed as he hooked his fingers around the edges of Thierry's socks and pulled them off. Thierry wanted to protest when Pietro began to rub between his toes, but it felt too good to stop him.

"I was angry that he was hurt in a way that meant he couldn't keep going."

At that, Thierry opened his eyes. "It's sports, no? You get hurt and you're done."

Pietro's smile was a little soft as he shook his head. "Not

always. Shit, baseball is full of players who defied the norm. Dudes with missing arms, missing legs. Deaf. Hell, there was even a blind guy who played in New York for years. But... even with all this long history of people making it work, Gabriel..." He stopped and took in a shaking breath. "He still lost it."

"Why?" Thierry asked, his voice barely a whisper.

Pietro squeezed his ankle tightly. "He was a pitcher—and he can't pitch without the use of that arm. I think...God, I think I held on to my anger longer than he did, and that most definitely makes me an asshole."

Thierry didn't quite know what to say. No one in his life loved him enough to be angry on his behalf. Hervé was in town to reconcile, but only to deal with his own guilt. To make himself feel better. His parents had been too eager to send him overseas because it was easier for them to deal with occasional updates rather than watch Thierry struggle hour by hour, day by day.

And maybe he'd feel differently if someone like Pietro raged on his behalf, but it was impossible to know.

The massage picked back up again, and the moment quietly passed.

"I know you wanted to be a chef," Pietro said softly a few moments later. "That was something I knew about you before, uh...before everything."

Thierry closed his eyes again and sank into the sensations. "*Ouais.*"

"Do you ever miss what you used to do?"

"Chasing after Hervé and his drunk friends?" Thierry asked with only a hint of scorn. "No. I just didn't realize how miserable I was until I was forced to leave it." He shifted, something sort of hot and not quite uncomfortable under his skin. He wasn't sure what it was—a familiar feeling, but he couldn't quite find the words for it. He didn't know if he wanted to lean in and chase or pull away.

Pietro's hands moved to the backs of his knees, and it got worse.

He shifted, then froze when he heard a strange noise, and flushed hard when he realized it was coming from him. A moan—chest-deep and wanting.

Pietro's hands stilled, but they didn't leave him. "You..."

Thierry wasn't brave enough to look, but he felt it now—the hardness pressing behind the zipper of his jeans. And fuck—*fuck*—it had been a long time since that happened. He'd tried to masturbate plenty of times since the accident and always failed. His erections had been involuntary and pointless.

Until now.

"It happens to me," Pietro said in a rush. He sounded embarrassed, but he still wasn't pulling away. In fact, he seemed to be holding on tighter, which was only making Thierry's situation worse because he was starting to actively want. "I can't tell you how many embarrassing boners I've gotten during massages after games and shit. Uh..."

Thierry licked his lips and waited.

"Is that what's happening? Do you want me to stop?"

It would be so easy to lean into the lie and just tell Pietro this meant nothing—it was just his body's way of reacting. And yet it felt almost cruel to deny himself, even if it meant Pietro throwing him out on his ass, because for so long, he wasn't sure he could want anyone again.

Not just physically, either. His life had changed so fucking drastically, and he'd come to realize that working for Hervé, the sacrifice he made all those years ago had been connection with anyone else.

And Pietro was sitting here offering him scraps of it, and he was too afraid to deny him the answer to that small, simple question.

"Don't stop."

Pietro's fingers spasmed, and Thierry finally forced himself to open his eyes and look at the other man.

"I'm hard because of you," Thierry went on.

Pietro swallowed thickly, and then he shifted in his seat. "Me too."

Thierry's ears rang for a second, almost like they were unwilling to believe what he was saying. "Are you…"

Pietro let out a high, tense laugh. "You can tell me to go fuck myself and, shit. I will, I swear. We'll never speak of it again. But fair's fair, and you were honest, so I should be too." He paused, then bowed his head. "I've wanted you for a little while now."

Not a long while, but somehow that made it better. He knew he wouldn't mind if Pietro had found him attractive before, but he didn't want to know if this man had wanted him when he was nothing more than hired muscle. When he was a man bitter and angry and wanted someone as kind as Pietro was to hurt.

Because that wasn't him anymore.

The bullet hadn't killed him, but it had most certainly set in motion the destruction of those parts of him he now desperately wanted to carve away.

"Do you," Pietro started, then fell silent.

Thierry waited on a knife's edge for the question he wasn't ever going to be brave enough to ask.

Pietro looked up. "Do you want to go upstairs?"

CHAPTER SIXTEEN

The moment the words left his mouth, Pietro felt like the biggest jackass in the world. It wasn't just the risk of rejection, which seemed imminent considering how on edge Thierry was, but also asking the man, whose legs were clearly refusing to cooperate, to go *upstairs*?

Fuck his fucking brain.

Fuck it for being such a...

"Yes."

Pietro froze, definitely buzzed and a little worried that his desire for Thierry was making him hallucinate the things he wanted to hear. He gently pulled his hands off the man's legs and looked up at him. "Yes?"

Thierry's face was unreadable, but there was a light in his eyes, almost amused. "Unless you didn't mean it?"

"I meant it. Shit," Pietro said in a rush. He glanced toward the hallway, then back at Thierry. "I don't have an elevator."

At that, Thierry laughed so hard, his head fell back against the cushions. "*Je sais.*"

"I mean..."

Very carefully, Thierry pulled his legs away, dropping them to the floor. He didn't move closer to Pietro, but his hands were curled in tension like he wanted to, and Pietro wished to God he would. "I know what you meant. I know what you're asking. I have had sex before."

If Pietro's face got any hotter, he'd burst into flames. "I. Uh. Is that what you want?"

"Is that what you were asking for?" Thierry countered.

Pietro realized he should probably be more direct. The worst mistakes in his life had come from lack of communication. "I want to do anything with you." It wasn't the first time he was profoundly aware that ADHD and drinking didn't mix well. His brain was ten steps ahead of him now, and his tongue was loose. "I really want to kiss you."

Thierry's hands uncurled, and then he lifted them, and Pietro found himself shifting closer without realizing it. In fact, he was so distracted by Thierry's movements, he hadn't realized they were about to touch until warm pressure hit the back of his neck, and he realized it was Thierry's fingers pushing up into his hair.

"Oh," he breathed out.

Thierry laughed, a soft sound mostly through his nose. Then there was no distance between them at all, and their lips were meeting in the space between. Pietro groaned and opened for him, and Thierry's grip on him tightened as he slid his tongue into Pietro's mouth.

They were both a little wine-sour, Thierry's own flavor a little salty from the food at the field, and it was the best thing Pietro had ever tasted. More than anything, he wanted to sling his leg over Thierry's, straddle him, and rut until he came, but he also wanted more.

He wanted Thierry in his bed—naked, writhing under his hands. He wanted to lower himself onto the man's cock and open himself up and just feel stretched and needy. His dick gave a firm twitch behind his pants, and he palmed himself with his free hand as he broke away from the kiss.

"So. Upstairs?"

"You might have to help me a little bit," Thierry said.

Pietro would do literally anything he had to in order to get that man into his bed. He wasn't strong enough to hope that this would ever happen again, so he was going to hold on with both hands and take every single thing Thierry offered.

"Promise me something," Pietro said as Thierry leaned on him. His movement was strong and steady, but Pietro sure as hell didn't mind the touch.

Thierry looked at him as he reached for the banister and carefully lifted one leg up onto the top step. "What is it?"

Pietro swallowed and felt like an ass for even bringing it up, but he knew they couldn't go further until he was sure everything beyond tonight would be okay. "Promise you aren't going to freak out in the morning and quit on me."

Thierry's hand spasmed against the wood railing, and he didn't meet Pietro's gaze for a long moment. "I wouldn't put our work relationship at risk. I know you need someone."

Pietro wasn't just thinking of himself. He'd get by—he'd been getting by for years, no matter how many medical professionals it pissed off. But he also knew that Thierry couldn't risk losing his job, and he didn't want pride or fear to take that away.

"I do need you," Pietro said slowly. "But I also like you. I'm...I don't want to lose any part of what we have."

Thierry seemed to relax at that, and he turned slightly, using his free hand to cup Pietro's cheek. It was warm and soft, and he couldn't help but think of the last time Thierry had touched his face. It had left him bleeding, and this almost felt like it was rewriting history.

Was he a fool?

Maybe, but it was impossible to care.

"I won't leave you," Thierry said. "I don't want the impossible. I just want you to touch me."

Pietro almost choked on his own tongue, but he managed to keep control of himself as he urged Thierry to take the first step and then the second. It was slower than he wanted but faster than he expected before they made it to the landing, and then Thierry followed with his fingers linked around Pietro's, and he opened the door to his bedroom.

It was messy, because his shit was always messy, but the housekeeper had been there recently enough that he didn't look like a total slob. His bed was unmade, but it just meant less work to do when he finally got Thierry between his sheets.

"Can you just...I'm gonna," he said, thumbing over his shoulder, trying desperately to grasp onto words.

Thierry smiled at him softly. "I'll undress. Go do what you need to do."

It was worded sweetly but almost like permission for Pietro to leave the room and have a quiet freak-out while he hunted down lube and his box of condoms. It was enough to settle some of the storming chaos in his gut as he moved into the bathroom, and he pressed his forehead to the closed door and took several breaths before turning back to the sink.

There wasn't a chance in hell he was going to remember where everything was, so he just hoped his past-self kept his shit somewhere logical. The medicine cabinet was empty, but he dropped to his knees and let out a sigh of relief when he saw a small, unopened box of condoms that came with a few packets of lube sitting under the sink.

Throwing it on the side of the faucet, he stared at his reflection and willed himself not to get lost in his head because Thierry was just outside the door, waiting for him.

Grabbing mouthwash, he swished it around and met his own gaze.

He was still buzzing, but the thrill of having Thierry here was enough to simmer the alcohol down into a faint white noise, making it just a little easier to say yes to everything he was being offered. He spat in the sink, then washed the blue tinge down with water before grabbing the condoms and heading back into his bedroom.

The moment his gaze set on Thierry, he regretted not having the attention span enough to undress, because the man looked so good, Pietro's dick attempted to burst through the front of his stiff jeans. He was lying on his back, half propped up by pillows, watching him. He had one hand curled around his cock, which was half-hard, and his lips were parted, eyes half-lidded and dark.

"I," Pietro tried to say. He tossed the condoms onto the pile of blankets at the foot of the bed, and then his hands began to work at his button and zipper. "You look fucking amazing."

Thierry chuckled quietly, his gaze trained on Pietro's hands, which were struggling. "Are you alright?"

Pietro laughed and dragged a hand down his face. "I'm so turned on, I can't focus." He rolled his shoulders back, then forced himself to get the damn jeans open, shoving them to his knees. He kicked at the legs as he made his way to the side of the bed and managed to get there without falling on his face. When his right leg was free, he pressed his knee to the edge of the mattress and laid a hand on Thierry's sternum, which was thick with black hair.

"Hello," Thierry said.

Pietro felt a shiver race up his spine, and he leaned in to kiss over Thierry's nipple. "Hey."

Thierry's hand flew to the back of Pietro's head, holding him there, and he took that as the nonverbal request for more that it was. He opened his lips, then closed them down hard with his teeth behind to bite—not stinging, but firm.

Thierry gasped and dug his fingers into Pietro's hair even harder. "Ah. *Putain.*"

Pietro grinned and licked at the nipple before fighting Thierry's grip and lifting his head. He managed to get the last leg of his jeans off, then swung it over Thierry's hips and settled himself down—not resting all of his weight on the man. His hands pressed against his chest, trailing down toward his stomach where there was a thick knot of scar tissue.

He knew what it was, and he couldn't stop staring.

"Three surgeries," Thierry said quietly. He reached between them and curled a hand around Pietro's wrist, dragging his hand over to the spot. "I can't feel very much there."

Pietro traced the jagged flesh with his thumb, then looked up. "Will it hurt if we fuck like this?"

Thierry's brows lifted, and color rose on his cheeks. "I don't know, but I want to try." He let Pietro's wrist go and grasped his hips, pulling him down so their cocks pressed together. Pietro's was still covered by the fabric of his briefs, but the friction was enough to send him racing toward pleasure.

"Jesus, fuck," he moaned. His head dropped low, and he began to rock his hips. It wasn't enough, yet it was almost too much. It had been too fucking long since he'd been in bed with someone he wanted this desperately, and he was going to humiliate himself if he wasn't careful. "Can you fuck me?"

When he was met with silence, he looked up to find Thierry watching him with an unreadable expression. "Are you asking me if I will or if I'm capable."

Pietro was hit with a rush of shame. "Fuck. I...I meant if you're able. I just...God, I'm sorry. I don't mean to be patronizing. I just don't know where you're at, and I want you so much, and..."

His words were cut off when Thierry grabbed him and yanked him into a kiss so rough, teeth scraped his lip, and he swore he tasted blood. He opened himself to it, wanting more, begging wordlessly for Thierry to take anything and everything he wanted. His body was alight with need, and every brush of Thierry's hands was an exquisite promise of torture as he raced toward the inevitable end.

"I need you," Thierry was murmuring against his lips. He pulled back but not far enough for Pietro to see his face.

He closed his eyes shaking his head. "I want it to be good for you."

"It will be." Thierry's nails raked his sides. "Take these off."

Pietro carefully lifted high on his knees as Thierry's fingers hooked around the waistband of his briefs and drew them down. It was a small struggle, but soon enough, the other man flung them across the room, and Pietro dragged the T-shirt over his head. As it fell off the side of the mattress, Thierry pushed up on one elbow and traced a touch from Pietro's throat, all the way down to where his hard cock was jutting from his thick, black hair.

"*Je suis très chaud.* Do you have...?"

"Yes," Pietro said in a rush, and he was careful still not to put too much pressure on Thierry's legs as he leaned back and groped for the box. He got it after a couple of tries, and he tore the corner with his teeth before letting the three condoms and the three packets of lube tumble onto the blanket.

The pair of them stared down before Pietro grabbed the lube and pressed it into Thierry's hand. "I don't want a lot of prep. I like to feel it. I have a toy if that helps, because I want to be opened up on a cock."

Thierry swallowed thickly, and Pietro felt him harden, felt him pulse beneath him. "I think I can perform."

There was an edge of teasing to his honest words, and

Pietro grinned as he watched Thierry roll on the condom, then coat his hand until it was slick and shining in the dim lamplight. He shifted back to give the man room to coat his cock, and then Thierry's hands moved to his hips again, drawing him forward.

When his fingers began to circle Pietro's hole, he froze. "I want..."

"I know, I know," Thierry said, like he was soothing a skittish beast. "I know. Just let me get you wet, *chéri.*"

Pietro's entire body shuddered at the sweet name, and he was helpless to do anything but lean forward and let Thierry dip two slick, fat fingers inside him. The burn was intense, eclipsing anything else he was thinking and feeling. He lost himself to it, the quiet murmur of Thierry's voice in his ear nothing but noise.

It ended too quickly for his liking, the sudden emptiness in his hole almost startling. But it didn't last. Thierry lined himself up, then gave a single, short thrust.

The head of his cock caught on Pietro's rim, and out of almost reflex, he bore down, taking it inside. A short groan escaped his chest as he stretched wide, and they both froze as Pietro's arms began to tremble with the strain of keeping himself upright.

"*Tu es très bon pour moi,*" Thierry murmured. "So good. Look at you take it."

Pietro had not been expecting dirty talk, and he was half-sure Thierry was switching between French and English to rile him up.

And shit, it was working.

He was hot all over, and desperate, pushing down slowly as he let Thierry's cock stretch him wide open. It was more than he expected—so much better than fingers, though he realized in that long moment of having those digits inside of him, he could have done that all night too. He could have just lain there and let Thierry finger him until he was loose and soaked and unable to do anything but cry the other man's name.

Maybe if the universe cared about him enough to give him this one more time.

His thighs started to shake as he bottomed out, then let himself rest on Thierry's hips, feeling the man pulsing inside of him. He found the courage to look down as Thierry pressed thumbs into the joins of his hips, and he found naked desire staring back at him.

"You good?" he managed to ask, his voice hoarse.

Thierry nodded. "Better than good. Can you move?"

"I just," Pietro said, the words almost getting stuck in his throat. "I need a second?"

Thierry said nothing, but he dropped his arms and pushed up onto his elbows. "A kiss?"

Pietro almost laughed because he hadn't realized how desperately he wanted that until the other man offered. He gasped as he leaned forward, changing the angle of Thierry's cock which hit just right. He clenched around him, making Thierry groan into the kiss, making him grip harder, take more.

"Yes," Thierry hissed as Pietro gently lifted up, then dropped back down. "Again."

Pietro didn't need telling twice. He was so fucking hot, all he could do was chase the pleasure being offered. He clenched hard as he began a fast, needy rhythm, letting Thierry's hands grab him by the hips, guiding his thrusts higher up, harder down.

He rolled his hips, chasing the angle again, and when he found it, he bounced, taking Thierry's cock deep inside him until his body threatened to give out.

"Ah, ah, ah," Thierry breathed out. His hips weren't moving much, but he made up for it in the strength of his arms as he guided Pietro through it. "*Mon amor, mon coeur. Je veux que tu jouisses.* Come for me, come..."

Pietro didn't realize he was obeying until he had already grabbed his cock, and he stroked himself fast and hard, his hand a blur until he was suddenly shooting all over Thierry's chest. In the haze of his orgasm, he could see Thierry staring down at it, and then the man let out a single, long moan just before Pietro felt him spill hot and heavy into the condom.

He lamented for a quick second that he wouldn't feel the man dripping out of him, but he was unable to complain after being so thoroughly fucked, he wasn't sure he'd be able to string words together. His strength left him entirely, but Thierry managed to ease his slide as he slumped over, grimacing as Thierry's cock popped out of him.

He couldn't see straight for a few minutes, but when he came to, Thierry's cock was naked and limp, resting in his curls, which were wet with the leftover lube and spilled come. Pietro lifted his hand, his wrist a little weak, and he dragged the tips of his fingers through it before rubbing the heel of his palm over Thierry's cock.

"Too much?" he asked when the man groaned.

Thierry shook his head and shifted a little closer. "No. I like it."

Pietro smiled, reaching between the man's legs for his empty balls, and he rolled them along his palm gently. They were hot and heavy, and Pietro wondered if Thierry would think he was a fucking weirdo if he asked to fall asleep this way.

"You're so fucking sexy," he murmured.

Thierry laughed, rolling onto his side a bit. Pietro lifted his head, expecting a kiss, but he was startled when the other man's lips pressed to his forehead, just above his left brow. "So are you."

Pietro didn't know what the fuck to do with that. No one ever kissed him like that—at least, none of his lovers. He wanted more—he wanted more so much he *burned*—but he knew better than to ask. Instead, he pulled his hand away and rested it against Thierry's hip.

"Look, I can take you home if you want, but you're gonna have to give me at least an hour to put my brain back in my head."

Thierry chuckled and brushed fingers through the side of Pietro's hair. "Where did it go?"

"Dude, you fucked it right out of me. It's somewhere on the floor," Pietro mumbled. He arched into the touch like a cat and gave no fucks about how he looked.

Thierry was quiet for a little while, then he sighed. "I can call a car, you know. If you prefer that I leave."

"I prefer you stay right here and let me cuddle the shit out of you," Pietro told him, unable to put up any emotional defenses. He felt okay about it though. He didn't think Thierry would be the kind of man to use that against him. No matter what happened in the future. "I'm also okay if you want to use a guest bedroom."

Thierry was quiet so long, Pietro peeled one of his eyes open to look at the man. There was concern on his face, but not disgust or distaste. When the man caught him staring, he rolled his eyes back up to the ceiling. "I would like to stay with you."

"Okay, though I'm sensing a but," Pietro pushed.

Thierry's lip quirked in the corner, and he shook his head. "I don't think I've ever done this. Slept in bed with a lover."

Is that what we are, he wanted to ask, but he didn't. Instead, he rolled fully onto his side and tucked one of his legs over Thierry's. "As bed partners go, I'm pretty fucking awesome at it. I run hot though, so if you need to shove me away later, I won't mind."

Thierry huffed a quiet laugh and nestled a little closer. "You're certain?"

"More than," Pietro mumbled. He was fading fast, and try as he might, he couldn't seem to keep the blackness from pressing in on the edges of his vision. "Wake me if you need anything, okay?"

He was asleep before he could hear Thierry's answer.

CHAPTER SEVENTEEN

When the alarm went off, Pietro woke alone, and it took about three seconds for his heart to jump into his throat and disappointment to flood his veins so hard he thought he was going to scream. The spot beside him where Thierry had been sleeping was cold—like the kind of cold that said it hadn't been occupied in hours, and Pietro wondered when he'd allowed himself to relax so much that he'd been able to sleep through someone sneaking away.

Part of him said it was a good thing. It was progress. He was letting his guard down.

The louder part of him said that he should have expected it because they'd been drinking and Thierry was vulnerable, and fuck's *sake*, Pietro was his boss.

So yeah, technically it was probably the least he deserved.

Rolling over, he flung his legs over the side of the bed and padded over to his bathroom. He was still kind of sticky from the spilled lube and from where his come had smeared over his dick. His ass was a little sore because it had been a while since he'd taken anyone, let alone someone Thierry's size. His thighs ached a bit too from how he'd tensed to hold himself up, afraid he was going to hurt the man.

And shit, maybe Thierry noticed that Pietro was being careful with him? Maybe that's why he ran?

Or maybe he was a garbage lay.

He should probably call his therapist to deal with that spiral, but it was easier to start the shower, take his morning meds with a palm full of water from the sink, then scrub away the evidence so he wouldn't have to smell it all over him as he wallowed. He didn't linger, though he half considered rubbing one out because remembering the way Thierry had grabbed him and guided him and fucked him into oblivion got him hard.

He'd be holding on to that night for a while, he knew.

His dick calmed down by the time he was done drying off though, so he slipped into sweats and checked the time to make sure he wasn't going to be late. The last thing he needed was to get reamed out when he got to the field because afternoon games always had kind of a weird vibe for him, and he didn't need anything else making it worse.

His socked feet padded lightly on the stairs as he hopped down the last three, debating about just grabbing something on the way. He wasn't sure he wanted to eat whatever Thierry had left him for breakfast, especially knowing he probably fucked it all to hell by being, like, clingy or whatever.

Running his hands through his hair, his thoughts going in a dozen different directions, he came to a skidding halt when he realized he was smelling something.

Coffee. Fresh coffee. And he could hear the gurgle of the percolator, and…shit, was that bacon?

His hands were on the verge of trembling as he came around the corner and into the kitchen, and he couldn't stop the punched-out laugh of utter relief when he found Thierry at the stove, sitting on his usual barstool, stirring something in a pan.

Thierry glanced over his shoulder with a tiny frown, setting the wooden spoon down on the counter. "Something's funny?"

A billion things, though funny wasn't the right word, but he also wasn't going to let this man in on his existential crisis. "Just didn't take you for a morning-after kind of guy."

"I'm not a monster," Thierry said primly, then went back to his work. "And anyway, you don't get to eat my fresh breakfasts most days."

Right. Because Thierry was his cook who meal-prepped for him.

Pietro swallowed past a lump in his throat and quietly told his feelings to fuck off because they had no place there. "You're a god," he said instead, reaching for a mug just as the coffee maker stopped making noise. "Have I ever told you that?"

"You might have said it after the lasagna I cooked for you," Thierry said, cocking his head to the side.

Pietro had kind of been angling for a sex joke there, just to test the waters. Message received. "What are you making now?"

"Breakfast burritos," Thierry said. "I make them for Sarah a few days a week so she can take them with her in the car. I figured they would be good for you too."

Right. Because he had to go. Fuck his *life*. Pietro gulped the too-hot coffee, then winced as he set the mug down and reached for his to-go cup. "I have a few minutes if you wanted to eat together."

Thierry shook his head, his smile almost apologetic. "I have an appointment with Chris. Maybe next time."

Next time. So did that mean... "Yeah, no. Cool." Pietro poured the rest of his coffee into his travel mug, then fished out the creamer from the fridge. It didn't take him long to get it all put together, but before he could say anything, Thierry was hopping off the stool and pushing a plate toward him as he checked his phone.

"My car is here."

Pietro scowled. "I thought I was paying for that shit."

"When I'm on the clock," Thierry told him. He smiled, then glanced at the garage door. "Do you mind if I get my chair, or...?"

"Oh. Fuck. Yeah, of course. We were...but then last night..."

Thierry held up a hand with a small, amused smile. "It's okay. Just close the garage behind me after I go?"

Pietro's mouth felt like it was filled with cotton. He wanted to plead with Thierry to stay, to draw it out a little longer. He could give him a ride—he'd happily be late if they could just not do...this. Whatever it was. This strained, uncomfortable small talk.

"Listen," Thierry said, and Pietro felt his heart sink to his feet. His gaze snapped up when warm fingers touched his chin though, and there wasn't rejection in Thierry's expression when he looked up. "We can talk later, yes?"

"I...yeah, of course. I have an afternoon game and presser. Then I need to watch tape, but I'll be home for dinner, if uh..." He stopped when he realized he was rambling.

Thierry's smile widened, and he didn't move his fingers from Pietro's face. "I had fun last night."

Pietro let out a huge rush of air. "Yeah. Me too."

"You don't need to be delicate, okay? I know things are complicated, and I don't have expectations. I enjoyed having fun."

Fun. Right.

"Me too," he said, and he was surprised that he managed to sound so honest.

Thierry's mouth softened before he leaned in and pressed his lips to the edge of Pietro's jaw. "Tonight?"

"Yeah. Stay for dinner. Um…with me," Pietro said as he took a step back, just to preserve whatever small bits of dignity he had left. "So we can talk."

Thierry's brow creased, and then he nodded. "Yes. Okay."

"Okay."

Pietro stood there rooted to the spot with his cooling burrito at his elbow, the coffee in his hand, and his heart on his sleeve. He'd never felt like this before, and he understood now why his brother had run so hard and so fast from love, until Ezra had caught up with him.

CHAPTER EIGHTEEN

"So. You finally got laid."

Thierry let out a surprised grunt as all the air was forced out of his lungs when Chris pushed his leg up. He was feeling weaker than usual, but that was likely due to a combination of the acrobatics he'd done in bed with Pietro and from the strain of holding himself together the next morning.

He also wasn't in the mood for an impromptu therapy session with Chris, which he could tell his friend was angling for. "I don't have to talk to you about this while you're on the clock," Thierry muttered, catching his breath as Chris eased his leg down.

Chris snickered as he settled onto the mat, then took Thierry's right foot into his hand and pressed his palm to the ball. "Push."

Thierry did. He was struggling to feel anything that morning, but the muscles were working okay on memory—at least, from what he could see. Chris' brow was furrowed, but he didn't look any more worried than he usually did on Thierry's bad days.

"Push," Chris said. Thierry obeyed again. "Did you pinch something?"

"Maybe," he couldn't help but admit. "He took it easy on me, but I didn't want him to. Probably a mistake."

Chris scoffed quietly, then switched legs. His left was a little bit stronger and a little bit more responsive. "Naw, I don't think you'll fuck yourself fully paralyzed or anything. And testing your limits isn't a bad thing. You've been worse."

"Comforting," Thierry said dryly.

Chris grinned at him over his knee, then began to work at his calves. "How was it?"

"No. We're not having this conversation right now," Thierry said with a grunt as the pain hit him for a second.

Chris laughed. "Afraid you'll get excited?"

Thierry raised his hand and flipped him off. "I don't..." He trailed off when Chris let him go, then sighed when the man patted his flank, urging him to roll onto his hands and knees.

"Come on. You'll thank me in a few months when you can get up to the real freaky shit without your legs crapping out on you halfway."

Thierry grimaced, but he still pushed onto all fours and tried to ignore the strain he felt in his back and hips. There were days he didn't mind. Hell, most of the time he was brimming with pride at how far he'd come.

But this morning, after the night he'd spent with Pietro, he didn't want to be reminded of his limitations. He didn't want to feel good about the fact that he could hold himself up like this.

"I know that face," Chris told him, lying flat on his back next to Thierry's body.

Thierry hung his head and sighed. "I don't think it was pity. I don't think he fucked me out of pity, but..." He licked his lips and trailed off.

"That man did *not* fuck you out of pity," Chris said. "You're hotter than burning. If I wasn't so in love, I'd be tryin' to get into those cute little shorts your ass wears even in the winter."

"My ass is not little," Thierry hissed.

Chris laughed and pushed himself up to sit. "Come on. Knees."

Thierry pushed up to his knees and felt his balance start to sway. Chris was there with his impossibly strong hands to keep him upright, and he let himself take the help because it was all he could do.

"He seem like he was unsatisfied after everything?" Chris asked, softer this time.

Thierry closed his eyes, but he shook his head because there was no point in avoiding his friend's questions anymore. "I think he enjoyed it. He was...enthusiastic."

"Hell yeah, man," Chris said, bumping his elbow.

Thierry opened his eyes and scowled. "He was strange this morning though."

"Not surprised. That dude looks wound up as hell." Chris put him back on hands and knees, and this time was harder to hold it.

The conversation died until Thierry was allowed to get back in his chair, and he strapped his legs down carefully as they began to tremor before rolling to the table to grab his water. He was feeling oddly low, which was unexpected after the night he had. Part of him wanted to call Pietro and tell him he needed the night off, then wallow in his bed until the feeling passed.

But he knew better than that.

The talk was important.

Chris dropped into a folding chair across from Thierry, then knocked his knee against Thierry's shaking one. "What's on your mind? Friend to friend," he added.

Thierry rubbed at his eyes, then shrugged. "What if he wants more than just hooking up?"

Chris' brows rose a little. "What if he does?"

Thierry swallowed thickly because he didn't know the answer to that. He never intended to act on his little—whatever he'd been feeling. He expected it to fade into nothing and for the line between professional and personal to settle between them again.

Friends was one thing, but more...

"What if he *doesn't* want more than just hooking up?" He had to give voice to that other ugly feeling that had settled in his gut. He wasn't sure which scenario he could handle. "Everything's so complicated. Hervé's still in town..."

"That fucker show up again?" Chris asked, his voice heavy with anger.

Thierry shook his head. "No. Well...he's sent a text or two, but I've put him on mute, so I don't have to read them. There's nothing he has to say that I want to hear."

"Nothing you need to hear," Chris corrected.

Thierry wasn't entirely sure that was true. It was possible Hervé had some magic words that would make all the ugly feelings left over from all those years start to heal. But he doubted it. And it wasn't like anything Hervé could say or do could erase what had happened.

Life had moved on. The world had moved on.

Thierry had moved on.

Staring down at his legs, he saw they'd calmed, so he undid the straps and let them stretch out in front of the chair. His muscles felt too weak to support his body, which was fine. He was in the mood to rest, considering his mind was on other things.

Like dinner with Pietro.

"You got that look on your face again. The one like you're all constipated by emotions," Chris told him.

Thierry offered him a flat look. "I just have things to think about."

"I get that. But do me a favor?" He paused until Thierry nodded. "Decide what you want, not what will be easier. Or what your boy wants out of this. You deserve to be happy."

It wasn't the first time Chris had said that. He and Sarah had been singing that song since they officially became friends. But it was harder to hear now that something like happy was just beyond his grasp, and all he'd need to do was reach for it.

"I haven't thought about what I want in a long time," he admitted.

Chris pushed up to stand, then dropped a hand on Thierry's shoulder and squeezed. "I get that. But maybe it's time to start putting yourself first."

Of course, Chris' advice was easier said than done, but Thierry was a master at avoiding emotional complications. Instead, he convinced his driving instructor to let him make the trip to the store that afternoon, and he felt surprisingly confident as he managed the hand brake, easing into the parking spot.

"Another week and I think you'll be good to go," Rod told him.

Thierry smiled and shrugged. He was ready to start reclaiming all the bits and pieces of his shattered independence and putting them together in whatever new shape they would form. He could do this, just like he could grab his cane and make his way to the front of the supermarket where the motorized carts waited.

The weather was starting to get colder and colder as they

crept toward October, and it was making him want rich, warm comfort food. What he'd love to do was serve a cassoulet, but he didn't have the time to prepare, and he wasn't quite sure Pietro would appreciate the significance of it. At the very least, he wouldn't be able to taste Thierry's childhood, sitting at his grandmother's table nibbling on saucisson and spicy mustard while she peeled meat from the duck legs.

Maybe someday, when—*if*—things worked out into something more defined. Even if he and Pietro could never become more than what they were now, Thierry could at least offer him some good memories to associate with their time together.

Turning the cart toward the butcher, he waited patiently in line as he decided on steak frites. It was the most basic comfort food, and he had plenty of ingredients and time to whip up some maître d'hôtel butter while he waited for Pietro to finish his afternoon game.

It would give him time to think, at the very least, and prepare for whatever it was Pietro wanted to tell him.

Taking the meat, he whipped over to produce for some potatoes, then wandered the aisles for oil. He came to a stop in the international section, and to his surprise, there was a very small European shelf—some escargot shells sitting on the lowest tier. He dragged his lip between his teeth and wondered how much Pietro would try and kill him if he used a few on the plate.

He almost laughed before he put them back on the shelf, then made his way up to the counter to check out.

Rod was waiting for him as Pietro parked his motorized cart, then slowly made his way across the parking lot with the bags hanging from his wrist. He stowed them in the trunk, then folded up his cane and tossed it in the back before sliding behind the wheel.

"Big date night?" Rod asked.

Thierry tried to keep a straight face because the reality was, he didn't know. But the prospect of it possibly being more—even if it was just fucking Pietro again—was too much to hide. He smiled, then shrugged as he started the engine and carefully backed out.

"It's definitely going to be an interesting one," he said, and he pulled out onto the main street to the sound of Rod's quiet laugh.

Although Rod insisted that Thierry was likely ready to make at least one drive on his own, Thierry still decided to accept Pietro's car service which was always at the ready for whenever he needed it. He tried not to think too hard about it, still trying to convince himself that Pietro would do this for anyone as he loaded up his carrying bag and waited outside.

The ride was quiet, the way it was always quiet, and he mumbled a quick thanks as he let himself out and headed up the driveway. His legs were aching from his long morning with Chris, and he lamented not having his chair. What he'd fucking give for a kitchen that he could work in without putting so much strain on his body.

Still, the stool was comfortable enough, and after he had the butter and herbs whipped up and cooling, he began a dry rub on the steak. There were hours before Pietro would be there, so he got to work on the man's lunches before finally washing, chopping, and setting his potatoes to freeze.

When he was finished, he realized there wasn't anything left for him to do but wait. It was strange being in Pietro's house like that. Normally, he'd leave. But that was before he was asked to stay. Before he knew what Pietro's mouth tasted like, how hot his skin got when Thierry worked him up—thrust inside him, fucked him open.

That sat both uncomfortable and welcome under his skin as he moved into the sitting room and collapsed on the couch. It was strange to be there—the place where it all began. Not just the night they finally crossed that line, but before, when Pietro had been lying there drunk and vulnerable.

He'd reached for Thierry then, and Thierry had reached back. In his mind, he knew there was no going back after that, but he hadn't been sure how far either of them would be willing to go. Hell, he still wasn't sure.

Grabbing the edges of his jeans, he helped his legs lift up, his feet resting against the low table. What he'd give for the ability to hop up and make a cup of tea. Or maybe to find Pietro's workout room and run. Or even just pace the house until his heart stopped trying to skip a beat.

It had been quite a while now since his body had felt like a prison, but he was feeling trapped and frustrated, with no way to break out of it.

Before he could do something drastic, like call a car and cancel the whole night, he reached for the remote on the table. He hit the power button and almost laughed when the sports channel immediately flared to life, silent, but he didn't really need the commentary. From the logo in the corner, he could see the Vikings were playing, and his pulse raced a bit. They were up by two, and it was the top of the ninth which meant it was almost over.

And they were close to winning, if they could hold off the Panthers.

Pietro wondered when the fuck he'd developed the ability to tell what the hell was going on, but he knew the answer. He'd been sneaking glimpses since the day he met Pietro, and it had only gotten worse since moving back to Denver. He just hadn't realized how much he was absorbing.

His finger hovered over the button to change it, but then the camera panned down onto the players—right onto Pietro, who was standing near third base, his knees bent in a slight crouch.

The other team was up to bat, and Pietro's eyes were narrowed down the line. His nose scrunched up and he looked fucking adorable for a second before he spit. Thierry chuckled and shook his head and wondered what the fuck was going to happen to them now.

The camera zoomed back out as the ball went flying, and Thierry found his heart thrumming just before Pietro ran backward—graceful and delicate with his glove extended. He hopped into the air, gaining nearly a foot as the ball landed neatly in his glove. The shot was just close enough for him to catch the proud little smirk on his face.

And then Thierry realized he was hard.

Fuck.

He'd seen Pietro in action—in person—but he'd been so far away it hadn't been a problem. His thumb twitched to change it again when his phone began to buzz in his pocket. The only man he wanted to hear from was currently playing a game, so he slowly dug it out, not really caring if they hung up.

When he looked at the screen, his chest went tight because in spite of there being no name, he recognized the number. Anger—he was feeling anger. He was tired of Hervé creeping in every time he was starting to feel settled.

He was sick of knowing the man existed.

His thumb was hitting Answer before he was consciously aware of it. "What do you want?" he barked in French.

There was a long silence, then a quiet sigh. "I thought maybe…"

"You thought wrong," Thierry told him. "I know I made myself perfectly clear the last time we spoke."

"You've been ignoring my texts," Hervé complained.

Thierry couldn't help a laugh. "Anyone else would have taken that as a goddamn sign they weren't interested in talking."

Hervé scoffed. "I told you I was stubborn."

"That's not the cute personality trait you think it is," Thierry told him. "And I don't know what the fuck you want from me. You showed up, said your piece, and I said mine. There's nothing left."

"I can't leave it like that," Hervé said.

Thierry laughed again. "You don't have another choice. I'm not going to give you anything else. I understand that you're fucked-up."

"I'm not..." Hervé began, now sounding actually angry.

"I understand that you are who you are and there's no changing it," Thierry went on. "But that's not my problem."

"I said I was sorry," Hervé said, more genuine than Thierry had heard him yet.

"I know."

"What else am I supposed to do? I'm trying to be better. I want to be better."

Thierry closed his eyes and rubbed at his temple with his free hand. "I'm glad to hear that."

"And yet, you refuse to let me," Hervé snapped—and ah, there it was. There was the exact reason Thierry would never give in. "How am I supposed to be better when you won't give me a chance to show you?"

"I'm not preventing you from being a better person," Thierry told me. "But I don't owe you space in my life. You want to be better—be better for everyone else in the future. What you broke with me can't be fixed."

"After everything we were?" Hervé asked.

Thierry opened his eyes and fixed them on the screen. They were showing Pietro again—now up to bat. The numbers in the corner said he was on strike two, which meant he was probably getting tired, but the score was the same.

They were going to win, and Thierry felt a rush of pride that couldn't be dimmed by Hervé's voice on the other end.

"*Thierry.*"

He snapped his attention back to the call. "You only kept me for as long as I could be of use to you. The moment I couldn't perform, it was over."

"I didn't mean..."

"Yes," Thierry interrupted from behind a tired sigh, "you did. And you regret it, and I'm willing to accept that regret. I'm willing to accept an apology. But I'm not willing to let you back in. I have nothing to offer you."

"I don't..."

"And you have nothing to offer me," Thierry went on, and he swore he heard a click from how hard Hervé shut his jaw. "Take this lesson and learn to be a better person for the people in your life now, and let me go."

He allowed another second of silence, and then he pulled the phone away from his ear and hung up. He contemplated turning the damn thing off, but if Pietro needed to send a message, he wanted to be available for it. His fingers tapped on the edge of the screen, and then it buzzed under his hand with a message.

Unknown: If that's what you want, fine.

It was in English, which was the most startling part. The rest was what it was—a vague threat, perhaps, or a promise.

Thierry didn't know, but he also didn't care. He let the phone drop to his side and turned his attention back to the screen.

He got lost in the push-pull of the game until it was over, and the Vikings were congratulating each other for the win. They were close now—so very close to making it to the playoffs. Thierry had never paid attention to things like championships. Not even when everyone around him was obsessing over the World Cup or the Olympics.

But now it felt personal. He felt this burning hot need to will Pietro and his team to victory.

A foolish, pathetic emotion, but he couldn't help it. Even if their relationship turned into nothing but physical comfort, he wouldn't be able to help it. He wasn't just falling.

He'd already fallen.

And it was too late to save himself.

CHAPTER NINETEEN

Pietro had managed to get his phone in his hand for a quick two minutes after the game. Once before his shower, he'd sent a text over to Thierry letting him know he was finished but had a shitload to do, and once right after he finished getting dressed to read Thierry's reply.

> Thierry: I'll have dinner waiting. Text me when you're on the road.

It was domestic, which sent strange feelings like fizzy soda bubbling through his veins as he made his way to the presser. The Vikings had secured their spot in the division championships, which meant there was so fucking much to do. And he wasn't going to let it get to his head yet. They had a long stretch in postseason to go, and he had his charity Little League game coming up and the auction dinner to follow.

And God only knew when he'd have time to think about what this thing was between him and Thierry, but he was determined not to let anything fall by the wayside.

He just had to hope and pray Thierry would be patient with him.

During the presser, he sat next to James, who fielded most of the questions, and Pietro was allowed to chip in with a couple of puns, but he didn't have to worry about keeping his thoughts in order or following the chaotic line of questions. His team had been backing his ass up like that for years, and he wasn't quite sure how to show them his gratitude.

They knew it was always worse when the stakes got higher, though, and when he was more exhausted. He could dedicate himself to one thing—and one thing only: the win. They trusted him to back their asses up on the field, so he let himself fall a bit into their hands with everything else.

They left the room laughing, with James slinging an arm around his neck and pulling him close as they headed for the parking garage.

"I'd fuckin' marry you if that wouldn't feel like incest," James said as they pushed through the doors.

"You're disgusting," Pietro shot back. He patted his pocket for the ninth time since they walked into the hallway, once again making sure his keys were still there.

James cackled, then shoved him toward his car. "I guess it doesn't help you're already fuckin' gone for someone else, right?"

Pietro didn't have it in him to deny it. He'd been almost distracted through their morning practice, and it was only the weight of what was on the line that kept him from getting lost in the memory of what it felt like to be stretched out around Thierry.

But now, it was impossible to hide, and James came to a skidding halt. "Wait, really?"

Pietro rolled his eyes and pulled his keys out of his pocket, thumbing the Unlock button on the fob. "We're not talking about this right now."

James cleared his throat, then took a few steps closer as Pietro reached for his door handle. "You fucked him."

"It's personal," he muttered.

"If it fucks with your game..."

White-hot anger rushed through him, and Pietro turned, fixing his best friend with a glare. "Are you serious right now?"

James immediately deflated and shook his head. "No. Look, I just..."

Pietro waited as his friend trailed off.

"You've been through a lot, and you've finally come out of a huge funk. I just don't want to see you miserable again."

It was hard to argue with the man when he genuinely gave a shit about Pietro. Most people cared, but not like this. Not like family. "I'm not being reckless," he said, finally opening his car door. It was late, and he was sore and exhausted, starving, and eager to see his would-be lover. "I just...I like him."

"So, are you together?" James pressed.

Pietro stared down at his hand, which was gripping the edge of the car tight enough that his knuckles were aching. "I don't know what we are, and I'm not really in a good place to define that right now. We can figure it out when all of us can think straight."

James made a small noise of protest, and then he let out a sigh. "He better treat your right, or I'm gonna knock his fucking teeth in."

Pietro looked up and grinned, shaking his head. "I know you will. See you in the morning."

James flicked two fingers off his forehead in a little salute, then headed off in the direction of his car as Pietro got behind the wheel, started up his car, and headed for whatever was waiting for him at the end of the drive.

Pietro remembered to text Thierry when he was at a stoplight, ten minutes from home. He felt a little bad about being late, but the guilt was immediately overwhelmed by the smell of cooking food when he stepped into the kitchen and dropped his keys on the counter.

Thierry was at the stove, standing next to a stool with a pair of tongs. The sizzling was so loud, he didn't think the man heard him come in, so Pietro took a moment to indulge in just looking. Thierry was standing straighter than usual, his shoulders back, his ass rounded and fit, his hair neatly ordered and softly curled at the ends.

He could only see his profile, but his nose seemed longer like that—hooked a bit at the very end, which complemented his sharp jaw, his full mouth, and the few days of dark growth along his cheeks. He looked fucking delicious, and if Pietro hadn't been so tired and hungry, he might have tried to skip dinner and the talk for something else.

He knew that was just asking for disaster in many ways though, so he cleared his throat and ignored the little bubbling restlessness that was creeping up his spine as his medication started to officially wear off for the day. "Hey, you."

Thierry's whole body twitched, and he glanced over his shoulder with a sheepish smile. "I didn't hear you come in."

Pietro smiled back. "I'm a sneaky fucker, what can I say."

Thierry rolled his eyes and turned his attention back to the stove which, now that Pietro had come closer, he could see were sizzling steaks. "Are you hungry?"

"Ask me in French," Pietro muttered, then flushed because he hadn't meant to say that aloud. He just…liked when Thierry spoke in his own language.

Thierry rolled his eyes. "*As-tu faim?*"

Pietro was close enough to touch the man now. "*Je suis faim.*"

Thierry gave him a look, and Pietro grinned.

"Means horny, right?"

At that, Thierry laughed and moved the steaks to the plate beside him, then set the tongs down and carefully turned. He rested his backside against the stool, then reached out with one hand and pulled on Pietro's belt loop.

"Not quite," he murmured, "but you have the right idea." And Pietro no longer wondered if Thierry still wanted him, because the man curled a hand around the back of his neck, drew him close, then kissed him.

It was hot, and he tasted rich like herbs with just a hint of spice. His hands were a little clammy from the steam coming off the stove, and it felt strangely nice as they kneaded into his sore muscles. When Pietro pulled away, his eyes were half-lidded and threatening to close, but he didn't want to stop looking at the other man's ruddy face.

"Miss me?" Pietro asked.

Thierry leaned forward and nipped at Pietro's lower lip, but he didn't answer. Instead, he knocked their foreheads together, then used both hands to ease Pietro back a step. "Do you need to shower before dinner?"

Pietro was slightly disappointed at Thierry's lack of answer, but he wasn't going to fight for compliments. He was too damn tired for that. "Nah. I had time after the game. Unless you're suggesting that I smell."

Thierry grinned and didn't answer that, either, but the playful look in his eye said he didn't mind whatever scent Pietro was giving off. "Can you drink wine right now?"

Pietro shrugged. "A glass won't kill me. Can't get shitfaced again though. Not until after playoffs."

Thierry nodded, then pushed up and reached for the two glasses that were resting on the drying rack near the edge of the sink. "Something red will go good with the steaks."

Pietro did as he asked, happy to have some direction and something to do with himself while Thierry finished plating the food. It was easy to pop the cork on a bottle of Cab he had in the little rack by the table and pour the glasses while he listened to Thierry humming to himself and finishing his work.

When he settled into the seat, Thierry was just a few steps away, holding two plates. "We haven't discussed what you'll need for playoffs. I imagine a lot of carbs and a lot of protein."

Pietro was proud of himself for not making a protein joke, but mostly it was because he was distracted by the plate in front of him. The steak was sliced, perfectly pink in the center, some herbed butter melting across the top. Beside that was a pile of fries that looked thoroughly seasoned, and his mouth started to water.

"Shit."

Thierry froze just after he plopped into his chair. "Something I forgot?"

"No. I mean, yes. I mean," Pietro said, then cleared his throat. "What's the French phrase for 'I'm horny for this food.'"

Thierry gave him a flat look. "Do you mean hungry?"

Pietro laughed and picked up his fork and knife. "I guess that works. This looks fucking amazing. God, I could die happy."

"I would prefer you live happy so you can continue to enjoy my cooking," Thierry said, his voice still deadpan.

Pietro grinned and stuffed a too-big piece of the meat in his mouth and began to chew. "Fuck," he drawled, the word drawn out. "You should open a goddamn restaurant."

"That's my plan," Thierry said quietly, taking a decidedly smaller bite.

For a second, Pietro swore everything around him froze. "You...that's. That's what you want?"

Thierry shrugged and looked somewhat uncomfortable, staring at his food instead of up at Pietro. "It's my goal. Eventually. I thought once I might work in a kitchen—work my way up to having something that's just mine. I can't do it that way anymore, but it's still a dream I have."

"So, what's stopping you? Why do this whole personal chef thing?" Pietro asked, trying to ignore the quelling fear of losing Thierry so soon after getting him and without having anything between them defined. With no claims, no promises, he could blink, and the man would be gone. But he wanted him to be happy.

Thierry smiled through his next bite, but it didn't reach his eyes. "Money's stopping me. I don't...I don't have much of a plan, and I certainly don't have collateral for a loan. I'm not a citizen of this country."

Pietro started to wonder if he'd ever quit making these goddamn faux pas about money. It was just so easy to forget he could write a check if he wanted and solve so many problems. And shit, he could offer it now, but he knew that was the fastest way for Thierry to turn tail and walk out of his life.

"If you ever want a silent partner, I happen to know a guy who can't cook for shit but definitely appreciates your skills and talent." He couldn't help but make that offer—the smallest compromise, and he hoped Thierry wouldn't hate him for it.

The silence was thick between them, and then Thierry sighed. "I'll keep that in mind."

Anything that wasn't a flat-out no or a go fuck yourself was almost like a yes. Pietro smiled and shoved a few of the fries in his mouth. "Did these come from frozen?"

Thierry looked as though Pietro had just asked if him he had served up deep-fried garbage.

"Sorry, sorry," Pietro said. "I was just saying because they're the best I've ever had."

"Clever save," Thierry said. He fell quiet a moment, eating a few more bites of his steak, and then he looked up. "I thought maybe some comfort food might be nice. I know this time of year is hectic."

"It's hell," Pietro said. He polished off the rest of his meat, then pushed his plate away. It was rich and probably too much for his gut after the game, but he felt warm and full and lazy. He wanted to pull Thierry into his arms and just drift away with him somewhere soft. "It's worth it though. And I can have my nutritionist forward you the meal plan."

Thierry nodded and started to stand up but froze when Pietro held up his hand. "You want something else?"

Pietro shook his head, then stood up and snatched both plates away. "Let me at least take care of the cleanup. You're off the clock," he added pointedly.

Thierry opened his mouth, maybe to argue, but then he seemed to realize what Pietro was saying, and he sank back down. "*D'accord.*"

Pietro smiled and scraped the plates before throwing them in the sink. He breezed past Thierry, grabbing his glass, and he downed what was left before swiping his hand over his mouth. "So. Want to talk? Or we can go fuck if you don't feel like having a whole entire discussion."

Thierry's eyes widened a fraction, and a thrill ran through Pietro when it looked like he was actually considering both options. After a beat though, his shoulders sank. "We should talk."

Pietro offered a hand, and Thierry didn't just take it, he also didn't let go as Pietro led the way into the sitting room. The place looked used—a coffee cup on the table, the cushions moved, the TV playing in the background on mute.

Something warm rippled through him as he realized that Thierry had been here for a while and had made himself comfortable. He wanted to turn Thierry around and cradle his face—to kiss him and tell him to do that all the time. To just... let it be a *thing*.

Instead, he followed Thierry to the sofa and sat as the other man propped himself against the cushions. Pietro watched him for a long moment, trying to spot signs in him that he was in pain or uncomfortable, but he didn't look much different from the man he'd always been.

Maybe a bit thinner than he was when he was working as a bodyguard, but not by much. Pietro was pretty sure he could still bounce a quarter off the man's abs—not that it mattered. He had come to realize over the last twenty-four hours that he didn't really give a shit what Thierry's body looked like, and that was an intense thing to deal with.

He did not have the space for it. Not yet.

"You look like you want to run away," Thierry said.

Pietro slapped a hand over his face and dragged it down with a groan. "Even if I did want to—which I fucking don't, thank you very much—I wouldn't have the energy. Today kicked my ass."

"And you won," Thierry pointed out.

Pietro wasn't sure if he should hate himself for the grin that spread over his mouth, but he didn't really care right then. "Yeah, we fucking did. We have the division championships, then the playoffs, and I'm going to want to die by the end, but this is the best part."

Thierry cocked his head to the side. "Is it really?"

Pietro shrugged. Sometimes it was, sometimes it wasn't, but it was always worth it. "Did you catch the game?" he asked, gesturing to the TV, which was on ESPN.

Thierry looked a little sheepish, but he nodded. "*Ouais.* I... for a little bit. Just the end."

"Fucking fanned that inning," Pietro said, flopping backward. "Won anyway."

"I watched the...euh..." Thierry shrugged, looking a little bit embarrassed with his tiny grin. "I don't know fancy slang for it. You caught the ball, and you kept them from scoring."

"Oh yeah. That. That's just called playing some good fucking baseball," Pietro said.

Thierry stared, then laughed and leaned in. His hands twitched like maybe he was going to reach for Pietro, but he didn't. "We should talk."

"Then sex?" Pietro asked.

Thierry's eyes darkened, and he licked his lips. "We're both in a complicated position. I work for you," he said, and Pietro bit back a groan because he hated the reminder. "You're in the middle of your season, and I know the stress is a lot."

Pietro bit the inside of his cheek, and then he nodded because both of those things were true. "I can't say I'm an expert at separating professional and personal relationships because I've never really done this before. I mean, sad as it is, Hervé was probably my most serious relationship, and that was a goddamn shitshow."

Thierry sighed and looked down at his hands. "I know. It's probably not easy since he's...well. I'm assuming he's called you."

Pietro's eyes narrowed. "Sorry, what?"

"He's here. He's been trying to get in touch with me," Thierry said.

Sitting up straight, Pietro couldn't decide if he felt anger because Thierry didn't tell him or guilt because Pietro had known and kept it to himself. "Has he been harassing you?"

Thierry was quiet long enough that it gave Pietro his answer. Before he could pop off about it though, Thierry took a breath. "I've told him repeatedly I have no intention of making amends with him."

"He apologized?" Pietro asked, a little shocked because that fucker only apologized when he was trying to manipulate a situation into his favor—and he never meant it. "Do you believe he's actually sorry."

"I don't know," Thierry admitted. "I think he may be dealing with feelings he's never experienced before. Guilt," he added with a small, humorless laugh. "Regret. Realizing that nothing he can say will change my situation."

Pietro ran his fingers over his mouth. "Do you want me to, like, I don't know…do something about it? See if I can find someone to get him to back off?"

Thierry smiled up at him and shook his head. "He'll… what's the phrase? Tire himself out? Like a little child."

Pietro laughed at that, rolling his eyes. "Yeah, I guess so. I'm fuckin' sorry though, babe. You shouldn't have to deal with him on top of all this other shit."

Thierry waved him off. "It's fine. It was almost refreshing to know I don't feel angry anymore." He went quiet, looking almost surprised at his own words. "It felt freeing."

Pietro wasn't sure he could ever be that man. If Hervé had caused his entire life to be tipped upside down and inside out, Pietro would be petty enough to hate him for the rest of his life. God, Thierry was too good for him.

"So, he hasn't called you?" Thierry asked.

Pietro felt his cheeks heat a little. "No, but um." He hesitated because he really wanted to kiss this man, and maybe put his mouth on Thierry's dick, and he wasn't sure if he'd be able to if he told the truth. But it was time. He liked him too much to lie. "He came to the club."

Thierry's brows flew up. "The club."

"Scooter's club. Scoot dragged me out one night, and Hervé was there. I basically told him to go fuck himself." And then it had gotten ugly, and Pietro had felt things he wasn't prepared for, and he didn't even get to punch the guy to even the score.

Thierry licked his lips again, then dug his hands into the cushions and shifted closer. "More complications?"

Pietro looked down between them. There was only enough space to fit Thierry's hand, and Pietro was done holding back. He laid his palm over the tops of Thierry's knuckles, then stroked upward until he was holding the man by his elbow. He still didn't lift his gaze, knowing he wouldn't be able to say anything else if he did.

"Things between us will always be complicated. I'm going to be your boss for as long as it takes for you to get on your feet. And we'll never be able to erase the past between us."

"That's something I've been coming to terms with quite a lot," Thierry told him. He twisted, and his other arm raised, and warm fingers pressed to the back of Pietro's neck. "My life has irrevocably changed, and right now, if I could go back and do things differently, I don't know that I would."

Pietro finally lifted his gaze, then dragged his hand up to curl against the side of Thierry's neck. He could feel his pulse racing, and it only got faster when Pietro dragged a thumb over Thierry's jaw. "That seems kind of foolish."

"It's not. Not when all of it gave me my freedom. Not when I ended up here." Thierry bit his lip, then let go, and Pietro couldn't stop staring at how it was spit-slick and a little puffy. "If I had never punched you, would you have looked twice at me? If we were just strangers?"

Pietro couldn't help a laugh because what the fuck was this

guy on? He leaned in so close, his nose grazed Thierry's cheek. "You are literally the hottest man I have ever seen. Yes, I would have fucking noticed you."

But maybe Thierry was also onto something because noticing him and having the balls to do something about it were two different things, and part of Pietro's courage came from the line Thierry had crossed once. Forgiving him for that night at the club had cost them both something—Pietro just hadn't realized what it was.

Until right then.

"I know it's complicated, but we can keep it simple for now, right? Until...until we have time to untie all these knots?" He held his breath, waiting for the answer because if it was no...his heart might not break, but it would get a little battered on his way down.

"I like simple," Thierry said.

Pietro started to pull away, but Thierry took matters into his own hands, grabbed Pietro by the face, and kissed him hard. Sharp teeth grazed his lips, and his breath was punched out of him as Thierry knocked him onto the cushions. The man's body was dense as hell, but the pressure was grounding as Thierry tried to hold himself up with both arms.

"I like it. I like feeling you on me," Pietro told him. "I liked feeling you inside me."

Thierry nodded, knocking their foreheads together as he released more of his weight. Pietro grabbed him by the hips and urged the contact. He was hard, but Thierry wasn't.

At Pietro's frown, Thierry tried to pull back. "Sometimes I... because of the injury..."

Pietro didn't let him go far. "I don't care. I mean...fuck. I mean, I *do* care, but if you want..." He flopped backward, knocking his head against the hard part of the sofa arm. "Sorry,

I don't know how to say this, and I don't want to sound like a dick."

Thierry was quiet a moment before he let down most of his weight and rolled to the side. The sofa was huge, but only just big enough to hold two grown men of their size. Pietro tried to shift over and give the man a bit more space, but Thierry stopped him by dragging a hand from his sternum to his dick.

"I still want to touch you. I want to get you off."

Pietro's eyes slammed shut, and he arched against Thierry's wandering hand, unable to stop himself. "Yeah, I'm...I'd be good with that. If you are."

"I still feel good," Thierry murmured as he leaned in to kiss Pietro's neck. "I like when you touch me too."

Taking that as tacit permission, Pietro rolled onto his side, hooking a leg over Thierry's hip. He shifted back to give the man's fingers room to undo his button and zipper, then let out a heavy moan when his dick was sliding against Thierry's warm, impossibly careful palm.

"You can go harder," he murmured. He leaned in, putting his mouth against Thierry's pulse, first with teeth, then sucking against the skin.

Thierry let out a soft grunt, nodding as he increased his grip, though he didn't start stroking yet. "So can you."

Pietro didn't need telling twice. He disrupted their position to get Thierry's shirt off, then his own, before he kicked his trousers down to his feet. Settling back, he wriggled his hips and whined until Thierry got with the program, the man laughing as he curled his hand back around Pietro's waiting dick, and he thrust into the circle of his fingers.

"Fuck. Yeah, fuck."

"You like it?" Thierry asked.

"More than." Pietro's own hand wandered to Thierry's chest, pinching at his nipples, then dragging downward. At the spot just above his scar, Thierry groaned, and his whole body twitched. "Good or bad moan?"

"Good." Thierry leaned into him harder. "That spot...sensitive." He seemed close to losing words, so Pietro didn't make him talk anymore. He just kept up a light touch, grazing fingernails across his stomach, kissing his collarbone, and alternately remembering to thrust against the hand that was holding him tight.

"Make me come," he breathed after a beat.

Thierry obeyed like he was just waiting for orders. Lifting his hand, he spit into it, then grabbed Pietro and began to jack him off with a firm, perfect rhythm. Arching into it and matching the speed with his hips, Pietro lifted his head just a little and surged into a kiss.

As his balls began to tighten and his skin heated up, he opened his mouth and let Thierry push his tongue in. The taste of him, the feel of him, it was just enough to send him toppling over the edge. He didn't have enough time to even take a breath before he was spilling, hot ropes spurting over Thierry's knuckles as he slowed his pace and eased him through the last of the trembling aftershocks.

Pietro realized his ears were ringing, and when the sound faded, he could hear Thierry murmuring soft French against the side of his cheek. He had no hope of deciphering the language with his head all muddled up, but he didn't really care. Thierry had moved his hand away from his dick and was now holding him so close, so tight, like he was afraid Pietro might disappear—and Pietro knew exactly how that felt.

CHAPTER TWENTY

Pietro asked him to stay again. He didn't say anything right away, but he walked Thierry to the door when the car appeared in the driveway, and then he pinned him to the window and kissed the breath out of him. "You don't have to leave, you know," he murmured against Thierry's lips.

And God help him, but he did, and that was the problem.

It killed Thierry to go home after everything, but he knew staying was out of the question. They weren't boyfriends, they weren't in a relationship. They barely spoke about what it was they were doing and only to make the single promise that they'd talk about it some other time.

When it was less complicated.

He almost laughed himself to tears in bed later that night because when the hell was his life less complicated?

Things were made worse the next morning when he woke up and realized he'd pissed the bed. His bladder was mostly in control, but not always, and especially not after his back was strained. PT, cooking dinner on his feet, then stroking Pietro off on the sofa had seemed to be exactly that tipping point.

It was worse when he tried to roll away and realized his legs would absolutely not cooperate. It was bad enough that he started to feel panicked, and he quickly found his phone, calling Chris.

"This is either for a ride home of shame, or something's wrong," Chris said, sounding far too chipper for how early it was.

"Are you at your office?" Thierry asked. He hadn't needed help like this in a long while, and humiliation crept up his spine because being alone made it that much worse.

"What do you need?" Chris demanded without answering his question.

"I think I hurt something. I think..." Thierry concentrated on his toes and managed to get them to wriggle—which was good. Great, in fact. But he couldn't lift his legs, and that was not a good sign. "I think I need to go to the hospital."

"Give me five minutes to redirect my appointments, then I'll be there." He hung up, probably knowing Thierry was going to argue with him and insist he'd find his own way. After all, he'd done it before, when he was still not quite walking on his own but deemed not disabled enough to need at-home care.

Pushing himself up to sit, he ignored the mess beneath him and got his feet off the bed. His chair wasn't close enough for him to reach, which was his own stupid fault for thinking this wouldn't happen again. His option was to sit in his mess and wait for Chris to arrive or attempt to use all the work he'd put into his body during PT and crawl his way across the floor.

The moment his knees hit the carpet and he felt nothing, he knew it was the wrong choice. He'd been warned about this by his doctors, but there had been no signs that his body was going to give up the goddamn walking ghost after a couple of rounds of unenthusiastic sex where he barely moved.

His arms were trembling as he got halfway to his chair, and

he almost sobbed out a relief when, three minutes later, he heard his front door open. He had his hands on the seat of his wheelchair when Chris walked into his room, and he ignored the man's tisk of disappointment in favor of letting Chris take him under his arms and getting him upright.

"Shower?" Chris asked.

Thierry bowed his head as he gripped his wheels and unlocked the brake. "I can handle that. Do you...could you..."

"I've got the bed, man. Don't even gotta ask."

Thierry didn't want to ask for his friend to clean up the piss in his sheets, and he could do it himself. He had done it himself, more than he wanted to really think about. But his head was a fucking mess, and he needed to clean up before they went in to see what was happening now.

Bitterness rose from his gut into his throat and stayed there as he soaped up and rinsed off, and he wouldn't let himself think about Pietro during any of it because he didn't want that man in the dark places of his mind while he struggled.

The bed was freshly clean, and new sheets were set with more pads by the time Thierry rolled himself out, naked save for his towel. He was grateful that Chris was trained in the mechanics of helping people with his injury level, because it saved him from having to give directions and ask for what he needed right then.

"I know what you're thinking," Chris said as he finished tying Thierry's shoe.

"You don't."

Chris laughed and slapped his calves. He felt it, but more like a tingling ache of sleeping nerves than real pain. "The fuck I don't. You're thinking you got a job, got some friends, got laid, and the good Lord still wants to make you look like his little bitch."

Thierry couldn't help the smallest twitch of his lip. "Isn't that blasphemy."

"I'm an atheist, and I don't think it would be anyway. Jesus damn well knows I'm tellin' the truth about this. Life sucks and it kicks your ass, but it's not to teach you a lesson." Chris straightened up and handed Thierry his hairbrush. "Your body's just doing what it does."

Thierry hated that, and yet, it made sense. It made more sense than anything else, anyway, and part of him wanted to cry. His eyes stung, but he managed to hold back the tears as he put himself as right as he could, then followed Chris to the living room.

"I don't know what I did. I...*putain*, I didn't do anything different."

"This might just be your body catching up with itself after taking this job," Chris told him—and hell, the man had warned him.

Thierry swallowed past a lump in his throat because if that was true, he wouldn't be able to stay working for Pietro. "I won't panic until I hear what the doctor has to say."

Chris didn't argue with him. He just stood by patiently while Thierry got his things, then followed him down to the car.

The drive to the hospital was short, and Thierry had done it enough times he had prepared himself for the long wait. He sent Chris home after checking in with the front desk since he wasn't emergent, and it would be a while before he was seen. It also wasn't very busy, and the nurses must have taken pity on him because he was triaged after only an hour and then wheeled back and helped up onto a bed just after that.

"The doctor's going to want a full workup," the woman told him, pushing a tray in. "Is your bladder control good enough, or would you prefer we do this with a catheter?"

Thierry sighed quietly. "Catheter. And I think I'll need some water. I haven't had anything to eat or drink yet."

He was grateful when she disappeared, then returned with a small plate of fruit and a large bottle of water. "Snagged this off Dr. Hannah," she said with a wink. "All of this comes from her backyard. I swear she's trying to create a tropical garden."

He took the orange and twisted it between his hands. "In this climate?"

Her brows lifted, and she leaned forward. "Right? She never listens. Anyway, drink up, and I'll be back in half an hour."

Thierry set the orange aside, then took the bottle of water and drank most of it with just a few gulps. He tried not to listen to the quiet bustle of work behind the little curtain, but he'd spent so much damn time in hospitals, it was hard not to listen. He recognized all the beeps of machines, and the quiet jargon of the nurses, and how he could tell when something was serious, and when the nurses wanted to throw the patient out for bullshitting their symptoms.

The half hour turned into an hour though, and in spite of not being able to really feel what was happening in his body below his injury, he felt the familiar, hot prickles letting him know his bladder was full. He started to feel a bit panicked and was just reaching for the cup when the nurse appeared again, looking a little harried.

"Sorry," she said, quickly slipping on her gloves. "Car accident."

Thierry grimaced, but he didn't ask for details. He was still struggling every time it was something serious like that. He didn't have many memories of the first few hours after being shot, but he knew they were locked away inside him somewhere, and the emotions always came out to play when things got intense.

He felt her wriggle his sweats down just as he dug into the

flesh of the orange, and he could feel it a little when she swiped the head of his dick with a cotton swab, and then he held his breath.

"Got much feeling here, hon?" she asked.

He shrugged. He'd know when she pushed it inside. "Just go for it."

The pinch was intense, and he decided that had to be a good thing, even as his hand spasmed and his thumb dug all the way inside the orange. It was over before it became too much though, and his body was instantly calm as his bladder was emptied out. He wiped his fingers on the edge of his shirt, then watched her pour some of his piss into the little jar.

"Blood will be next. None of it needs fasting, so you eat up," she told him, then gave him a little pat and wandered away.

Lying back, he finished peeling the fruit without another incident, then wondered if this was going to be his life forever. Settling into a comfortable void of routine, only to have it disrupted and his job abandoned thanks to circumstances outside of his control. With a quiet sigh as he ate, he thought about calling Pietro, but he decided that there was no point until he had actual answers.

<hr />

"It's a herniated disc, which isn't uncommon in your situation. It's causing a lot of pressure on your already injured spine. The only solution," the doctor said as he went over Thierry's scan, "is surgery."

Thierry nodded, the faint buzzing of panic in his ears just quiet enough that he could still make out the man's words. "Is there...risk?"

"There's always risk when it comes to spinal surgery, and more so when the patient is paraplegic. However, you're a good candidate for a full recovery, and this may actually increase your mobility."

It wasn't a promise, because Thierry had come to realize there were no promises that anyone could keep, but it was something. It was far better than he'd heard when he'd first been injured.

"How long for the recovery? And...there's a matter of payment," he started, because his bank account was running on fumes, and nothing with Pietro was solid.

The doctor gave him a look full of discomfort. "The recovery for someone with your injury will be at least two months, but probably not much more than that. Once we relieve the pressure, you should start to notice a difference within the first few weeks. Maybe even days. As for the payment, well, that's not my department."

Thierry had heard that one before too. His options were to remain there and figure it out or to fly home—and there was no guarantee his life would be waiting for him when it was over. He swallowed thickly and nodded. "*Merci.*"

"I'm sorry it's complicated," the doctor started, but Thierry waved him off.

"It's always complicated."

Silence settled between them, and then the man pushed to his feet and showed himself out without another word. The bedside manner in the US was kinder, but when it boiled down to care, to finances, to hope, it was all the same. The burden would always rest on him.

His fingers twitched, and he wished he knew what Pietro's schedule was because he wasn't sure he wanted to leave this on a voicemail. But the doctor had told him that he wouldn't be back up on his feet again. Not without this procedure—and that it was likely to happen again too, because that was his life with his injury.

Squeezing his eyes shut, he took a breath, then forced himself to be a damn adult. Gazing down at the phone screen, he allowed himself only a single moment to feel all the chaos raging inside him, and then his finger tapped over Pietro's name, and he waited, not sure if he was praying for the man to answer or to ignore him.

"Hey. Are you at the house? I had to leave super early, so I don't want you to worry about—"

"I'm at the hospital," Thierry said.

He heard a slight hitch in Pietro's breath, and then he cleared his throat. "Fuck. What happened?"

"Something that happens with my sort of injury," Thierry said, flopping back onto his pillow. He tried to wriggle his toes, but they refused to budge, and he wanted to scream in frustration. "I think I might have to go back to France."

Pietro made another noise, this one panicked. "What? Why? What's going on? Look, I can be there in like ten minutes if you..."

"Don't," Thierry snapped, then reined himself in because he knew Pietro only wanted to help. Pietro liked him, at least enough to care that this was happening. "I can't afford the surgery here. And before you start to offer—"

"No," Pietro interrupted, and his voice was heated. "Abso-fucking-lutely not. You're not turning me down this time."

"Pietro..."

"No," he snapped, and Thierry found his jaw clicking shut as if his body was obeying the order. "You are my employee—even if we haven't filled out the paperwork. You are also my fucking friend, and my..." Pietro let that sentence die off, and Thierry was glad for it because he couldn't handle thinking about that shit, either. "I would do this for anyone. Do you understand that?"

Thierry breathed out, his lungs trembling. "It's a lot of money."

"I have a lot of money," Pietro said. "I'll get the insurance thing worked out, but...shit. Do you want to go back to France for this surgery?"

At that, Thierry had to laugh, even if the sound was bitter. "No. I want to have it here so I can recover in my apartment and get back to work. But the doctor here is certain this will probably happen again with...with my level of activity. It's just the nature of my body now."

"You need to quit," Pietro said, all the life draining from his voice.

Thierry pinched the bridge of his nose. "Without finding a way to keep me off my feet so much, that might be the only solution. But I don't...it's not what I want."

"Okay. We can figure this out. One step at a time, right? Problems are nothing more than a list, and we can start checking them off."

Thierry laughed again. "Where did you learn that?"

"Therapy," Pietro said, like it was the simplest thing in the world. "I don't, uh...yeah. I don't talk about this a lot, but I have pretty severe ADHD, and the only way I can deal with life is by making lists. And they help. So we can try that, right? Because I don't want to lose you."

Thierry wanted to make a sudden vow that Pietro would never lose him, but he couldn't seem to form the words. "I don't know what to do."

"Well, good news for you, buddy, because I do. Make the surgery appointment, then forward the details to my assistant. She'll get the financials handled, and I'll have her handle the insurance stuff. And the rest, we figure out as it comes up."

"Thank you," he all but whispered.

Pietro made a choked sound. "Don't...fuck. Thierry, don't

thank me. Jesus." He went quiet again, then sighed. "But also, you're welcome. Now, can I come see you?"

"I think they're sending me home," Thierry said quietly.

"Fine, then I can come see you tonight at your place," Pietro pressed. "I'll bring dinner this time."

Thierry's eyes went hot, and he stared up at the white ceiling—at the little stain of water that looked like half a cat's face. "As long as you don't cook it."

Pietro chuckled very quietly. "Swear. I'll text you when I'm free, okay?"

"Okay." Thierry went quiet after that and waited until he was sure the silence on the other end of the line meant Pietro had ended the call. Letting his arm flop down to the bed, he closed his eyes and wondered if letting Pietro take over like this was surrendering his pride…or if it was Thierry finally embracing it for himself.

CHAPTER TWENTY-ONE

Finally home, Thierry let Sarah help him to the sofa, which was a lot closer and more comfortable than his bed. She fetched his weighted blanket, which helped with some of the tremors in his legs, and she put all of his essentials within arm's reach.

"I feel like I should stay," she said, shifting her weight from one leg to the other.

He offered her a small smile but waved her off. "It's not that I don't appreciate it, but I think I need some time to myself."

She still looked torn, but she didn't argue, instead leaning down to kiss his cheek. "Fine. But call me if you need anything. Or just...scream. These shitty-ass walls are so thin, I'll hear you."

Thierry laughed—a genuine huff of amusement—and he gave her cheek a pat as she pulled back. "*Merci, ma chérie.*"

"Mm, you know I love it when you French at me."

He gave her the finger instead, and she winked before showing herself out. He knew she was probably waiting just outside the door and would be for a little while, listening and holding her breath. He was well aware he seemed fragile and on edge—and really, he was. He wasn't expecting such a sharp setback, and he couldn't let go of the fear that after all this was over, he wouldn't have a life to get back to.

There was still no good solution for working in Pietro's kitchen. Sure, there was high-tech equipment like standing wheelchairs, but he had barely managed to afford the one he used now, and he still had to eat. He still had to pay rent, and his utilities, and he couldn't rely on Pietro's good graces for everything.

He didn't want to let it get to him, but it was hard not to feel defeated when there was no solution in sight. Yes, Pietro had probably been serious about wanting to partner in a restaurant—and yes, Thierry hadn't hated the idea. Not really. But he had nothing to contribute now, and it would be years before he was stable enough to even consider it a viable plan.

So...what was left?

Leaning back and getting as comfortable as he could, Thierry switched on the TV and turned it low before changing it over to baseball. The local channel always showed the Vikings' afternoon games when they were in town, and from how Pietro sounded, he wasn't surprised to see him on TV now.

He wasn't up to bat though, and Thierry didn't see him until the camera panned over to the dugout. Pietro was there, standing near the fence with his fingers curled around the links. He had his hat low over his brow, black smudges under his eyes, his mouth tipped down in a frown. Thierry wished he could see the rest of him, but watching the curve of his bicep was enough to spark the memory of how damn strong Pietro was.

He wanted that again—wanted to feel the weight of him

pressing Thierry into the mattress, feel his hot mouth pressing biting kisses along his neck, his collarbone, to his nipples. Pietro hadn't blinked twice, hadn't found it strange when Thierry just wanted to feel touch right above his scars. He hadn't questioned him—he'd just read his body signals, and he'd given everything he had to make Thierry feel good.

Maybe this wasn't going to last, but Pietro was proof that Thierry wasn't necessarily destined to be alone for the rest of his life. If a man like Pietro wanted him, surely there would be others.

He just wasn't quite sure why that feeling left a dark pit in the hollow of his stomach.

The thought chased him as his eyes got heavier, and eventually, as he watched the small players on the screen, sleep claimed him.

THIERRY WOKE, groggy and sore and immediately aware he wasn't alone. He was curled up against the cushions, and though the feeling in his legs was all but nonexistent, he could still feel something. Pressure—weight—contact. He peered one eye open and saw Pietro lounging back, one hand wrapped around Thierry's exposed ankle, his other one scrolling on his phone.

Thierry swallowed through a painfully dry throat, then cleared it. "How did you get in?" When Pietro frowned at him, Thierry realized he wasn't speaking English, and he tried again. "I left my door unlocked?"

Pietro's mouth curled into a smirk. "Your neighbor let me in. She's either really shitty at guarding you, or she has great taste."

"Or she knows how rich you are, so she would get a nice

payout if you kidnapped me and caused her mental distress," Thierry muttered. He pressed his hands into the sofa cushions and shifted so he was on his back. Sneaking a hand under the blankets, he tried not to look obvious as he tested the bag taped to his leg, which was attached to his catheter. It was partially full and would need a change, and he wasn't sure he was ready for Pietro to see that yet.

The man's eyes were keen though, and they narrowed. "Everything alright?"

"Apart from the obvious?" Thierry asked. He rubbed his fingers over his eyes, then stretched. "They gave me a little something for the pain, and it hit harder than I thought."

Pietro offered him a sympathetic grimace. "I brought pho. I figured it would be the best kind of takeout since it would keep until you woke up. Are you hungry?"

He was. He was starving, even though his stomach felt a little cramped. "I could eat. Do you mind, ah...helping me a little bit? Just a boost into my chair." His arms felt like wet noodles from the drugs, and he desperately wanted them to wear off. But he found he didn't mind that Pietro was here for that.

Gently easing his legs to the floor, Pietro offered a hand, which Thierry used to help right himself, and then he allowed the man to lift him under his arms and swivel him into his chair.

Casting one quick look at Pietro, Thierry quickly wheeled to his bedroom, shutting the door behind him before grabbing his bag of supplies that Sarah had left on his bed. He'd have the catheter until the surgery—and maybe a bit longer, which meant he'd only have to worry about the bag until that was done.

It wasn't much of a comfort, but it was some.

Rolling into the bathroom, he quickly took care of everything, then debated about changing into a fresh pair of sweats that didn't smell like hospital bed starch, but without his legs having much functionality, a one-minute task turned into ten, and he just wanted to eat some damn soup and enjoy the fact that Pietro was there.

It was that alone which had him rolling back into the living room, where he found Pietro at the coffee table setting things out on a tray. He looked up at Thierry with an almost sheepish smile and shrugged.

"I actually didn't know the best way to do this. I thought maybe a tray on your lap?"

Thierry huffed a quiet laugh and shook his head. "If I get tremors, we'll be taking a soup bath. I think the table will be fine."

Pietro didn't seem bothered that he had to transfer everything back into Thierry's little dining nook. He just set everything out and moved a chair aside, then pushed the Styrofoam container of ingredients toward Thierry's hand.

"Add what you want, then I'll pour the broth," he said. "Also...drinks...?"

"*Juste l'eau*," Thierry muttered, then looked up. "Water," he clarified.

Pietro winked. "I remembered that one too."

Thierry busied himself with the bean sprouts, noodles, meat, and herbs, refusing to listen or dwell on how sweet and helpful Pietro was being. And yes, all of Thierry's friends were helpful—just like the nurses and carers he'd dealt with over the past year and a half.

But Pietro just made it feel...normal.

He wondered if that was the thought responsible for that squirmy feeling in his gut. Or maybe it was the smile Pietro offered him, like he was happy to be there. Like he didn't want to be anywhere else.

"Man, I fuckin' love pho," Pietro said, clapping his hands together and rubbing them as he sat. He tipped every single thing into his own bowl before destroying his wedge of lime and scraping every last speck of the spicy sauce over the top.

"*Heathen,*" Thierry muttered.

Pietro gave him a look of full offense. "Am not. This is how you eat it, dickhead." He grabbed the pot of broth, then carefully tipped it over Thierry's bowl before adding the rest to his own. It was hot, a little pool of fat melted and glistening on the surface, the meat instantly going from pink to brown. "It's not proper pho if your brain doesn't try to drip out of your nose halfway through."

Thierry shook his head, but he smiled all the same, and he felt a warm, almost intense comfort as he dug in. Silence settled between them, but words weren't necessary. For the first time in a long, long time, he was content.

By the time they were finished, Thierry felt almost sick with how full he was, but he wouldn't have changed a thing. He groaned and felt his belly slosh as he rolled back a bit, and when Pietro laughed at him, he flipped him off again.

"Thank you for this."

"Mixed messages," Pietro scolded.

"You give me mixed emotions," Thierry shot back. He bit his lip, then dropped his hands to his wheels. "I do appreciate it. And I don't want you to worry. I can take care of myself."

Pietro eyed his kitchen, which had lower counters than his own, but not by much. "Listen..."

Thierry shook his head. "No. I appreciate what you're doing, and I'm accepting your help because I want to stay here. This is home now, and I believe you when you say you'd do this for anyone." And that he thought maybe was a small lie, but he wasn't going to call Pietro out on it, because if the situation were reversed, he'd feel the same way. Pietro was firmly in the column with people Thierry loved: Sarah, Hailey, Chris, his parents.

He might not bend over backward for a stranger, but he would for those people, and he could accept he was that to Pietro.

"But you and I both know you don't have time to fuss over me," Thierry went on, and he watched understanding dawn in Pietro's eyes. "I was taking care of myself just fine before this. Before I could walk again."

Pietro let out a slow breath, then nodded. "It *is* super-shit timing. I mean, not that baseball doesn't kick my ass pretty much year-round, but playoffs..."

"I know," Thierry said quietly. "This is enough."

Pietro rubbed a hand down his face, then pushed himself up to stand. "I've got tonight. I need to watch tape, but I brought my laptop for that. I was kind of hoping...I mean. I'd like the company."

Thierry honestly couldn't tell if Pietro meant that for himself, or for Thierry's sake, but the idea of not spending the night alone wasn't unwelcome. "Even though my place is shit?"

Pietro gave him a flat look. "I know you're hung up on the fact that my house is...whatever. Big. Fancy. But I like it here too. I chose spending hours at Ezra's apartment over my brother's place way before they moved in together."

Thierry frowned. "Ezra...?"

"His boyfriend. Not important," Pietro said, though Thierry doubted that with the way Pietro talked about those two. "It's not that I just don't mind, okay? It's that I like your place. It's small and it's cozy and...fuck. *You're* here."

Thierry didn't think he could make words if he tried. He dragged his tongue over his lower lip, then nodded. The pain was back—insistent and refusing to be ignored. It was pinpricks of fire racing up and down his legs and making his calves tremble and making him want to jump into a frozen lake just to make it all stop.

"I need to take something and lie down," he admitted.

"Then let's do that. I'm assuming me staying is a yes, since you haven't told me to fuck off."

Thierry laughed very quietly and shook his head. "I'm not telling you to fuck off. Meet me in my bedroom."

"Which one is that?" Pietro asked absently as he started toward the living room for his stuff.

Thierry huffed in quiet amusement. "It's the only other room besides this one."

"Aw, hell." Pietro looked over his shoulder with a sheepish smile. "I don't mean that the way you think I do."

"I know," Thierry said...because he did.

CHAPTER TWENTY-TWO

Crack! Pietro watched the ball hit the fence, then looked down the line at James, who was tossing another one in his hand. The bucket next to him was full, and he looked powerful and dangerous with the sunset as his backdrop. For a moment, he wondered if James would ever fall in love.

He kept his heart on his sleeve but his cards close to his chest, and anytime Pietro tried to get up in his business, the man shut him down. Hard.

Pietro didn't want to let him get away with the hypocrisy considering how often he meddled in Pietro's life, but it was hard to say no to his face. His own might be considered a baby face, but James had a sort of aggressive good look that made it impossible to do anything but try and make him smile.

"Okay, so you're not living with him now," James said. He drew his arm back, and Pietro adjusted his stance when he realized a curveball was coming his way.

He swung and missed, cursing as he tapped his bat on the edge of his shoe. "No, I'm not fucking living with him."

"You just stay over there," James said. He bent over to grab another ball, tossing it in the air.

"One fucking night," Pietro said. He swung too hard and missed again. "I stayed over a single night."

"Get your head on straight, and hit the fucking ball," James ordered. "This is batting practice."

It was unofficial batting practice, but it was better than vegging on his couch watching tape and trying to convince himself not to think about Thierry all alone in his apartment, waiting for Friday when his surgery was scheduled.

He squared his shoulders, adjusted his knees, then nodded. The pitch wasn't quite as low to the ground as his normal submarine throws were, but it was low enough he almost missed.

Almost.

"Atta'boy."

"Fuck off," Pietro muttered. "It's normal to worry, okay?"

"Especially after your heart got dicked down," James called out. He tossed another ball in the air, but instead of pitching it, he began to toss it between his legs, then picked up a second and third, picking up a juggle.

Pietro took that to mean they were either done or on a break, so he set his bat down and dropped to the grass, letting his back sink against it. "I like him."

"Man, you keep saying shit everyone knows," James said. There was a sharp sting as he whipped a ball along the ground and it smacked into Pietro's thigh.

"Fuck you, dude. Those are my running legs."

James cackled, but eventually, he sank down next to him and let his knee rest against Pietro's. It was grounding, and it was kind. "Is this one of those 'he's probably going to make it, but he could die on the table at any time' sort of surgeries?"

Pietro pushed up onto his elbow and stared at the last rays

of the dying sun sinking below the top of the mountain. "I think it's more like, he's probably going to be fine, but there's a terrifyingly high risk he'll never walk again if that surgeon so much as hiccups during the procedure." He didn't need to be looking at James to know the man was making a horrified face.

"Thierry thinks it's worth the risk."

"Well, he's up the same creek either way, right?"

Pietro thought so, but he also hadn't asked. It felt too invasive, and the last thing he wanted was for Thierry to have to explain it again to some dumbass who'd forget the details ten minutes later.

"You're not a dumbass," James said very quietly. "You know you're not supposed to call yourself that."

Pietro groaned and flopped back down, annoyed that he was talking out loud. Again. "I know," he finally said. "I don't actually think I'm dumb. It's just so fucking frustrating when I want my brain to do other things."

"Is he asking you to focus on him?"

Pietro pursed his lips, then sighed hard through his nose. "No. And...shut up."

James laughed and knocked his knee into Pietro's leg harder. "Never. But I'm not gonna come down on you for worrying about this guy. I mean, I was pretty pissed off that you had to go get hard up for the guy who fuckin' punched you. But I think I get it."

"He's not the same man."

"He is," James said, but before Pietro could argue, he held up a hand. "No, listen. We don't get to become different people, we just get to become better, you know? The little shitstain sneaking booze and robbing my overworked single mom and blaming her for how crappy my decisions were? That guy still exists because those things I did still exist. Even if they're in the past."

James never talked about his childhood. Once or twice, when he was shitfaced after a good win on a long roadie, he opened up. But never with such heart, and never details like that.

"All I can do now is be better to her and better for her. And anyone else that might come along." James rubbed the back of his neck, tipping his head forward. "This guy will always be the one who lied about you cheating and punched you for it. But he's also the guy making your life easy and making you smile. I got no room to tell you to let him rot, you know? If the worst thing I ever did was punch someone, I'd walk out of here with my head high."

"You should do that already. You're my best fucking friend," Pietro said, his voice quiet but hard. He went silent again, then stretched his arms above his head before sitting up. "I want to build him a kitchen."

James choked on a laugh. "No shit?"

Pietro punched him in the thigh, hoping he gave him a charley horse. "I want to buy him a restaurant, but I know he won't take that. Not yet. So instead, I'm gonna build him a fucking kitchen he can cook on without ruining his back."

"And without leaving you?" James asked.

Pietro rolled to the side to kick him in the ankle, and he didn't answer. "Scale of one to ten, how ridiculous am I being right now?"

"Solid six," James told him. "So…no more than usual." He propped up on his elbows and looked over at Pietro. "I like this for you."

"Shut up," Pietro said, but there was something warm blooming in his chest, and James shook his head.

"He'd better not fuck up again, or I'll kick his ass myself." When James settled back down, Pietro reached out and took his hand, feeling safe no one else was watching his moment of utter vulnerability, and knowing James would always have his back.

The rest...well, they were just details.

Usually, postseason was a blur. Time was nothing more than counting hours and minutes between practice, and travel, and games. His head was filled with numbers and statistics and strategy. He ate like shit, and slept like shit, and upped his meds because they were the only thing that took the edge off the swirling chaos in his brain.

This season was no different, except at the end of that first week. That Friday, he checked the time, then left the field early because Thierry would be wheeling back into surgery, and Pietro would be damned if he left that man to face it alone.

He had a car drive him to avoid dealing with parking, and it took him a little cajoling and eventually a call to Thierry's bedside to have him approved to come back. But it wasn't long before he was seated at his would-be lover's side.

Thierry was in a single room, an IV hooked up to his hand, looking like he hadn't slept in days, which was probably the case. Pietro hated himself a little for having stayed away, but he knew it was for the best. He would have been too anxious, and Thierry would have been fixated on making sure that Pietro was feeling okay, neither of them would have relaxed.

Now, with Thierry's hand firmly in his own, Pietro allowed himself to breathe. "Someone will call me, right. If...well."

Thierry rolled his eyes. "I'm not going to die."

Stranger things had happened. Big, terrible, tragic things, in fact. Pietro wasn't going to focus on that though. Thierry had enough on his plate, and he'd been through this more than once. "I'm going to come back right after the game."

Thierry stroked his thumb over the back of Pietro's hand. "No. You're going to go home and do whatever it is you need to do because you have a game tomorrow, and you'll be on the road."

Pietro squeezed his eyes shut and hated that the man was right. "This fucking sucks, you know."

Thierry laughed. "*Ouais, je sais.* But there's one thing you can do for me. If you want."

Pietro straightened up and squared his shoulders, making Thierry laugh again. "Anything."

"Try to win."

Pietro scoffed as he settled back down in the chair. "*Try?* Bitch, this game is in the bag." His overconfidence had been one of his postseason coping mechanisms for years, and having something to promise Thierry made it even easier. "I'm not worried about the game."

"Alright," Thierry conceded, "but you still need to focus on it."

Pietro knew that, and he was prepared to compartmentalize and push Thierry into a little box while he was out there making sure he didn't let his team down. It would maybe be one of the biggest challenges of his career, but he wanted it. He was craving it because it was proof that if he finally did let someone in, let someone close, he wouldn't fuck up his game or his personal life.

"Is someone going to be here when you get out?" Pietro asked after a beat.

Thierry nodded, his eyes growing heavy, and Pietro wondered if they'd already given him something to relax or if the stress was just finally taking a toll on him. "Chris and Hailey, and Sarah will be around to take me home when I get released. One of them should be here soon."

Pietro checked the time and realized he only had a few

more minutes before he was due back. He had an oatmeal muffin in the car to stuff into his face, which would have to sustain him for the rest of the night—and it would. He was too wound up to eat anyway.

"You need to go," Thierry said, his words cutting into Pietro's thoughts.

Pietro hesitated, but he knew there was no point in trying to delay. Thierry still had surgery, and he still had a game to win. He carefully detached his fingers from the other man's, then gripped the bed railing with one hand, cupping Thierry's cheek with the other. "I will see you when this is all over."

Thierry blinked sleepily at him. "Mm."

Running his thumb over the man's cheek, he gave in to his impulse and bent over, pressing their lips together in a soft, chaste kiss. Thierry smelled like mint and hospital. The first part he could get used to, the second he hoped was more rare.

"Be good," Pietro whispered.

Thierry laughed sleepily. "Always."

Turning on his heel, Pietro forced himself to leave. He felt off-kilter, but he had just managed to pull himself together at the elevators when the doors opened, and a familiar man walked out. Tall, broad, gorgeous with dark brown skin and closely cropped hair. Thierry had sworn Chris was engaged, and happily so, but he couldn't help a small twist of jealousy at how close they were.

Chris looked startled to see him, and after a beat, he stuck out his hand. "Hey, man."

Pietro gave him a quick shake. "Hi. I, uh..."

"Stopped by to wish him luck?" Chris chanced.

Pietro wanted to smack his hand over his face, but he maintained his composure. "Something like that." His arm tensed as he went to reach for the button, but he froze and turned back to Chris, who had taken a step to the side. "Can I get your number?"

Chris turned slowly and raised his brows. "My number?"

"I need to know that he's alright. I'm...fuck. I have a game today, so I won't even be able to check it until later, but...yeah."

Chris' face softened. "Ah. Yeah, no worries." He held his hand out, and Pietro quickly opened up his own to a new contact and passed it over. As Chris was typing, Pietro saw him glance up after a second. "You really like him."

Pietro felt put on the spot, but there was no sense in lying because there was no other answer than the truth. "Yeah, I really do."

Chris said nothing as he finished adding his contact, and Pietro watched him send himself a text. "Good. He likes you too. I know you two worked out all that shit from before—and I don't know what kind of man he was before he moved here. He won't talk a lot about his past, and I know he gets down on himself. But he's a good guy now."

"He's better than good," Pietro said quietly. "You don't need to give me the shovel talk. I already know he's better than he thinks he is."

Chris laughed and shook his head. "Nah, man. This isn't the shovel talk. This is me just telling you to be patient because this shit ain't easy. The surgeries, the recoveries, the limitations. It's gonna be hell on his self-esteem, and more than anything, he just needs someone who can weather it without pushing him to get over it."

Pietro nodded. He felt time nipping at his heels, reminding him he needed to go, but he didn't move yet. "You sound like you know from personal experience."

"My dad was quadriplegic," Chris said with a shrug. "That's why I got into the business, you know? Growing up with that shit. He and my mom almost split up more times than I can remember. Every time he got angry..." Chris closed his eyes and shook his head. "It was different. Different attitude, different generation. But the needs are the same."

Pietro licked his lips and took a step back because he realized what Chris was saying. He had to make damn sure he was capable of being what Thierry needed—not just what he wanted. "Tell him I'll see him soon" was the only response he could give, and from Chris' smile, he realized it was probably the right one.

In the elevator, he carefully tucked all of his feelings into those small boxes and stashed them in the dark corners of his head. He let everything sink back into game mode as he waited for his car, and the moment he arrived at the field, he immediately went to work.

CHAPTER TWENTY-THREE

Thierry was one of the unfortunate people who didn't do well with being put under. He always woke like he was on a boat in the middle of a raging storm, and even with having no food and water for more than a full day, his stomach still heaved itself up into the little tray the nurses left behind for him. His eyes refused to open, and when they finally obeyed, he had double vision accompanied by vertigo so powerful, he didn't know how he wasn't falling out of the bed.

Maybe it was from the fact that he had no feeling at all in his lower half that kept him rooted, but that didn't make him feel better.

With a tiny groan, he tried to lift his hand, and he heard the sound of someone shuffling at his side. He was drifting on a sea of darkness, only the occasional pop of orange from the sun hitting his eyelids, and he wanted…someone.

Something.

Comfort.

He didn't really know what he was asking for, and language seemed beyond him.

Cool fingers brushed over his brows and words started to penetrate the fog. "...got you. Just rest. Do you want something for your throat? How about some ice? The nurse left it here for you."

His lips parted and a plastic spoon pushed past his teeth, depositing small cubes on his tongue.

"That's good. Just rest."

It took Thierry a moment to realize the person—the man—was speaking French. He was desperate to open his eyes and ask how—ask who—but he was too far gone.

THIERRY HAD no real concept of time as his body purged the rest of the drugs pumped through him, but it felt like days had passed since he'd risen toward consciousness that first time. His memory was patchy, but as he struggled toward awareness this time, he was far more alert. He was profoundly aware of the pain in his back, that he was slightly elevated, and that his whole body felt heavy.

He didn't even try to test the movement in his legs since he wasn't really sure he had a lower body, but that wasn't abnormal. It had been like that after every procedure on his spine.

He dragged his tongue over his lips and groaned, and that voice was back.

"Want more ice?"

Thierry used what little strength he had to peel an eye open, and his heart thudded in his chest so hard, he heard the beeping machine to his right start to jump. Hervé was there, sitting in a chair and leaning over his thighs.

Thierry blinked several times, wondering if it was some sort of hallucination, because it wasn't possible. "How did you get in here?"

Hervé chuckled quietly. "Is that any way to greet the man who's been taking care of you?"

Thierry wished more than anything that he could leap from the bed and take the little fucker by his throat. "How did you know I was here?"

Hervé let out a sigh when he realized that Thierry wasn't going to let it go. "Look, you don't need to worry about that right now, okay?"

Except, he did, because Hervé shouldn't have known where he was, and he shouldn't have been able to get into his room. His hand moved—slow and steady across the sheets until it touched the edge of the railing where the call button was, and he pressed his knuckle into it.

"Get out."

Hervé scoffed. "Really? That's how you're going to treat me after everything I've done?"

Thierry knew better than to sit up or try to move, but he wasn't above reaching for the little tray on his rolling table and flinging it at the man. "I don't want you here. What could you possibly want?"

"I told you, to make up for what I did," Hervé said, his voice rising. He shot up from the chair and gripped the railing on Thierry's bed. "Why can't you just accept that I want to make it up to you?"

"Because I don't care," Thierry said. His throat was sore from being intubated, and he couldn't raise his voice which was just another frustration. "I want you to leave me alone."

"Not until you let me prove that I'm better," Hervé said through clenched teeth.

In spite of himself, Thierry laughed and shook his head, closing his eyes again because the effort of looking at Hervé wasn't worth it. "Do you even hear yourself when you talk? All you care about is yourself—how you feel. If you need to make peace with God, do it without me."

Hervé leaned in to say something else, but the nurse walked in just as Thierry opened his eyes again. Her face was pinched, and her gaze cut from Thierry to Hervé.

"I'm glad to see you're awake, Mr. Bourget. How's your pain?"

"Terrible," Thierry told her. "Can you please remove him? He's not supposed to be here."

The woman looked a little startled. "Your boyfriend?"

At that, Thierry nearly sat up. He would have, if his body was capable of obeying his brain. "That's what you told her?" he demanded in English.

Hervé looked nervous now. "They wouldn't let me see you."

"Get out," Thierry snapped, louder this time. "Please, if you need to call security..."

"No," Hervé said. "I'm going." He marched out without looking back, and Thierry let out a breath the moment the door swung shut.

The nurse hovered for a moment, then shook her head. "I'm sorry. We had no idea." She took a step closer, then began to adjust his monitors, though he was pretty sure it was just nervous fidgeting. "Do you have a partner we should know about?"

"Ah. Yes," Thierry said, though he wasn't quite sure why that answer felt both right and wrong. Everything felt so complicated. "He's American. His name is Pietro Bassani."

"I'll make a note, and I'll be sure that security is aware that man isn't allowed into your room again," she told him. She fussed with him a little more, then checked a few more things behind him before showing herself out.

The adrenaline was enough to combat the lingering fatigue

from the anesthesia, and he realized there was no hope of him going back to sleep. His fingers were trembling, but his arms were regaining strength enough to reach for his little pitcher filled with half-melted ice.

It took him a few minutes, but he managed to get the top off, then tipped some of the cubes on his tongue. What he wanted was to take huge gulps of the cold water, but he knew throwing up would wreck him like nothing else would.

Patience was not his strong suit, but the relief from waking up without panicking doctors in the room was enough to get him through.

He gazed at the clock on the wall and saw that it had been nine hours since he'd been wheeled back.

Losing time like that always hit him hard, and as he laid there, he realized he still had no answers. Had it gone to plan? Or had the damage been too much for them to repair anything?

He'd live, whichever way the fates turned him on the path, but he hated the not knowing.

A soft knock on the door interrupted him, and Thierry braced himself, letting out a small sigh when he saw Chris' head poke around the corner. He looked tired but chipper, and he gave Thierry a wink as he walked in and took the chair Hervé had abandoned.

"Yo. Do you know why they gave my ass such a hard time at the check-in desk?" Chris asked, leaning back and crossing his legs at the ankle.

Thierry tried to shift himself a little and immediately regretted it. Pain like fire raced through his lips, and he had to breathe through it. "Ah," he said, ignoring Chris' worried stare, "Hervé was here."

At that, Chris sat up straight. "I'm sorry, he was what now?"

Thierry licked his lips, then reached for his ice again and

crunched down two cubes before he answered his friend. "I don't know what he said, but the visitor's desk gave him a badge and let him in. I think…I think he was here when I was first coming out. I remember someone speaking French to me."

"Well, you know that wasn't me," Chris said, his voice hard. He clasped his hands hard and let them hang between his parted knees. "You have him thrown out?"

Thierry nodded. "He wasn't happy about it. I think he might try to come back."

"Man, I am gonna kick his ass so hard…"

Thierry held up a hand, then set his pitcher down and rubbed at his face. Everything felt kind of sticky and itchy, and he wanted a bath and to sleep in his own bed. Of course, he'd get none of those things. He'd be lucky if a nurse brought him a washcloth to wipe away his post-surgery sweat. "I'll deal with it if he does."

Chris didn't look happy about that, but he settled back anyway. "Your boy was here earlier too. Before you were wheeled back. You remember that?"

Thierry didn't want to smile—didn't want to give himself away—but he couldn't help it. Yes, he remembered Pietro holding his hand, and talking quietly, and kissing him just before the drugs really took hold. "Did he say anything to you before he left?"

Chris rolled his eyes. "Like some fuckin' high school cafeteria gossip? Shit." He winked through and shrugged. "He was worried about you. I told him I'd send him a text to let him know you got through okay."

"Did you?"

Chris shook his head. "Wanted to check first. How are you feeling?"

"Can't move," Thierry admitted, "but I didn't expect it right away. The doctor hasn't been in yet."

Chris looked mildly annoyed. "Yeah, alright. I'll just send him a thumb's up, then give him details later after someone comes to check on you. You mind if I hang out?"

Thierry waved him off. "I'm not going anywhere."

"Cool. Because I heard there's a game on, and I wanted to catch the score." Chris winked again as he snatched the TV remote from the little place where it was hanging on the bed, and Thierry found himself drifting once more to the sight of the man he was falling for on his TV screen.

THE DOCTOR WOKE Thierry from his doze, and he wasn't totally surprised to find the room was empty. He didn't know if the man had kicked Chris out, but he was a little grateful for it. If it was bad news, he wanted a moment to process on his own.

Swallowing thickly, he elevated his bed a little, then let the doctor check him over with sensation tests before he took a seat. "Nonresponsive right now, but that's not anything I was expecting this soon. Do you want to tell me how you're feeling?"

"Same as before," Thierry said, trying not to sound irritable. "How did it go?"

"As far as I can tell from the technical side, it went just fine. Very little bleeding, and we managed to alleviate the pressure. You were fairly responsive during the surgery, and as the swelling goes down over the next few days, we'll get a better idea of how successful it really was."

So, no real answers other than to say that Thierry wasn't a worst-case scenario.

He could live with that.

"When can I go home?"

The doctor laughed. "What, you don't like our hospitality?"

"Bed's soft, but the food's shit," Thierry answered him, and the man laughed again.

"Fair. Let's give it forty-eight hours and reassess." The doctor clapped his hands softly, then rose from his chair and set it back against the wall. "Is there anything I can get you for now?"

Thierry shook his head. All he wanted was to rest, to heal, and to get back to his life when it was all over. Long weeks would stretch in front of him before any real progress would be made, but it was a lesson in patience he was willing to learn.

He waited for the man to show himself out, and when the door was closed, he pulled his rolling table closer and grabbed the juice a nurse had brought him earlier, and his phone. Pietro's game wouldn't be over just yet, but as much as he appreciated Chris keeping the man updated, he wanted to offer something himself.

> Thierry: I'm awake. Surgery went well, but I won't know results until later. Good luck on the game, *chéri*. Knock one out of the park.

He could only hope that Pietro saw the message for what it was: a subtle way of saying he was here, and willing to cross some lines if Pietro wanted him too.

CHAPTER TWENTY-FOUR

Pietro sometimes wondered why one game's victory felt worse than another game's loss. It happened sometimes, where the mood was just somber and while on the outside, they were patting each other on the back and grinning at the crowd, the weight of what was to come was heavier on their shoulders.

There was no real time to celebrate considering they still had a long flight ahead of them and another game to win. He had no doubts about a Vikings' victory this year, but it almost felt like his career was on the line. But maybe it wasn't that at all. Maybe it was knowing that he had important information to read, and that could define what his future looked like.

Pietro sat on the bench, staring down at the phone in his hands, daring himself to turn on the screen.

"Petey."

Pietro closed his eyes as James took a seat next to him.

"Want me to do it? You know someone would have called if shit went wrong." James nudged him, but Pietro didn't move because no—he didn't know that. It wasn't like he was Thierry's emergency contact. He wasn't even his boyfriend.

Hell, they weren't even friends, at least as far as they had defined their relationship. Thierry was his employee, and they'd fucked twice.

No strings.

Jesus, it was a mess.

Forcing himself to nut up, he finally tapped his thumb on the screen and saw two messages waiting for him. His heart was in his throat, but not in a bad way, because the second message was from Thierry himself.

> Chris: All good, man. He's up, waiting on the doc. Talk soon.

> Thierry: I'm awake. Surgery went well, but I won't know results until later. Good luck on the game, *chéri*. Knock one out of the park.

Pietro found himself laughing so hard, James actually started to rub his back. "Yo, are you having a freak-out?"

Pietro shook his head and ran a hand down his face, trying to catch his breath. "Shit. Shit, no. I'm...he's fine."

"That's good," James said slowly.

Pietro bit his lower lip until it stung, and then he let go. "He told me to knock one out of the park."

"Aww, you gotta disappoint that little French face of his. You took the fucking collar tonight."

Pietro knocked his elbow into James' side, but he was still smiling. Most of the tension drained away from him, and he was a little wobbly as he pushed himself to stand. "Okay. I need to get the hell out of here."

"First you need to shower because you smell like my fuckin' high school jockstrap," James said, standing up and giving him a small push toward the showers. "Then you call your man so you can put yourself out of your misery."

James was grinning all the way to the stall.

He got through the postgame routine as quickly as he could, and it took everything in him to follow through with his promise not to show up at the hospital and sleep in the chair next to Thierry. It wouldn't do either of them any good though, and he kept that thought running around his head as he microwaved some of the leftovers Thierry had thrown together before everything went to hell.

He eyed the bottle of wine sadly but forced himself to curl up on the sofa with his laptop and all the videos Weber had sent over for him to watch. His finger hovered over the trackpad, but instead of hitting Play, he dropped his hand and picked up his phone instead.

Feeling like a bit of an asshole, he held his breath as he hit Thierry's name, then waited.

"You could have been interrupting my beauty sleep," came a groggy voice.

Pietro laughed, his throat kind of thick, his eyes a little hot. He hadn't realized how glad he was to hear the man's voice, and fuck, what did that say about him? "Sorry, Aurora."

"You think I don't get that reference, but I've been to Disneyland," Thierry said, his voice a little stronger now. "Is everything alright?"

"I feel like I'm supposed to be asking you that," Pietro pointed out. He blew on the wedge of sweet potato speared at the end of his fork, then shoved it in his mouth before speaking again. "So really, how are you?"

"I'm fine. Are you eating?" Thierry demanded.

Pietro rolled his eyes and settled back, letting the too-warm container rest on his stomach. "Yes, Mom. Fuck. I'm eating some of that roasted veggie thing you froze for me."

Thierry made a quiet noise of contentment that Pietro swore went right down to his toes, making them curl. "Ah, *bon*. That will be good for you before your game tomorrow."

Pietro scoffed as he shoveled a few more bites into his mouth. "Yeah. Gotta get on a plane at ass o'clock tomorrow too, which sucks. I just uh…I just didn't want to leave without seeing how you were."

"I sent you a text," Thierry complained. His tone was softer now, like he was drifting, and Pietro knew he was going to have to let him go soon.

"Yeah, but your phone might have gotten kidnapped by a well-meaning nurse trying to avoid drama, you know?"

Thierry snorted. "Too much television."

"Or not enough. You know how fucking busy I am." He scraped the container, then swallowed the last bites before throwing it on the table. "They feeding you okay there?"

"It's all shit," Thierry told him. "Hospital food, always shit." He let out a long string of French after that, then laughed.

"Sounds like someone got his morphine cocktail," Pietro said with a small grin. "Wish I could be there to see it."

"Wish I could kiss your face," Thierry murmured.

Pietro went hot all over. "Jesus, don't say shit like that when I'm not there to make good on it."

Thierry laughed. "I like your face. Very beautiful face. Even when I punch it."

"Oh my God," Pietro groaned. "I hope they let you bring those drugs home. This is gold, and I want to be a part of it where I can record you."

"Do you like my face?" Thierry asked.

Pietro softened and closed his eyes. "Yeah, bud. You have the best face. You should get some sleep, okay?"

"See you in the morning."

Then the line just went dead, and Pietro stared down at the phone in his hand before a laugh rushed out of him. It was on the verge of turning into a sob though, and he swallowed it back before he could get too out of hand.

Turning his screen back on, he switched to his messages and sent out one to his brother because he just didn't know what the fuck to do with this big, hot, uncomfortable feeling in his chest.

Pietro: I think I might be dying? Can love kill you? Asking for a friend who is me. Don't respond to this. I'm being a jackass.

He hit Send before he really thought about it, then threw his phone to the other end of the sofa before he could do anything else that could potentially ruin his life or destroy his rep. He hit Play on the video instead, leaning forward—so close, his eyes were almost crossed. Play after play, minute after minute, he absorbed as much as he could until he swore he would go mad with all the information in his head.

Bong! Bong!

Pietro nearly flew a foot off the sofa before he realized the obnoxious sound was his doorbell. He made another mental note that he knew he'd immediately forget that he needed to hire someone to come and change it, and he shuffled off the sofa and to his door.

He was only half-surprised to see his brother standing there with his arms crossed and a scowl on his face. Gabriel had looked like a grumpy old man, even when they were kids, and it was worse than ever as he stared at Pietro.

"Why are you worrying about your dick during playoffs?" Gabriel demanded.

Pietro sighed and waved him inside. "Definitely not

worried about my dick. My dick is fine. Little Pietro is getting all the attention he needs."

"I hate you so much," Gabriel complained as he led the way into the sitting room. He made a noise that almost sounded pleased when he saw the tape on Pietro's laptop, but he rounded on him, and his bitch face was on high. "Why are you worried about your heart?"

"Because it doesn't give a shit that I'm trying to get my happy ass back to the World Series and decided to fucking fall in love with my chef?" Pietro said with a groan. It was the first time he said it aloud like that—just sort of out there and blunt without trying to soften the edges or make excuses for what that emotion was. It rocked him a little, and he found himself collapsing into his sitting chair and putting his hands over his face. "I'm so screwed."

"Probably," Gabriel agreed, taking a seat on the sofa. "Could be worse. Does he want to be with you?"

"I...I don't know. I want to say yes. We fucked a couple of times," Pietro added.

Gabriel looked thoroughly unimpressed.

Pietro licked his lips. "I want to build him a kitchen."

"You have a kitchen. And unless he's living in some sort of tiny house situation, I'm assuming he also has one."

Pietro gave him a flat stare. "I want to build him a kitchen he can work in that doesn't destroy his back and make him go in for more spine surgery."

Gabriel softened. "Is that what happened?"

Pietro shrugged. "I guess. I think it was a combination of several things, but I think working here made it worse. There's this company that can, like, totally reno kitchens so the counters can raise and lower, but I don't have fucking time to arrange it. I sent the info to Allie, but I forgot to follow up."

"Let me help."

Pietro's jaw snapped shut with an audible click. He swallowed. "Seriously?"

"Why do you think I'm some monster who wouldn't want to help you with something like this?" Gabriel asked, and he sounded honest-to-God hurt.

Pietro winced because it was his own self-esteem issues that felt he was unworthy, but he realized how it looked by putting that shit on Gabriel. "It's my fault. I...hell, I know you want me to be happy."

Gabriel nodded. "You're in the middle of something big and serious. Just give me your damn black card, and I'll make sure it gets done."

"You know I have an assistant for stuff like that," Pietro said weakly.

Gabriel shook his head, then rose and stuck out his hand. Pietro took it, and he didn't protest when his brother swapped their positions and made Pietro pick up his laptop again. "I'll work with her. This is your home," he said, sitting down and immediately getting on his phone. "This guy is important to you. I know you want it done right, and you know I can make that happen."

It was true, and Pietro was feeling so grateful, he almost wanted to put his fist through the damn wall. "Charity Little League thing soon," he said, hitting Play on the video again.

Gabriel grunted in response.

"You and Ezra are coming."

Gabriel grunted again, and Pietro let himself take that as a yes.

Before he was really aware of it, Pietro's Little League charity was on him. He had to check his playoff shit for twenty-four long hours so he could focus on those kids. But try as he might, his heart wasn't completely in it, and it wasn't because of the game.

A small part of him had imagined a scenario where he'd sweep into Thierry's apartment with tickets and an invite on bended knee. Maybe they'd make out a little bit, maybe Thierry would help Pietro forget how awful things felt.

But none of that happened.

They weren't on radio silence, but Pietro's schedule was so full, he hadn't been able to make time for anything more than a few texts and two late-night phone calls over the long weeks of Thierry's recovery. So, in a moment of blind panic, he acted.

He sent a suit over to Thierry's along with the invite to the auction, along with a quick text explaining what the hell it was. Then he had a total freak-out because that was probably a dick move. It probably would have been better to at least ask Thierry to come over and invite him in person, but Pietro's kitchen was torn to pieces with the remodel, and he didn't want his would-be lover to see it until it was done.

So. His bed was made.

He managed to show up for the Little League game and cheer his kids on to their win, even with the knowledge that Thierry still hadn't responded to his invite. They raised, according to his PA, a buttload of cash, and it was all Pietro could ask for. The auction would fill in the gaps that the tickets left behind, and Pietro could forget just for one night all the stuff waiting for him with the sunrise.

And he could only hope that at some point that night, he'd look up at the doorway and see Thierry there. Even if it was just to tell him off for being an insensitive ass-clown.

Before the presser, he managed to slip into an empty room to take a breather and get his head on straight. He tapped his fingers on his phone in his pocket, then finally pulled it out and held his breath when he saw a message waiting for him.

Thierry: What is this package?

Pietro: Info's on the invite. Please don't hate me. You don't have to say yes. I just miss you.

There was no response, and Pietro didn't have time to really freak out because suddenly his assistant was there dragging him back in for the last interview, and he had a whole speech to give about inclusivity in sports. Someone touched his elbow, and he flinched hard, pulling away before walking up to the collection of mics.

He didn't recognize any of the reporters, but over their heads, he could see Gabriel was there, leaning in and speaking softly into Ezra's ear. Ezra was smiling, his eyes half-lidded, and Pietro felt a small stab of jealousy because God damn it, he wanted to be that happy.

And it was just out of reach.

"...the purpose of the game tonight, is that correct?"

Pietro blinked and cursed himself for not at least attempting to focus. But he'd done this before, and he'd learned how to bullshit through his media training. "The purpose of this particular league is to encourage sports to be more inclusive. It needs to stop being some inspirational story when a disabled kid is included on their school team. There are plenty of ways for people to play whatever type of ball they want." He fought the urge to rub his face, and instead he jammed his hands into his pockets and began to fidget with his phone.

"Do you feel a lot of this was brought on by your brother's accident?" someone asked.

Pietro felt the ripple go through the room, and he used every ounce of his self-control not to look at Gabriel because half the people there did. "I've said this before, and I'll say it again—you shouldn't need to know someone personally to be invested in allyship or accessibility. People deserve to follow whatever dreams they have—going to space, becoming a doctor, or an engineer..."

"Starring pitcher for the Huskies?" someone called out, and at Pietro's scowl, they all laughed.

"Yeah, you wanna make me a mortal enemy, go for it," he quipped. He took another breath, then shrugged. "I've met enough people in my life—long before Gabriel was injured—who were left out for reasons that were frankly bullshit. And I hope I'm talking slow enough for your censors, but I'm not sorry for swearing because it is. I'm not doing this because I want points. I'm doing this because it's fair, and I should be able to use my platform to make a difference."

There were a few more questions punted his way, and then he was saved by Allie, who quickly got him out and into a private corridor where the press couldn't follow. He breathed out, his chest a little tight, then pushed fingers through his hair.

"You should have just told them you cried yourself to sleep every night because you couldn't cut off your arm and give it to me so I could still kick your ass in playoffs," Gabriel said from behind him.

Pietro hadn't heard him come into the hall, but he also wasn't surprised that Gabriel had followed him. "Eat a dick."

"Every night," Gabriel said with a grin.

Pietro groaned and turned. "You're no fucking fun since you met Ezra. I'm tired of it. I want a goddamn refund."

Gabriel smirked, but then the expression melted into something serious, and he dropped a hand on Pietro's shoulder. "Do you need to bail tonight? You know I can cover for you."

Pietro bit the inside of his cheek, then shook his head. "I might have fucked up. I sent Thierry an invite like literally last second. Like the thought popped in my head this afternoon, so I had someone go pick up a suit for him and drop it off with tickets to the dinner, and I think..." He trailed off, and Gabriel stayed silent for a long time. "I think he's pissed about it."

"Did he know about the dinner?"

"Technically?" Pietro said quietly. "I told him I had the dinner coming up. I was going to invite him before his surgery, but everything got so busy, then suddenly it was here...and..."

"Then he was probably not completely surprised by the invite."

Pietro scoffed. "Yeah. I guess I can blame playoff brain, though I'm not sure he'll let me get away with it."

Gabriel stared at him a minute longer. "You really like this guy."

"More than," Pietro said miserably. "We've barely spent any real time together, but it's...I don't know. It's different. I think it could be good, but I don't trust myself."

"I know you don't, and that's probably your worst personality trait," Gabriel said, squeezing his shoulder tighter.

Pietro scoffed. "Jesus. Tell me how you really feel."

Gabriel shook his head with a slight smile. "You're your own worst enemy. You're the only person in your life who doesn't think you're worth so much more." Gabriel drew his hand away and pushed it into his pocket. "If Thierry doesn't show up tonight in that goddamn suit which probably won't fit him because that shit needs to be fitted, I'll pay for your entire kitchen reno bill."

Pietro's mouth dropped open. "Don't be an ass."

"I'm not being an ass. I'm being confident." Gabriel cuffed

him again, then took a step back. "Go get ready. You look like total shit."

Pietro was left standing there with his mouth half-open and a dangerous amount of hope pulsing to the beat of his heart.

CHAPTER TWENTY-FIVE

"I don't know what to do."

Chris laughed from his spot, leaning against the wall as he watched Thierry stare at the suit hanging on the back of his closet. Thierry found himself tense, like he was almost afraid the suit was going to blow up or turn sentient and start dancing the gavotte around his damn bedroom.

He'd been staring at it since it arrived—except for the five minutes it took to text Chris and Sarah. Sarah was working a long weekend shift, though, at a teen group home, so Chris had to shoulder the burden of Thierry's freak-out.

"You could, I don't know, try putting it on," Chris said.

Thierry scoffed, shaking his head, though that thought had occurred to him no less than twenty-five times since it arrived on his doorstep. He *could* put it on. It probably wouldn't fit, and he'd look like a fool, but he could put it on and show up and punch Pietro right on the dance floor again because what the hell was he thinking?

"I can't go," Thierry said. He was surprised at how flat his tone was considering how he was feeling inside. "I can't...how can I go?"

"Well," Chris said slowly, "you get dressed and comb your fucking hair because it looks like shit—you white boys need to brush your hair at least once a day. Then you get behind the wheel of your car and drive your happy ass down to the very fancy venue. You eat expensive rich people food and drink a lot because you know that shit got an open bar."

"It's not that simple," Thierry said quietly. "What would I do about Pietro?"

Chris laughed again. "It damn well is that simple. You can punch your boy, or you can hold his hand. Hell, you can drag him into an empty hallway and suck his dick, if you really want to."

Thierry's whole body felt hot, and his legs twitched from the sudden tension in his muscles. "I...it's. He can't just do this. He can't just send me a suit and a ticket for a dinner and just assume I'm going to be there."

"Is that what he did?" Chris asked, his tone a little quieter.

"Yes," Thierry insisted, except...it wasn't. Not really. He thought maybe that was Pietro's intention when the suit first arrived, but his text after? Thierry could hear the man's adorably confused stammer like he'd done something without thinking and was now trying to figure out why. "Actually," he added, because Pietro knew he deserved better, "he probably wasn't thinking. He probably meant to invite me, but then I had my surgery and..."

"And the fucker's busy trying to set world records in baseball and shit?" Chris tried.

Thierry groaned. "I can't go."

"You keep saying, but I know you're just lying to yourself. You can go. I'll even drive you if you want."

Thierry's hands were sweaty as he gripped his wheels, then rolled forward and touched the edge of the trousers. They were soft and almost stretchy...and hell, maybe they would fit.

"Try them on," Chris murmured. "What have you got to lose?"

"Time?" Thierry muttered. It would take him forever to get dressed because yes, he had sensation back and range of motion, but he had no strength, which meant everything was still taking just short of forever. "Pride?"

And yet, the very idea of a night out with fancy food and free drinks, and finally seeing Pietro—even if it was just for a moment—it was almost impossible to pass up.

Who the fuck was he kidding.

"Let me help," Chris said. Thierry opened his mouth to argue, and while normally Chris would let him have it, this time the man shook his head. "You get frustrated tonight and we both know you're gonna give up. And that's not good for you. He wants you there, and you want to see him."

Thierry bowed his head and reminded himself for the thousandth time that accepting help was not accepting defeat. And Chris was right—he wanted this badly enough he could taste it. "The trousers. Just the trousers."

Chris grinned at him. "Grab the suit. We're gonna make you look fly as hell."

It was easy to turn himself over to Chris' hands after that. It was mostly to save himself from sliding into a panic about showing up and facing Pietro without knowing what the hell either of them really want from this...he couldn't really call it a relationship, but a friendship wasn't right, either. And Pietro might be his boss, but it was so much more now.

The confusion had him swearing quietly in French as he held on to Chris' shoulders and let the man manipulate his legs into the loose, very expensive clothing. He got zipped up after that—and the trousers were big, but that was going to help since he'd be in his chair for the entire night.

The shirt fit a lot better, and he didn't hate how he looked as he held on to Chris with one hand and examined himself in his full-body mirror attached to the back of his bedroom door.

"Down with you," Chris told him, giving him a gentle push back into the chair, then quickly went to work on his hair. Thierry tried not to count down the minutes to when he was supposed to arrive. He was going to be late considering it had taken him several hours to get his head out of his ass and make a decision in the first place.

Thierry also wasn't going to be hard on himself about his indecision. It had been a long couple of weeks in recovery—in waiting to see if his body would start to function like before, and lying around lonely and alone, not sure what the future was going to hold. It had been a lot of introspection and debate about whether or not he was willing to put his heart on the line.

Then Pietro had sent this ridiculous gift and his nervous text, and Thierry realized he was in too deep to say no now.

"Your boy's on TV."

Thierry blinked, shaking himself out of his thoughts, and he looked up to see that Pietro was on his bedroom TV. Without asking, Chris reached for the remote and turned up the volume, and Thierry let the sound of Pietro's exhausted voice wash over him.

"...enough people in my life—long before Gabriel was injured—who were left out for reasons that were frankly bullshit. And I hope I'm talking slow enough for your censors, but I'm not sorry for swearing because it is. I'm not doing this because I want points. I'm doing this because it's fair, and I should be able to use my platform to make a difference."

"Shit," Chris said when the interview cut off and the screen moved back to the two reporters at a long desk. He hit mute again, then dropped the remote. "He's an alright dude."

"More than," Thierry said quietly. He glanced at himself in the mirror, and while he still looked thin and tired, he also looked determined and ready. "I want to be with him."

"Tell me something I don't already know," Chris said with a laugh. He spun Thierry's chair and adjusted a few locks of his hair before stepping back with a nod. "*Mm.* Hot like burning."

Thierry rolled his eyes, but oddly, he believed it. It had been a damn long time since he'd seen himself as anything but hired muscle or a sad sack just trying to get his life back again. But he knew he was more—he knew he'd always been more. It had just taken him this long to break apart all those walls he'd put up and erase all those words people had thrown at him over the years trying to make sure he was put down and stayed down.

"You want me to drive you?" Chris asked.

Thierry shook his head. "I think I need to do this myself."

Chris smiled, clapping him on the shoulder. "Then get your skinny white ass out the door before they don't let you in."

Thierry found himself trailing after his friend with a laugh lodged in his chest and a massive grin on his face.

THIERRY HADN'T QUITE CONSIDERED the logistics of showing up to the event or how chaotic it was going to be. He was two hours late, but there was still a massive line of cars, and he inched forward, terrified he was going to hit one with his slower reflexes. He didn't, of course. He trusted himself to get there safely, and eventually he made it to the valet, who gave him a skeptical look when the door opened and Thierry started to take his wheelchair out.

"Uh...evening...sir? Do you have your ticket?"

Thierry fished around for it, then handed it off before pulling his chair from the back seat. He was just reaching for the first wheel when the kid cleared his throat. "Problem?"

"Can I, uh...will I be able to drive that, sir?"

Thierry frowned, and then his brows shot up when he realized what the kid was scared of. "It won't be an issue. Give me a second." He finished putting the second wheel on, then transferred to the seat before leaning forward and removing the pedal box on the floor. "Just don't touch the hand controls and you'll be alright."

The kid bit his lip again, nodding, then slipped behind the wheel and adjusted the seat. Thierry rolled back a bit, then was hit with a sudden wave of trepidation because every car in front of him, and every car behind, was some luxury brand. They were shining and new and looked important.

And he was there with his shitty little Honda that was beat to hell from shopping carts ramming the sides, and the paint was peeling in the back. He had half a mind to call the kid back and tell him never mind, but then he remembered that Pietro honestly didn't give a single fuck about those things.

He wanted Thierry for who he was.

The rest were just details.

Wiping the sweat off his palms, he gripped his wheels and momentarily regretted not bringing gloves with him as he made his way to the front. There was a man at the door looking at him like he was almost afraid to ask Thierry for his ticket, so he quickly put the stranger out of his misery and produced the embossed invite Pietro had sent him.

"Is there a plus-one, sir?" the man asked.

Thierry shook his head. "Only me. Is...are there stairs?"

The man looked confused for a second, and then his shoulders relaxed. "The party's on the third floor, sir. Elevators to the right."

Thierry took his ticket back, then wheeled into the lobby. In spite of the long line of cars that had been queuing to let out their passengers, Thierry found himself waiting alone as he watched the numbers on top of the elevator doors slowly tick down to G. His heart was beating a little fast, and he started reaching for his phone to text Pietro and let him know he'd actually made it when a hand fell on his shoulder.

He jolted so hard his leg slipped off the footrest. "*Merde!*"

"Sorry, oh my God. I'm so sorry," came a voice from his right.

Thierry looked over and saw Pietro's friend James standing a foot away, his face drained of color. "You scared the shit out of me."

"I know. I'm sorry." James said. "Can I help?" He gestured toward Thierry's leg and made a motion like he was going to lift it.

Feeling a surge of irritation, Thierry grabbed the edge of his trouser leg and flexed his muscles, heaving his foot back into place. "I'm fine."

"Yep. Yeah. And I'm still an asshole," James said, holding up his hands in surrender. "Want me to get another elevator?"

Thierry scoffed as the doors opened, and he rolled forward. "Just get in."

At that, James smiled and followed, slamming his finger over the Close Door button when a smartly dressed couple headed for them. When Thierry gave him a look, James shrugged, unrepentant. "I hate sharing with strangers."

"You don't know me," Thierry reminded him.

James waved him off. "I don't *not* know you."

Silence fell, heavy and awkward, before Thierry took a breath and asked, "Is he still here?"

James laughed and rolled his eyes. "He should be in bed watching tape before he passes out considering we're flying out tomorrow at the ass-crack of dawn. But yeah, he's still here."

"And so are you," Thierry pointed out.

James cackled again as the doors opened, and he held an arm against them to let Thierry pass in front of him. "We're all dumbasses."

That startled a laugh out of Thierry as he followed James down a long corridor, the sound of music, talking, and laughter getting louder the closer they got to a massive set of double doors. He faltered a little, his anxiety getting the better of him, and after a beat, James noticed and stopped.

"You good, man?"

Thierry licked his lips and nodded, but he couldn't make himself move. "I...it."

James' brows furrowed. "You want me to get him? He's probably in there dancing like a loon and all fucked-up from getting no sleep in the last week. He'll be happy you're here."

Thierry squared his shoulders. "He invited me, but I didn't know..." He picked at the edge of his lapel.

James softened and took a couple steps closer. "If it helps, the only thing on his mind these last couple weeks besides kicking ass was worrying about whether or not you were too lonely during your recovery."

Thierry felt a punch of relief, and right behind that, a punch of guilt. Because in reality, he hadn't thought about Pietro much. Only in the quiet hours lying in bed when the pain made it impossible to sleep. But his days had been filled with PT and existential crises about what he needed to do after he was back up on his feet.

It wasn't that there hadn't been room for Pietro, it was just that the man had been a whole other bag of emotions he wasn't ready to deal with.

He felt cruel, almost.

"That didn't help, did it?" James pressed.

Thierry laughed softly and rubbed a hand along the back of his neck. "Knowing he wants me here did. I just don't want to make a scene."

"Don't punch him in the mouth again, yeah?" James said, and there was only the slightest edge to his tone. "I think that's all he really gives a shit about."

Thierry winced, but he deserved it. One day he could demand that people moved on from that incident, but it was still too soon—too fresh. "I would never hurt him again."

"Lies. We all hurt each other—especially the people we love," James countered.

Thierry rolled his eyes. "I don't love him."

"Eh," James said and waved him off. "Maybe not yet, but you will, and that's pretty fucking close enough to make my point. I'm not saying don't hurt him, okay? But he's lonely, and he's fuckin' delicate, which he'll probably kill me for saying, but I don't care. He's been through some shit, and he hasn't always been the greatest guy, but he deserves better than he's gotten in the past."

"I know," Thierry said quietly.

James took one more step closer. "From what he's said, you do too. So that's why you're gonna march—wheel, whatever—your ass through those doors and go find him. It'll make his night."

That was enough for him. It was enough to fill those gaps of doubt that had been growing larger and larger since he pulled up to the curb in his shitty little car. He nodded, then looked at James' face once more before pushing past him, and he didn't argue when the man took quick strides to hold the door open.

Inside, it was a mess of bodies—people standing at high tables with glasses of wine, champagne, and martinis. It was loud enough to make his head spin a little with both conversation and music. There were people in the middle of the room dancing and a buffet along the far wall, though the only people there were a group of kids picking at the dessert trays.

Thierry felt eyes on him, giving him a quick look up and down, but then they moved on. He didn't know if it was because he was just so uninteresting he wasn't worth looking at or if they were trying not to care, but he wasn't going to make that his problem.

He had one person to find.

He maneuvered his way through the crowd, which wasn't easy. People were definitely drunk and not paying attention. He clipped a few calves, ran over dress trains, and squashed a couple of toes, but he let those moments pass with a waved apology and determination to find the man he wanted.

The small cluster of people right in front of his dance floor eventually parted, and when Thierry's gaze fell on the people dancing, it was like the room stopped. Hell, it was like the world stopped.

Pietro was there, looking gorgeous as ever in a suit that was made just for him. His soft curls were artfully tousled, his eyes tired but shining bright in the lights overhead. And he was dancing.

With his ex.

With Hervé.

Thierry swore the floor had opened up beneath him and he was falling. He swore some black void was just below, waiting to envelop him. The couple spun, and Pietro's back was to him, and that's when Hervé saw him. His lips curved into a smile, and just before Thierry turned to go, Hervé leaned in and whispered something into Pietro's ear.

He couldn't possibly move fast enough, cursing half in his head and half aloud when he realized he couldn't just get up and run. He'd have to roll across that godforsaken hall, sit at the elevators, wait for the damn doors to open so he could get the hell out.

He felt like a fool, his eyes burning hot as the doors closed behind him. He should have known. He should have fucking *known* that Hervé hadn't come to apologize. He'd come to make an effort so when he went crawling back to Pietro, he'd have something to show for it—proof he'd changed.

And Thierry would be the bad guy for not accepting Hervé's olive branch.

Pietro was kind too. He'd let Thierry keep his job. He'd wait a while before he felt comfortable being with Hervé in front of him—as though time might make that easier to bear. Or maybe he'd let Thierry go after finding him a new job.

Thierry found himself in the bathroom instead of waiting for the elevators. It was almost like he'd gone into a momentary fugue state because he didn't remember making the conscious choice to go in. But as he sat there in the middle of the empty room, surrounded by echoing pale tiles and open stall doors, he thought maybe he would cry.

He hadn't really done that since after the accident, when the reality of his situation sank in, but he was close now. Heartbreak for a totally different reason—but ultimately it was the same outcome. It was his life going off the rails, and he was powerless to do anything about it.

He curled his hands into fists, arms shaking, then wheeled up to the sink. Grabbing the edge of the counter, he stood up and braced himself. His legs felt weak but better than they had in a while. He kept his balance as he turned on the water, then cupped his hands under the spout and splashed his face.

It was cold enough to shock him out of his spiral but not enough to take the edge off his pain. Why had Pietro sent him the tickets and the suit if he was just going to fall back in with Hervé? Was it some kind of sick joke? Was it some sort of misguided apology?

His phone buzzed, and it startled him enough he almost fell over. Turning to rest his back against the counter for balance, he dug the damn thing out of his pocket and stared at Pietro's name on the screen.

> Pietro: Where r u? Scooter said you were here. Can't find u. Shit got weird.

Thierry's hands shook as he contemplated his reply. He didn't want to lie to Pietro, and maybe...hell, maybe it wasn't what he thought. But he knew he couldn't be there. He couldn't watch whatever the hell was going on play out in real time. He was still hurt, still recovering.

> Thierry: I had to leave. I'm sorry. I can't do this with him here.

> Pietro: Fuck, you saw him? Where are you now? I'm coming to you.

> Thierry: Gone.

> Pietro: Go to my house. I'll meet you there. We need to talk.

And those four words were enough to nail a coffin shut. But as he slipped his phone into his pocket and began to head toward the elevators again, a small voice started to wonder if maybe those four words, right then, meant something else entirely.

CHAPTER TWENTY-SIX

Pietro was done with James' disapproving look. He knew he was exhausted, he knew he should be home, but he had obligations. And it wasn't like he was the only player in the MLB who did shit like this. Hell, he wasn't the only man on their team that pushed himself too far from time to time.

Orion had his own thing going on, and the season before, James had disappeared for three days before anyone could find him, only to learn he'd been working in a teen shelter trying to get it up off the ground. But he couldn't deny he was exhausted, and he was stressed because he hadn't heard a word from Thierry, and he wasn't sure the man was going to show.

Maybe he was having a bonfire with the suit and tickets.

It would probably serve him right for just sending them over there and expecting Thierry to drop whatever he was doing and show up. He hadn't seen the man since before the surgery, and if he hadn't been so tired, maybe he'd have been able to think of a better way to show his interest.

He felt like a disgruntled alley cat who was finally being

given attention. He didn't know how to say thanks other than shoving dead birds under the pillows of people who were kind to him.

Passing a hand down his face, he desperately wished he could drink. Instead, he stuffed his face with cream puffs and ignored the smiling, laughing faces and checked his phone every ten seconds.

"I'm going downstairs to that bakery for cookies," James murmured in his ear as the night began to wear on. "You want me to get you anything?"

"Valium," Pietro muttered savagely.

James snorted. "Cute. Seriously though…"

"Seriously though," Pietro repeated, turning to face him, "ask the valet if they've taken a car from an absurdly hot man using a wheelchair."

"Or," James countered, grabbing his shoulder, "you could fucking call him and put yourself out of your misery."

He could do that. He *should* do that. But that would mean facing a definitive rejection, and his heart wasn't ready for that yet. He preferred being trapped in Schrödinger's box alongside the poor cat. He watched James walk off, then he turned back to the dessert table and resolved to stay there with a couple of the sticky-fingered kids until someone forced him away.

He was halfway through stuffing his cheeks with the last of the cream puffs when he heard the smallest scoff. Turning, ready to tell off anyone who wanted to judge him in that moment, he froze and nearly choked when he realized it was his ex standing a foot away.

"What the," he started to say before realizing he had to chew and swallow. He was too shocked to really be humiliated as he wiped chocolate from the corner of his mouth, but he didn't think that was going to last.

"What am I doing here, you want to ask?" Hervé chanced.

Pietro's eyes narrowed. "Almost took the words right out of my mouth," he snapped. "Because I was going to ask what the actual fuck you think you're doing here."

"I thought it should be obvious," Hervé said.

At that, Pietro rolled his eyes. "That what, you're still an asshole? Congratulations. Anything else?"

Hervé's shoulders slumped. "No. I'm...I'm sorry. I didn't come here to argue."

When Hervé took a step closer, Pietro ducked out of his reach. "Seriously, how the fuck did you get in here? This is an invite-only event."

"I have connections," Hervé said with a shrug. It was his standard answer every time Pietro had ever asked him that question—and it was more annoying than it had ever been. "And I wanted to see you."

"Well, here I am. Now, if you don't mind, I'm waiting on—"

"Thierry?" Hervé said.

Pietro stiffened. "How the hell do you know that?"

"We've been talking since I arrived here." Hervé smiled when Pietro's face went a little white. "He didn't tell you? He had me over at his place for a long talk. I've been helping to take care of him after his surgery."

"You're a fucking liar," Pietro hissed. There was a tinge of doubt in his voice, though, because maybe it was possible. It was just hard to imagine Thierry forgiving Hervé enough to let him that close.

The other man shrugged and spread his hands. "It is what it is. I just wanted to come here to make amends with you. If he and I are going to be together, and he's working for you..."

Pietro's ears began to ring, and it was the shock that had him not protesting when Hervé took his wrist and drew him onto the dance floor. He moved to the beat without being consciously aware of it, but when he came to, he tried to pull back.

Hervé's grip on him tightened. "Don't make a scene, *mon amour*."

"Fuck you. You don't get to call me that," Pietro spat, but he knew Hervé was right. He couldn't make a scene there. Everyone was watching him.

Hervé sighed and gently ran his fingers over the side of Pietro's neck. "I don't want us to be enemies. I didn't come here to steal your boyfriend, you know."

"He's not my boyfriend." The words came automatically, but they sounded like a lie because he'd thought...no, he was so damn *sure* there had been something more than just friendship. The last time they'd talked, the last time they'd kissed, and he definitely felt something between them.

Hervé laughed. "I know what you look like when you're in love."

At that, Pietro couldn't help but smile, couldn't help his laugh. "No you don't, because I was never in love with you. I was caught up with the chaos, and I didn't know what it meant to be with a good man until I got rid of your ass."

Hervé stiffened, then turned Pietro gently and leaned in to whisper in his ear, "Is that what you tell yourself every night?"

Pietro shook him off. "I don't need to. The moment you were gone for good, I could breathe again. You're a bad person, Hervé. You're cruel, and you only care about yourself, and the reason I know Thierry wouldn't give you the time of day is because you're not worthy of forgiveness. Not his. Not mine. And the only thing you are right now, showing up here like this trying to cause drama, is pathetic."

With that, he turned on his heel and stormed off, refusing to give a shit what Hervé did after that. He was almost at the door when a hand darted out to catch his sleeve, and he relaxed the second he realized it was James.

"Dude, where are you going? Thierry's looking for you."

Pietro froze and glanced around wildly. "What? He's here?"

James frowned. "Yeah. He didn't find you?"

"No, I was..." Fuck. He was on the dance floor with Hervé. That mother*fucker*. Hervé had done it on purpose. He'd seen Thierry and... Oh, he was going to murder him. "Get security and have Hervé thrown out. Then call Allie and tell her I want a restraining order and to get legal on the phone. I'll sign everything when we get back."

James frowned. "What happened?"

Pietro pulled out his phone, firing a text off to Thierry. "Hervé fucked up this whole night."

James sighed. "Look, you want me to find a way to get him thrown back to France for good? Because I probably have a guy for that."

Pietro glanced up from his phone, his heart beating wildly after reading Thierry's reply, and he managed a choked laugh. "No, but ask me after tonight. I have to go save this relationship so I don't lose him before I actually get him."

James reached out and cupped his cheek. "He's in love with you. Or, well, he's close. Just breathe. It's going to be fine."

Pietro curled his hand around the back of James' neck and brought their foreheads together. "Thank you. I'll call you later tonight."

"Just text. I feel like once you catch Thierry, you're going to be busy with some freaky, filthy sex."

Pietro laughed, flipping him off as he tore out of the dance hall, then went right for the stairs as he raced toward the lobby. He wasn't quite sure what to expect, and he said a small prayer that the valet wouldn't take too long getting his car.

He knew timing was important on this because the more

space Thierry had to think about what he'd seen, the less chance Pietro had of making it better. He wanted to cry, or scream, or maybe punch something. Instead, he fumbled for his ticket, then came to a skidding halt when he saw a figure hunched over a few feet away.

The light glinted off the edge of Thierry's wheels, and he looked both gorgeous in the suit Pietro had sent but also tired and defeated. Pietro's heart began to thud in his throat, but he ignored the attendant and walked over.

"Hey."

Thierry's entire body jolted, and his head snapped over to look at him. His eyes went wide. "What..."

"So, Hervé is a dick."

Thierry was quiet, then after a beat, he laughed. "I am so tired of hearing his name."

"Me too." Pietro licked his lips, then walked over and knelt down because he needed to look that man in the eye. "Whatever you thought you saw..."

"Dancing," Thierry said, his voice hoarse. "And for a second, I convinced myself that you were together and trying to be kind to me with the suit. You...gave me a plus-one."

Pietro squeezed his eyes shut. "I thought you might want to bring a friend since we haven't seen each other in a while. I wasn't sure if you were, you know, still into this."

"I was," Thierry murmured.

Pietro felt that like a physical blow. "Right." He moved to stand, but Thierry's hand shot out and touched the side of his face.

"I am."

Pietro bowed his head, then nuzzled into the touch and laughed. "Yeah? He fucking told me that you two are together. He said he's been spending time at your place helping you recover."

Thierry let out a long string of French swears that Pietro didn't have a hope of understanding, but from his tone, they sounded creative. "He was at the hospital when I came out of surgery. I had him banned when I realized he was there. He told the nurse he was my boyfriend."

"Oh, I'm gonna kill him. I'm gonna kill him, and we're gonna sue the hospital for letting him in, and..." Pietro started to stand, but Thierry grabbed his wrist. Turning pained eyes to his lover, Pietro wanted to fall to his knees and beg for...something. He wasn't sure what, but the feeling in his gut was getting worse.

"Did you believe him?" Thierry asked quietly.

Pietro bowed his head. "I don't think so. I think whatever I felt—whatever doubt—was just there because I still don't feel like I'm good enough for you. But I also know *he's* not good enough for you."

"He's shit," Thierry said fiercely.

Pietro found himself laughing again, and leaning in, and letting Thierry hold him as close as they could manage in their awkward positions. "He *is* shit." He knocked his head against Thierry's. "God, can we get the hell out of here, please? I need to take you home."

Just then, a car pulled up to the curb, and Pietro's eyes widened as the attendant got out and exchanged Thierry's ticket for a wad of cash the other man was holding.

"You're driving?"

"I finished my classes," Thierry said with a shrug. "Just before the surgery."

Pietro grinned. "That's...oh. That's great!" He glanced over at the attendants, who were pretending like they weren't watching, and he had a feeling some shit was going to end up on Twitter by morning. "It's gonna take forever get my car, but we can..."

"Come with me," Thierry said. His hands dragged down Pietro's arms, linking their fingers together as Pietro stood. "I can drive you. You have a fancy assistant who can pick your car up while you're away, right?"

Pietro laughed and shook his head, but he wasn't saying no. "Yeah, I guess I do."

"If you don't mind riding in my...well, Sarah calls it a shitbox..."

Pietro cuffed him on the arm. "It's a cute car."

"It's mine," Thierry clarified. "And I'd like to take you home."

Abandoning every single fuck he had left, Pietro reached down and gripped Thierry by the shoulders, then leaned in to kiss him. "Take me home."

Thierry smiled against his mouth, then kissed him again.

CHAPTER TWENTY-SEVEN

The mood wasn't like before, and there was also no hope of getting Thierry up the stairs, no matter how many steps he could take. He did show off his newly acquired progress by walking from the car to the garage door, but he was using his chair for support, and Pietro wasn't about to push it. Besides, he really did have to be out the door at dawn, and he didn't want to have to drag Thierry out of the bed and down the stairs that early even if he did manage to get him up.

It was just one more thing he'd have to change. A master bedroom downstairs was more work—but he wanted to make the effort.

"So, I figure we can set up on the couch or even in the guest room. I have one down the hall if you want to..."

He was cut off by another string of curses in French, and he turned to see Thierry staring wide-eyed around the kitchen. "What did you *do*?"

Pietro's face went molten hot. "Uh."

"You've ruined it," Thierry said, his voice trembling. "Pietro..."

"It's just going through a remodel. It'll be totally back to normal by the time you're ready to work again," he defended in a rush. "I swear, it just looks bad."

Thierry sank into his chair, looking like he needed it for more emotional support than anything. "It was fine. It was beautiful. Why would you..."

"Because it was hurting you," Pietro snapped, and then he sagged forward on a bit of counter that wasn't torn up or covered in plastic. "The counters were too high, and you couldn't cook in your chair. This job was making your life so much worse."

"I don't understand," Thierry said quietly.

Pietro licked his lips, then shook his head and gestured toward the hallway. "Down the hall, third door on the right. Not as comfy as my bed, but not bad, either."

"You're not getting out of this so easy," Thierry warned.

Pietro put up his hands in surrender. "I know, but it's better to talk in there."

Thierry narrowed his eyes, but he gripped his wheels and pushed himself out of the kitchen. Pietro took the chance to take in a full breath, then snag a couple of water bottles from the fridge before he followed. Anxiety was still racing up and down his spine, sort of cold and clammy, but he forced one foot in front of the other until he was through the guest room door.

Thierry was there, sitting on the edge of the bed with his chair off to the side. He was still dressed, though his shoes were off, and he was twisting his hands in the space between his knees. Pietro had never seen him look so uncertain, and part of him wanted to race back to the party and make Hervé pay for how badly he'd managed to disrupt this fragile thing between them.

But maybe it wasn't really Hervé's fault.

Maybe it was the fact that they'd never really talked or bothered to define anything.

"Thirsty?" he asked.

Thierry looked up, then shook his head, so Pietro put the bottles on the nightstand.

"Tell me about the kitchen," Thierry said, and Pietro's cheeks went hot.

"I hired a company to adjust the counters so you can cook in your wheelchair. I don't totally understand how it works, but I'll show you the brochure if you want."

Thierry looked at him, his expression almost tired. "You shouldn't have."

"Yes, I should have, because I don't want to lose you, and I'm not going to just sit back while this job is making your life harder."

"You wouldn't have lost me," Thierry started to argue, then stopped when Pietro stepped between his legs.

"I know. You would have stayed in spite of how much you were hurting, and…" Pietro went quiet, because he didn't want to say aloud how he knew it would make Thierry resent him, and the job, and how they'd fall apart before they really even began.

Thierry swallowed thickly, then looked up at him. "Would you help me undress?"

Pietro let out a sigh of relief because mostly, he just wanted something to do. He wasn't sure if Thierry actually needed the help, or if he'd just seen the signs of Pietro's distress, but either way, he wasn't going to question it. He dropped to his knees, ignoring the pops in his joints, and he carefully unbuttoned the trousers.

"Not a bad fit," he commented as Thierry leaned back on his elbows, and Pietro managed to slide the waistband over his round, sizable ass.

"It was adequate," Thierry said. When Pietro shot him an indignant look, he grinned. "It would be better next time if you tell me before so I can get something proper to wear."

"I thought you looked hot, even if I didn't get to fully appreciate that ass in a suit," Pietro admitted.

Thierry's cheeks were a little pink around the edges, but his smile didn't quite reach his eyes, and Pietro knew they weren't quite there yet. "I wish you had called."

"Me too," Pietro said. "Not just because that dickhead fucked it all up, either. I'm...God, I'm such a disaster, you know? I forget things until the last minute, then I overcompensate or I just don't think. My therapist told me I was like a boulder rolling downhill some days."

Thierry looked at him a long time, pausing as he worked through his buttons, and then he went back to the task. When his shirt finally hung open, he dropped one hand to his thigh, the other lifting to cup Pietro's cheek. "I understood what you were trying to do."

"I can't promise I'll do better because it's just this disconnect in my brain. And I've only been doing this therapy thing for a short time, so it will get better, but..." He blew out a puff of air, nuzzling into Thierry's palm before pushing away and standing up. "This is who I am."

"I like who you are," Thierry told him. "I would have liked it more if I'd known Hervé was invited..."

"Oh, that little fucker was *not* invited," Pietro said, anger rising in his tone. "That shit-starter was definitely not on the guest list."

Thierry let out a small breath, but there was relief in his face after that. "I didn't know. I thought maybe you two were trying to work something out?"

"No. Never. I...he..." Pietro wrung his hands, then quickly started to strip as Thierry shuffled back on the bed. It took a collected effort to get the covers back and have them both lounging against the headboard, but it was worth it when Thierry rolled toward him and laid a hand on his waist.

"Tell me," he murmured.

Pietro closed his eyes. "If Hervé belonged with anyone, it was with the man I was—the one who was angry and dealing with an uncomfortable diagnosis, and still not quite over my brother's forced retirement. I was hurting, and I wanted to hurt someone, and he was there. He was happy to give it as much as he took it. It was fucked-up, and it was toxic. And he was never kind to me."

Thierry bowed his head. "He was not a good friend to me, either. I don't know that he's ever been one. He was so afraid of letting go of what little power he'd managed to gain over the people in his life—like he knew if they stopped for even a second and saw the person he really was, they'd abandon him."

"I kind of get that," Pietro admitted, because he did. He'd been like that once—but being cruel like that had never felt good. It never felt right. He had a long road ahead with Thierry, but he was willing to walk it—to fight anything that came up along the way, because he wasn't going to let this go. "I want to start over, without him hanging over our heads."

Thierry nodded. "Tonight?"

Pietro grinned, then lifted his head, and Thierry was there to meet him with a kiss. "Tonight."

Arms wound around his waist, and Thierry tucked him in close. "I'm falling for you," Pietro admitted.

Thierry laughed quietly. "You redesigned your kitchen for me, *chéri*. I had a feeling you might like me a little."

"You don't think I'd do that for anyone?" Pietro asked.

Thierry looked at him for a long time, then urged Pietro to lie down. Facing each other, Thierry traced a touch over his features, passing over his eyes, his nose, over his mouth. He followed it up with a long, slow kiss to his lips, then his jaw, then just under his ear before pulling away. "I think you would do a lot of things to help a lot of people. I think you would fix your kitchen for anyone because you're kind. But I think you did it because you're in love with me."

"Am I really that transparent?" Pietro asked.

"Were you trying not to be?"

Pietro gazed at him, then surged in for another kiss. "No," he said right up against Thierry's mouth. "Not to you."

Thierry held him tight and didn't stop kissing him, even as he answered. "*Bon.*"

Pietro laughed, and laughed, and kissed him, and laughed.

EPILOGUE

"Come on," Pietro whined, leaning half his body on the counter. "Not even for a World Series champion?"

"You have four rings," Thierry said with a sniff. "The magic is worn off."

Pietro whined again. "But... *cake*."

Looking over his shoulder, Thierry smiled in a way that might look sweet to someone else, but Pietro knew it was full of denial and torture. The counters were currently lowered, and Pietro was enjoying the feeling of the cool marble against his overheated skin. He was freshly returned from Arizona and happy to be back to a Colorado spring instead of the desert's pre-summer heat.

"I only have a couple weeks where I can get away with cake for dinner," Pietro said, speaking against the counter. "You're so mean."

"And yet, you love me," Thierry told him.

Pietro grinned. He never got tired of this—fucking around in the kitchen, the banter, the way Thierry would eventually give in. They were approaching their anniversary—that autumn when playoffs started looming, it would also signal another turn of the world in which he and Thierry were disgustingly in love and the past was nothing more than a bad memory.

Neither of them had heard from Hervé after the night at the banquet hall, and when Pietro had quietly asked James if he was responsible for it, his friend had just smiled and shrugged. Of course, James was also the kind of asshole who was willing to take credit for shit he didn't do, so Pietro didn't trust him.

But frankly, he didn't care, either. It didn't matter why Hervé had disappeared from their lives and eventually from the conversation. The point was, he was gone, and Pietro was happier than he thought he could be.

He let out a quiet moan when warm fingers suddenly started to ruck up his shirt, and he twisted so he was a little more facedown when he felt a body press against his.

"You really up for this, tiger?" Pietro asked, the sentence ending on a gasp when Thierry reached between his legs and palmed his balls that were hanging low in his jogging shorts.

"Trust me, I'm up for it." Thierry punctuated that sentence with a thrust against his ass, showing him just how hard up he was. "I took a Viagra."

Pietro grinned, a little feral and desperate, as he spread his legs wider. "Tell me you have something besides olive oil for lube. That shit was *disgusting*."

Thierry laughed, then kissed the side of his neck as he reached for the hem of Pietro's shirt and pulled. The marble was even cooler now against his overheated skin, and he groaned when Thierry shoved him down again. "I'm prepared."

"Fucking liar. You wanted to bone on the plane last month, and you forgot lube then," Pietro started, then immediately lost his train of thought when sharp fingers pinched his nipple. "Oh, fuck."

"Mm." Thierry used his free hand to tug Pietro's shorts down, and a bare cock immediately thrust between his ass cheeks. "You want me?"

"I always want you," Pietro said. He writhed, trying to get Thierry's cock to line up against his hole in spite of not being lubed up or prepped at all. "Babe, come on..."

"Patience," Thierry told him.

"Fuck patience," Pietro said, then gasped as a slick finger pushed against him, and he screwed his eyes shut at the sound of his lover's gentle laugh.

"I think I can make you wait."

Pietro thunked his head against the counter because he knew Thierry could—and would. The more he pushed, the slower Thierry would go until Pietro was a shaking mess. And yeah, okay, he liked that a lot, but he'd just gotten back, and he wanted to be fucked into oblivion.

"I'll take care of you. Don't I always take care of you?" Thierry finished his sentence by dragging his palms up Pietro's back, then tugging him to the very edge of the counter. His cock slid between his legs, the head nudging Pietro's balls, and he laid a biting, openmouthed kiss to the back of Pietro's neck. "*Je t'aime.*"

Pietro squeezed his eyes shut. The feeling in his chest was too big to name, the need in his body too great to ever be sated. But that was okay. He hoped they both died trying. Spreading his legs further, he willed his body to relax as Thierry finally slipped a finger inside him.

A muffled shout rang out, and he only realized it was him as another one crawled up his throat to follow, and he bit down on his arm as the burn of two fingers hit him.

Thierry wasted no time, gave him no space to breathe, as

he added a third. Of course, he knew Pietro liked this, to be barely prepped before Thierry was pounding into him. It was different from the way Thierry liked to be taken—slowly stretched apart for a long forever of tongue, fingers, and toys.

It was only when he was loose and close to gaping that he liked Pietro to thrust inside, and Pietro fucking loved doing that to him. He adored their dynamic, and he adored the man who was now adjusting his hips and pressing the head of his cock against his waiting hole.

"Ready for me?" Thierry asked.

Pietro shifted his hips, restless and desperate. "Always. Always. Babe, *please.*"

Thierry chuckled, but the sound turned into a groan as Thierry pushed inside him. Strong hands lifted Pietro from the counter, pulling him back against Thierry's broad chest. His legs were still weaker—and always would be—but his upper body could bench Pietro if he let him.

And he had, once or twice.

That wasn't as sexy as this though—as Thierry holding him up with one arm and bracing himself with the other. And Pietro was overwhelmed with his lover's strength and his competence, and his ability to just take him with spread legs and snapping hips.

It didn't last long, because fucking upright never did with the two of them. But Pietro sure as shit wasn't going to complain when Thierry dropped into his wheelchair and Pietro landed straight down on his dick. He bottomed out without being able to take a breath, and he wasn't sure if it was on accident or on purpose, but the angle was perfect.

Thierry's cock rammed right against his prostate.

Head leaning back, Pietro let himself shout toward the tall ceiling as Thierry grabbed his hips and urged him to move. He felt boneless and helpless against Thierry's urging. He lifted his hips and slammed back down, over and over until he felt the heat rising under his skin.

"Close," he gasped.

Thierry held him down hard and used his hands to circle Pietro's hips. It was slow, erotic torture, and Pietro found his legs spreading, looking down with half-lidded eyes at his painfully hard cock, which was leaking a stream from the tip.

"Touch...touch me," he begged.

Thierry growled, biting at his neck as his hand moved from Pietro's hip to wrap around his length. He was slow there too, dragging the orgasm from him inch by inch until Pietro was crying, stuffed full and on edge and ready to promise anything if he could just come.

Thierry was muttering soft French in his ear, and Pietro lost himself to the rhythm of it as his orgasm finally slammed through him. His entire body racked with shudders as he felt his balls tighten. He came in pulsing ropes over Thierry's fist, only half-aware as he watched. He felt like he was outside of his body for long seconds, and then he slammed back in as Thierry wrenched his head to the side and claimed him in a rough kiss.

"I love you," Thierry repeated, in English this time.

Pietro whined, unable to speak as Thierry suddenly pulsed, then filled him. His eyes fluttered shut, and he leaned back hard against Thierry's chest as they both tried to regain their breath.

"How was that, World Series champion?" Thierry murmured, kissing along his jaw.

"Fucking perfect." Pietro laughed, then grimaced because they were naked and sticky and come was everywhere. Leaning his head fully back on Thierry's shoulder, he turned his head to mouth at his lover's jaw. "I love you too. You know that, right?"

Thierry let out a small hum, and he was smiling as he pressed his face against Pietro's lips. "I do."

"I'd love you even more if we could have cake for dinner," Pietro added.

Thierry growled, but the smile on his face lingered, and he threaded his fingers through Pietro's hair. "You seduced me for cake?"

"I seduced you because I adore the absolute shit out of you." He twisted, pulling a face when Thierry's half-hard cock slipped out, but he made no real move to get off his boyfriend's lap. "And *also* cake."

"I can accept that," Thierry told him.

And Pietro grinned and kissed him once more.

THE END

Curious about Gabriel and Ezra? You can read their story now. Nothing Ordinary is available on Amazon and free to read with Kindle Unlimited.

COMING THIS SUMMER

Hit and Run Book 2: Line Drive
A bisexual awakening, single dad romance, coming to Amazon and Kindle Unlimited.

"Can I get your number?" James asked suddenly, and Ridley startled in his seat.

"What for?"

"So we can be friends," James said with a wink. Ridley thought the man was joking, but then he pulled out his phone, unlocked it, and passed it over. "Tell me to fuck off if I'm overstepping."

Ridley willed his fingers not to shake as he typed in his name and number. "You're not. I'm just surprised considering what a colossal fuck-up I am right now."

James took the phone back and tapped the screen, then Ridley felt his own phone buzz in his pocket. Shit, James wasn't kidding.

"I wasn't kidding the other day when I said that I didn't have parents who gave a shit about me. I know you love your kid, and I know you're trying. We all fuck up." James' smile, if possible, went even softer. "You're actually trying. I want to be friends with people like that."

Ridley nodded, then stared down at his hands which were curled around his cup. "Thanks for this. I needed a kick in the ass, and I didn't know who to ask for it."

James threw his head back, his laughter rich, making Ridley light up under his skin once more. When he looked back at him, his eyes were shining, and his grin transformed his entire face. "Any time man. And I mean that."

In spite of himself and his mood, Ridley managed to smile back. The moment felt almost final, in a way. Or, at the very least, important, and when he walked out with another tea in his hand, he realized there was a warmth behind his ribs he couldn't easily explain away.

ACKNOWLEDGMENTS

I would like to take a quick moment to thank Jay and his husband for sensitivity reading Thierry for his injury and recovery experience, to Mariel for your assistance with Thierry's French, to Luke for your help with Pietro's late diagnosed ADHD, and to Cindi for your keen eye on proofing and making sure all my Baseball facts are correct.

MLB TEAMS:

Eastern:
New York- Blues
Boston- Hounds
Providence- Mavericks
Vermont- Rockets
Raleigh - Knights
Durham- Panthers
Salem- Canons
Pittsburgh- Blue Jays
Savannah- Bolts
Miami- Marlins

Central:
Louisville- Boulders
Chicago- Cavalry
Detroit- Hawks
Ann Arbor- Sliders
Miwaukee- Lightning
Green Bay- Eagels

MLB TEAMS:

Cleveland - Tigers
Knoxville- Raiders
Nashville- Trackers
Fargo- Reds

West:
Phoenix- Wasps
Albuquerque - Devils
Denver- Vikings
Las Vegas- Sharks
Seattle- Spartans
San Francisco- Flyers
LA- Strikers
Portland- Royals
Vancouver- Saints
Provo - Warriors

ALSO BY E.M. LINDSEY

<u>Kindle Unlimited Books:</u>

Broken Chains

The Carnal Tower

Hit and Run- A Baseball Romance

Irons and Works

Love Starts Here

<u>Wide Novels:</u>

On the Market

Malicious Compliance

Collaborations with Other Authors

Foreign Translations

AudioBooks

ABOUT THE AUTHOR

E.M. Lindsey is a non-binary writer who lives in the southeast United States, close to the water where their heart lies.

Where to find EM Lindsey:
  TikTok
  Instagram
  Facebook
  Website

Printed in Great Britain
by Amazon